MW00815583

*Katherine L. Whaley*

# BIBLE STORIES

# FROM THE OLD TESTAMENT

*Stories that uplift, educate, and inspire*

PREP PUBLISHING

FAYETTEVILLE, NC

*For Coco Smith*

*fondly,*

*Katherine L. Whaley*

PREP Publishing
1110 ½ Hay Street
Fayetteville, NC 28305
(910) 483-6611

Cover design by David W. Turner

Library of Congress Cataloging-in-Publication Data
Whaley, Katherine L.
      Bible stories from the Old Testament : stories that uplift, educate, and
      inspire / Katherine L. Whaley. — 1st ed.
         p.   cm.
      Rev. ed. of: Bible stories from long ago.
      ISBN 1-885288-12-3
      1. Bible stories, English—O. T.   I. Whaley, Katherine L.  Bible stories
      from long ago. II. Title.
      BS550.2.W39 1999
      221.9'505—DC21                  98-48429
                                          CIP

Printed in the United States of America

*This book is lovingly dedicated to Fr. Lincoln Taylor, O.H.C., who, since this book's inception, has gone to join in heaven the Christ he so clearly reflected to us on earth.*

# CONTENTS

# FOREWORD

KATHERINE WHALEY is of the company of scripture lovers who, rather than using the Bible simply as a rich treasury of proof texts, ponder quietly, carefully, and deeply—all elements of prayer—the Old Testament Holy Writings as an infinite source of delight and enrichment as well as of pathos, unfaithfulness, and dereliction. In her case, I believe, this book became increasingly inevitable. Even with no contrived promptings of others, its telling of its stories in a fresh vocabulary of understanding bursts from her heart and lips in a manner that reflects the unmistakable authenticity of the original Author. She cannot do otherwise than share the treasure abounding in her own heart and mind.

The stories are for adults; some of them are definitely rated "PG," but as Katherine says, "They are surely to be shared with children, and really want reading aloud, and not in a 'stained glass voice.'"

Through the channels of her association with an Anglican Monastic community, I have been privileged to observe the radiance and inward rejoicing with which she spoke of these tales of fear and wonder, of the disciplined care necessary to preserve the accuracy of the Old Testament text, yet the inescapable manner in which they reflect unchanged human virtues and vices as old as the Garden of Eden, as new as tomorrow.

She once remarked that the emphasis of the stories is on the fact that, for example, only the accident of time kept David and Bathsheeba out of "Dear Abby." (II Samuel 11)

There is nothing of heavy foreboding or measured compulsion in these stories. The free-moving atmosphere is probably shaped by the fact that many of them impetuously unfolded as the attention of the narrator was lost in the creative beauty and intricacy of fashioning the stitches of holy vestments. Much, I should say, as the rugged elements of St. Paul's theology must have pressed upon him as he was about his tentmaking.

There are unforgettable moments of soaring beauty. One of them of characteristic delight is in her story of Creation. "Then in a moment of pure merriment, like a child throwing handfuls of confetti, God spangled his firmament with stars to finish his day's work."

Beneath these confections awaiting the reader there is nevertheless an inescapably sober consideration. A suspicion has grown in my mind through the years that as a consequence of the propriety of the Episcopal church at the dawn of the nineteenth century, insisting in the very First Article of Religion that: "There is but one living and True God, everlasting, WITHOUT BODY, PARTS, OR PASSIONS," the popular mind would absentmindedly assume that the people of the Bible, fashioned in the image of that God, would also be, to a degree, deprived of the same lively essentials. The result could only be the unhappy misfortune of having to labor to catch the fire of truth, of scripture, spelled out with a cast of strange, listless, and unemotional figures moved by some opaque compulsion, yet not quite daring to risk committing a full-blooded sin. The God of the Old Testament himself was manifestly unlike such creatures and would never be guilty of designing them.

No, the God whom Katherine came upon in her stories was of a gloriously massive stature, but he is quite willing to sit down on a hot day, and like a proper Jew, patiently bargain with Abraham over the fate of Sodom.

The effect of this little book of Bible stories is that under the hand of the lovely storyteller, the characters of the Old Testament, in an almost startling fashion, come alive and to a rewarding degree fulfill her stated intention: to make their characters as familiar and accessible as a next-door neighbor.

LINCOLN A. TAYLOR † O.H.C.

HOLY SAVIOUR PRIORY

PINEVILLE, SOUTH CAROLINA

# PREFACE

The stories in this book begin with the Creation story and continue through the reign of Solomon. They are told, as far as is possible, chronologically, and they are told as myth. The language and choice of material is aimed at adults, but many of them are appropriate to read with children. I want to share their delight with you and perhaps lead you to look again at the books of the Old Testament that are their source. (There is much more there. I haven't told it all, by any means!) To the devout Jew or Christian they are the saga of God's dealings with his people, but to *anyone* who loves a good story, they should be enthralling.

They are tales of people whose fascination is not in their difference from you and me but in their sameness. Even God in these ancient tales thinks a lot like other folks we know. He gets a kick out of making things and watching them work. He yearns for Adam's friendship. He is sad and angry when it goes wrong, but that doesn't stop his loving Adam and Eve all the same, and giving them gifts in their banishment.

The villains have good in them (Cain kills his brother, but in fatherly love builds a whole city to name after his son), and the virtuous men are imperfect (David spares Saul's life twice over, and then has Uriah killed so no one will discover that Bathsheeba, his wife, is bearing David's child).

The women are wonderfully various. Esther is lovely enough to seduce the king into saving her people from destruction. Leah is so plain Jacob rejects her and works an extra seven years to have her sister. Deborah is known for her wise judgments and Hagar taunts Sarai with her barrenness until she is driven out.

These are tales of adventure. God walks with men. Angels run messages. Rivers and seas part to make pathways. Kingdoms and champions rise and fall on the faith of a boy or the perfidy of a monarch. And through the whole story, like a scarlet thread, runs the love of the God who longs for his creation's response—who punishes or forgives, rewards or deprives. The details of the stories are retold with a fidelity to truth as it was seen by their first ancient tellers. The emotional responses are my own twentieth-century involvement with these people whose desires and fears seem hardly different from those I experience today. Where two versions of the same story exist (as in the creation accounts), I have combined elements of both with no attempt to reconcile the inconsistencies that are characteristic of myth. No attempt is made to pronounce on the "truth" of the tales. That is left to the reader.

My thanks to the people of Holy Trinity and St. John's Episcopal churches in Fayetteville, North Carolina, who have listened to these tales and laughed and wept. To the monastic community at Holy Saviour Priory of the Order of the Holy Cross for their nurture and encouragement. To my family, who has shown such interest and delight in this work as to convince me that I really *am* an author. To my husband, Frank, whose unshakable confidence kept me from chucking the whole affair every time I got a case of writer's cramp. To all these and God only knows how many more good folks, I owe this book. I offer it to them all with love and joy!

—KLW

# BEGINNINGS

# The Creation

ONCE UPON A TIME, before time (for God is not of time, but of eternity), there was God, and that was all. There was God and no other thing or creature or world or wisdom. Only, there was God. And God put forth wisdom and power and created a void, and darkness over the deep, and his spirit hovered over the water, and he called forth light. And God said, "I like that! I'll call it day!" and then, because he found his darkness lovely too, he named it night. The evening came, and the morning, and that was the very first day and the real beginning of once-upon-a-time.

The second day began, and God said, "I'll fashion an arch with waters above and waters below and I'll call it heaven." And seeing his day's work he was delighted. The third day he separated the waters below his vault and called them seas, and the dry part he called Earth, and he rejoiced, "I've made myself a world; and I think I'd like some green things on it; something alive and growing!" and with a flourish he added a wonderful touch. "These are so good," said God, "that I'll fix it so they happen over and over," and he gave each growing thing its own seed, and the day ended with his rejoicing in it.

You may well have noticed by now that none of these days *dawned*, but the fourth day God said, "My earth needs warmth and light and joy for all the creatures I'm putting there," and he set the sun in the heavens to make his day glad and golden. "Still," said he, "I love my night, and it should be dressed with no less splendor," and he hung the cool, soft moon. Then in a moment of pure, holy merriment, like a child throwing handfuls of confetti, God spangled his firmament with stars to finish his day's work.

Now, green things and plants are lovely enough and all very good in their own way, but God suddenly had a longing to make things that would swim and fly and creep and crawl and croak and sing. He began his fourth day filling his sea with whales and whelks, with abalones and octopi, with all manner of things that swim and float and flourish in the deep salt sea. Then he turned to his skies and created eagles and egrets and robins and rooks, and then he thought to himself that it would be marvelous to have creatures that belonged to *both* water and air, and he created all manner of waterfowl. Last of all that long day's work he created the songbirds, teaching the lark to rise toward the sun on the ecstasy of her song and the nightingale to haunt the night with liquid loveliness, and he saw that it was good, so he blessed them all and said, "You too shall have life and procreate with me like the green growing things."

The next day God filled the earth with all manner of delights—tiny green chameleons and big gray mastodons and every other sort of thing that creeps or crawls or walks or runs or skitters or scampers, and to each he said, "Bring forth! Multiply in your own kind and cover the face of my earth with life." And so he ended the fifth day.

God began the sixth day in a thoughtful mood. He looked on all his good creation and was glad, but it seemed to him it wanted something more to make it complete. God watched and pondered and then he said "I know! I want something capable of loving as I love! Someone to be my friend!" So God created Adam in his own image. With his own hands he took the dust of the earth and molded it into his very special creature, and he breathed his own breath into Adam, and called him "man."

Now, after God created Eve (but that and what came of it is another story), he looked at his whole world and found it very good. Then God spent the seventh day in peace and joy, resting from his work and contemplating with delight all that he had made, so ever since, that day is set aside as holy and blessed!

# Eve's Temptation

GOD WANTED TO MAKE a very special place for the man he had created to be his friend, so he planned and planted a garden for Adam to live in, with all manner of luscious fruits and succulent herbs, and he set Adam there to be a gardener of it and enjoy the fruit. "Only, Adam," said God, "there's one small thing I ask of you." "Of course, God," said Adam. "What's that?" "See those two tall, glittering trees right there on that little hill at the garden's center?" "Yes, God, I surely do, and they're really splendid!" "So they are, Adam, so they are! But listen, those two trees I reserve for myself! All the rest I give you, but if you eat from those, you will most surely die."

God sounded really serious, and Adam couldn't see that he needed that particular fruit anyway, and so he readily agreed. And God said, "*Good*, Adam, that's the way a friend should be! And now, how about another friend for you? One to love and help you all the time when I'm not always close by?" That sounded fine to Adam, and presently there began a real parade of God's marvelous menagerie. Each animal in Eden was brought to Adam to be admired and named and each time God showed him a new one, Adam would say, "Yes, that's *nice*, God, that's really clever." But each one lacked something. The cat was cozy and soft, but too small to be much help; besides, just as he was patting it, the cat took off after a mouse.

The horse whinnied and nuzzled him with its velvet nose, but it was such a big, angular beast and it flicked its tail and galloped off.

The dog took Adam's fancy especially, and he must have spent the better part of a day frolicking with it and scratching behind its ears, but then when he'd try to talk with it as he did with God, it would wag its tail and make that odd sharp noise that Adam came to call barking, and finally Adam tired of that too.

After Adam had seen and admired and named all the animals and all had been not quite what was wanted, God said, "I'll tell you what, Adam. Why don't you take a little nap and let me think on it some. You need a help really right for you."

So Adam curled up under the tree of knowledge and God made him fall into a deep sleep from which only God himself could waken him.

While Adam lay sleeping, God took one of his rib bones (and to this day, menfolks are short one rib). God took that rib bone, and out of it he made a woman—the prettiest, softest, brightest-eyed little creature you ever *saw*, and the first thing she did was *laugh*, and the second thing she did was begin to chatter! And God smiled and he said, "That's good! But hush, child! I've lifted my sleep and you'll wake Adam." But it was really too late. Adam rolled over there on the soft grass, and he looked up and saw God holding Eve by the hand. By now Eve was quiet, like a girl will be when she's about to meet someone she very much wants to have like her, and when Adam stood up, God put her hands in his. Adam took one look down into her lovely face with the eyes lowered demurely, and he ran a wondering finger across her smooth, round cheek, and then he burst out, "Oh, God, she's beautiful! This, at last, is bone from my bones and flesh from my flesh! I'll call her 'woman' because she is truly a part of me." (And ever since that time, this is how it has been when God joins a man and a woman.)

Adam and Eve lived together in the garden in great joy, and God used to come and walk with them sometimes, and take delight in that friendship. All went well until one day when Adam had gone for a run with Dog to a far part of the garden and Eve decided she'd rather sit under the tree of knowledge and enjoy its fragrant shade. It was her favorite spot in the garden because here God had first put her hands in Adam's.

As the sun grew hot, toward midday, Eve became half drowsy in the heat, and she hardly noticed that Serpent had come walking down the tree trunk (for you must know that at the start, Serpent walked on legs like the other creatures). She gave a little scream when his cool skin touched her hand; not out of fear—for that emotion was unknown to her—but because he was so very cool against her fingers, and *such* a bright yellow-green. "Oh, Serpent! You startled me!" "It's almost lunchtime, Eve. How come you're sitting here half asleep? Shall I run up and drop some fruit for you?" "Oh no, Serpent! Not from this tree. Adam says God told him we mustn't eat this fruit… or… what *was* it he said would happen?!" Old Serpent chuckled condescendingly. "I suppose he said you would die of it, Eve. Was that it?" Eve was relieved he'd remembered it. "Yes, that was it, Serpent, that was it exactly! He said we were not to eat it or even *touch* it on pain of death!"

Serpent got that look on his face you always hated on your older brother's when he was about to tell you just how dumb you were, and he said, "*Honestly*, Eve!" and Eve said defensively, "Well, he *did*!" And Serpent said, "Do you really believe that, Eve, you little ninny? You're not really very old yet, you know, whereas *I* who am much older and more experienced can tell you, God is simply being sneaky! *He* knows if you eat that fruit your eyes will be opened and you will know good and evil and you will be like gods yourselves! All that nonsense about dying is simply scare tactics!"

Now, the serpent wasn't all that much older than Eve, if she'd stopped to think about it, and she might just have wondered how *he* knew so much about God, but Eve panicked and she said, "Do you really think so? Is that a good thing? To know all about good and… and…" "Evil!" said Serpent. "Good and evil! And of course it's good! Just think how much more fascinating you would be to Adam if you knew all that! And why do you suppose he goes off and leaves you all alone like this? He's losing interest!"

If Eve had thought a minute she would have seen through this just as easily as you do, but Eve was rattled! She didn't even notice that Serpent had scurried back up the tree and was peering at her from the lowest branch. That's why it seemed so fortuitous when one of those lovely reddish-gold fruits fell right in her lap. Almost as if it were meant to happen. I wasn't there, and maybe I'm giving the serpent a worse name than he deserves, but the fruit had never fallen off that tree before. Eve didn't think of that either. She just closed her hand around that perfect, fragrant fruit and took a big bite. It was delicious!

# The Fall

EVE ATE SLOWLY AT FIRST, savoring the taste of the forbidden fruit. It *was* delicious, but it had an odd, bitter aftertaste, as if … Just then Adam came up.

"Eve! *What are you eating?*" he cried in horror.

But the fruit had begun to have its effect on Eve and she had a heady feeling of power, so instead of bursting into tears as she might have done earlier that day, Eve pursed her lips in a pretty pout and curved an arm around Adam's neck and coaxed: "*Try* it Adam, it's—it's good!" She pressed the half-eaten fruit against his lips. So Adam ate a bite too, and then he reached for another fruit and another, and they both gobbled that fruit as if they'd never stop (and ever since, men have been greedy for knowledge without considering its consequences). But even in Eden there was a limit to how much you could stuff in, and at last they stopped their eating. Eve daintily licked the last of the juice off her fingers and for the first time since she began to eat looked—I mean really *looked*—at Adam, and found him looking back at her with the strangest look on his face. He looked as if there was something, well, not *nice* about her, for with the eating of that proscribed fruit, shame had entered the garden in all its ugliness. Without a word, they sneaked off into the nearest thicket and found the largest leaves they could lay hands on and began to cover their bodies to hide them from each other.

The rest of the day they simply avoided each other. It wasn't like it had always been before, and there was no joy in being together. But that evening, when God came to walk in the garden's coolness, as he often did, by common consent they hid in the deepest thicket clutching each other's hands guiltily.

Presently, as he walked, God called, "Adam! Adam, my friend, where are you?" and Adam slunk out of the bushes to face God. He'd

7

always loved God's presence before, but now… God said, "Adam?" And Adam said, "I heard you, God. I knew you were here, but I was afraid because I am naked, and so I hid." And God said, "You're *what*?!""Naked," said Adam, "You know…""Adam!" said God. "Where did you learn *that*?" Adam just looked shamefaced and squiggled one toe in the dust. "Adam, have you eaten the fruit you promised not to?" God's voice was stern and sad.

"I… I…" Adam felt *awful* and then he thought, "It's all *her* fault! I'd never have—" and so he said, "God, it wasn't *my* fault. It was that woman you gave me. She tempted me and—well, she's absolutely irresistible and so I ate it!"

By this time Eve had come out of her hiding place and God just gave her one sharp, sorry look and said, "Well?"

And Eve said, "It wasn't *my* fault. Serpent got me all confused, and he *is* older than I am, and he made fun of me and—well, yes, I ate it."

"Serpent!" called the Lord God in a voice like cold stone. And Serpent slithered down the tree on his belly, all his lovely delicate legs *gone*. And God said, "That's how it's going to be from now on, Serpent, and Eve's offspring will be your implacable enemies, where you might have lived together in mutual kindness, and you and all your brood will hate and attack them in return."

And to Eve he said, "You will have children in pain, and you will long for your husband, but there will not be the loving understanding between you that there was before, and he will seem hard and distant and heavy-handed to you."

Finally God turned to Adam. "Because you have listened to the woman and broken your promise, our friendship can never be quite the same, and now I must protect my other tree from you, so you can't live in my garden any more. Food will come hard for you now, and you will sweat and labor until you die and your body returns to the dust from which I made it." Then the Lord God made clothes of skins for Adam and Eve, for he loved them still, but he banished them from his garden and put cherubim with flaming swords at the gate to secure the tree of life. So Adam no longer walked with God as friend with friend.

# Cain and Abel

WHEN ADAM AND EVE first wandered out from the garden, what held them together mostly was raw fear. In the garden they had lived in such innocence that they didn't even have a *word* for danger, but now every beast and sound was a potential enemy. Darkness brought no rest because it was haunted with fears, and daylight brought scorching sun or chilling rain to add to the misery of trying to find food. For a time that's all there was to existence and it was bitter— bitter as the aftertaste of that fruit. Finally Adam remembered something. In the first flush of the new knowledge gained from eating the fruit (for knowledge is, of itself, good), he had looked at the woman and named her Eve (the mother of all living things). Now, as he watched her deft hands plucking berries from the bramble he noticed, again, the enchanting curve of cheek and breast and thigh, and when she tore a finger on the thorns and cried out in pain, for the first time since they were turned out of the garden, Adam thought of someone besides himself. He put his arms around Eve to comfort her, and as she turned her body against him, the hurt was forgotten and that aching desire for each other which was one of God's special gifts overwhelmed them, and like all their fellow creatures, they rejoiced in the act of procreation.

They watched Eve's body bloom and swell with their child, and in the wonder of it their exile became a little less bitter. Finally the day of Cain's birth came, and Eve, holding her firstborn to her breast, exulted, "I have got a man with God's help!" And Adam, watching her, felt his heart strangely moved at God's gift. It seemed, somehow, to bring God's friendship back a little. Presently Eve conceived a second time, and they called the second son Abel.

You know how fast children grow up, and it seemed no time at all until the boys were old enough to take a man's place in the world.

9

Abel became a shepherd and Cain a gardener, raising food for the family by tilling the soil. The garden of Eden seemed almost a dream now, but Adam and Eve took care to teach their sons of God's friendship. That's why, one day, Cain and Abel decided that it was high time they themselves approach God in their own right, so they built an altar and Cain brought some of his new grape crop and some mighty fine turnips and squash and a lovely russet pomegranate and laid it on God's altar. After he stepped back, Abel laid down the firstborn of his flock—the whole of it—even the fat, which was considered particularly special.

I don't know what the problem was—whether Cain had held back his best fruits or whether he really didn't honor God, but only went through the motions, or whether a brother's rankling envy of a younger brother marred his gift, but God *did* know, and God rejected Cain's offering but he received Abel's cordially.

Cain was simply furious! Ever since Abel had been born he had been the fair-haired boy! Mother always babied him and Dad gave him lighter tasks because he was the youngest and now even *God* was surely playing favorites! That's how it looked to the sulking Cain, anyway, and he simply refused to hear God's admonition that if he would just settle down and resist the temptation to jealousy he could master it and be as secure as his brother.

Not only did Cain not struggle with his evil desire, he nursed his grudge and plotted until they were alone together, and then he said, "Come on Abel, let's walk out and see how my barley crop is doing." And the unsuspecting Abel trailed good-naturedly along until they were well out of sight or possibility of discovery. Cain had always been the stronger of the two when they tussled as boys, and besides, Abel had no idea he needed to defend himself, and it wasn't a minute's work for Cain to knock him unconscious with a heavy boulder and cut his throat like a sheep's so that his lifeblood flowed into the ground. Last of all, he scrabbled a hole in the soft earth at the edge of the barley field and hid his brother's body.

After he'd killed Abel, Cain went on home. When his mother asked about Abel later that day, Cain, who had always been taciturn, grunted something about not being his wet nurse and went out to hoe in his garden. God wasn't so easy to deal with, though, and when he asked, "Cain, where is your brother?" Cain tried the same tack. "How should *I* know? Am I my brother's guardian? After all, God, he's a grown man and surely can take care of himself."

But God wasn't put off as his mother had been, and he said, "Cain, what have you done? Do you think I can't hear your brother's blood crying out to me from the ground where you spilled it? Surely I who give life know when it is taken away!"

Cain hung his head, speechless, and God continued, "The ground that has been your joy and your livelihood shall be accursed to you for your brother's sake. When you cultivate it, it won't produce for you, and you shall be a wanderer over the face of the earth, and a fugitive."

Looking down the length of the life ahead of him and both desiring and hating it, Cain cried, "God, I can't bear the weight of my doom! See, you drive me from home and kindred and from the sight of your own face, and whoever finds me will surely kill me!"

So God took pity on Cain and put a mark on him, saying, "If anyone kills Cain, sevenfold vengeance shall be taken for him." But the sentence of banishment remained, and Cain left God's presence to settle in the land of Nod, east of Eden.

# Adam's Descendants

WHEN CAIN WENT OUT to live in the land of Nod, the place was awfully empty. Eve grieved for her son Abel's death, but Cain's departure was a constant sore spot in her heart. Dead is *dead*, and one learns, however unwillingly, to accept finalities, but as long as a woman lives, and knows her child to be alive, she will yearn toward him. Was he hungry? Did he have clothes to wear? Was the misery of his loneliness more than he could bear? And it was so quiet around home with both boys gone. The lines deepened in Adam's face and he was short-spoken and kept to himself a lot, grieving in his own way; but Eve was inconsolable.

Finally God stepped in. Eve could hardly believe it, and she hugged it to herself secretly lest she somehow should have mistaken the signs, but somewhere around five months along, when her body began to swell with it unmistakably, Eve said, "Adam, how would you like another son?" and she laid his hand against the bulge and smiled.

Ten years slipped off Adam's face and *he* smiled for the first time since Cain's furtive leave-taking. The expectation of this child was like spring at the end of that first winter when they had almost given up on the hope of seeing blossom or fruit again.

Eve still thought of Abel and she still fretted about Cain, but more and more her thoughts turned to the child she carried in her womb, and when he was born, she said, "God has granted me a son to replace Abel whom Cain killed!" She called him Seth, and he was dearer to Adam than life. When Seth grew tall, he too had sons and daughters, and the house was merry again with the sounds of children's voices. Eve never forgot her other sons, but she took comfort in Seth and his brood.

Cain may have had it hard at first, but by the time we take up his story again, he too has a wife and a son called Enoch, and has taken up the contracting business. He has, in fact, built a whole town and named it after Enoch. He too lived to see his children's children, and some of them were real "chips off the old block." One in particular was called Lamech. Lamech married himself two wives at once (which was considered acceptable at that point); when we meet him he is bragging to his wives that he killed a man for wounding him and a boy for striking him and while the vengeance for killing his ancestor Cain was to be sevenfold, if anyone lays a hand on *him* vengeance will be seventy-sevenfold. Nice guy, Lamech, and undoubtedly of the blood of the sulky and hot-tempered Cain.

All Cain's progeny were builders, and I suppose it was bound to happen, sooner or later. As the generations advanced, they built larger and larger cities, and wickedness flourished until finally God got fed up with it and flooded the whole thing out (but that's another story).

Even after the flood, the survivors still had this urge to build and clump together, and they laid plans, finally, for the city to end *all* cities. It was to have, among other modern delights, a tower that would "reach all the way to heaven." One of the big selling points for this city was that it would really get all mankind organized and confirm their power and invulnerability for all time. No one seems to have given God much thought in the matter, and that was their mistake.

God came down to inspect this town and tower. After all, he could appreciate creativity. That was right in his line. But the longer he looked, the less he liked what he saw. God went back to his heaven and thought it over and he said, "Mankind is at it again! They are right back in the 'greed and grab' business I had to throw them out of Eden for. If they wanted to reach heaven to be my friends I might just let them, but they've forgotten me altogether. They only want power and more power, and that's got to be stopped."

God had already wiped out mankind once with his flood, and he had decided then that he never meant to do that again, so this time, chuckling at the idea, he invented a new subtlety. Next day when the workmen all got together at the tower, each heard strange sounds from the others' mouths, and each shouted at the other for talking nonsense. The louder they shouted, the less it helped; and finally they threw their tools down in disgust and scattered. To this day, the children of men speak many and diverse tongues, and even when they speak the same one, nations rarely understand one another, and the Lord God settled back in his heaven to wait for his mankind to grow up.

# Noah and the Ark

I MEAN TO TELL YOU, the world was in a *mess*. The flocks were being stolen in the fields. It wasn't safe to walk out alone at night. Babies died of starvation in the public paths, and gangs of sharp-faced, hungry children made swift raids on fruit orchards and grain fields. It was all the *war,* said the graybeards—all that money going into arrows and spears, and so many young men being killed and leaving widows and orphans. No, said the others, it was this generation's youth. They were always wanting more (a wild, greedy lot), and all they could think of was drinking parties and clothes and sex. (And they sighed righteously as they settled their fat paunches a little more comfortably and took another sip of wine or popped another honeyed almond in their mouths.) The kids said it was the way their elders had loused up the world, and what could *they* do with such a mess, and the young men went out to find "meaningful relationships," much as their fathers before them had made concubines of the prettiest of their slaves.

It was a mess, all right, and God, looking it over, thought so too. He didn't talk much about whose fault it was. God just said, "It's *got* to go! I never intended this stinking mess when I made men a present of my world, and I won't have it." So God came to see his friend Noah. Noah lived out a ways from the city with his wife and three sons and their three wives—kind of out on the edge of the desert, it was. The grazing wasn't as good as down in the valley where the cities were, but it was quiet, and a man could raise a decent family, and Noah had done just that. He had a few grapevines under cultivation for his own wine and raised enough barley for bread, and what with goats for milk and cheese, it wasn't a bad life. Then God said, "Noah, build me a boat," and Noah, who was always ready to do what God asked, said, "Sure, Lord—whatever you say, I'll... a *what*?" And God said, "*Boat*, Noah, a *big* one. Three decks, so you can carry enough food for the livestock and yourselves. Since you haven't had much experience as a shipwright, here are the plans."

"But Lord," pleaded Noah, "that's *crazy*! There's nowhere within ten days' journey of here where you could sail anything that size." And God said grimly, "There *will* be, Noah. Just get going on it and stop puttering with those grapes. They're going to be under a couple thousand feet of water before they ripen. You might pack a few cuttings, though. This earth is *bad news*, and you and I are going to start over!"

Noah still couldn't imagine the whole thing, but he called the boys to start building, and told the women to get the food in shape to be stored. They killed all but their best breeding stock, and salted and smoked the meat and tanned the leather, and the girls spun the sheep's wool into great skeins of yarn. They pickled and salted and preserved everything that was ready, and one day they put all of it in the ark—that great pitch-smeared monstrosity sitting there in the middle of that dry plain. Then the animals came in, more than could possibly fit, but somehow they did—I guess God must have taken care of that.

Finally, God said, "Now, Noah! It is time!" And the eight men and women who lived in that lonely place trudged through that door into the dark, crowded hold of the boat, and God shut the door. No more free sight of the sky or open space—just the cramped little upper deck room and the uneasy sounds animals make before a storm. There was a crack of lightning and an earthshaking roll of thunder and the skies opened. When they told it later to their children's children, they were to say that even the deeps under the earth rose up to aid that mighty flood. The queer half-light of the storm through the small window holes faded into a night of such blackness you could hardly *breathe* in it. They clung together in silence.

Sometime that seemed like three days later, the ark began to move uneasily, as if it were coming to life, and by the time the black gave way to the leaden gray of a new day, they were afloat on a sea of water where the south meadow had been, and away to the east Mount Moriah swam up out of the desolate waste and the water poured like doom. No wind, no lightning now, or thunder, just a sheet of relentless buffeting rain. Well, Mrs. Noah stirred herself, being a practical woman, and said, "Boys, if you'll just see to the animals and bring up some fresh milk for us, we will make shift to fix some breakfast." And she began bustling serenely around as if she were cooking in her own tent again, and so began that first of many long, slow days during which the family talked and quarreled and prayed and worked at what they could find to do and occasionally peered out at that inexorable rain. There were some different days.

There was the black early morning forty days (by the careful notches Noah carved in the cabin door to keep track) after they had embarked when Shem's firstborn came squalling lustily into the world by the light of a carefully held oil lamp. And as they watched the marvel of his firm round body and touched his tightly clenched fists, somebody noticed that morning was somehow different. It was *still*; deafeningly still. The sky was still lead gray, but there wasn't a drop of water falling.

Then there was the night the boat began to rock gently in a rising wind, and day dawned clear with all the clouds blown from the sky and they knew God was starting to dry up the waters. But that was no ten-minute job! And month followed month in the same routine. Shem Jr. was up on his hands and knees rocking and all but ready to crawl when Ham's little girl was born. That was the week they sent the raven out to see if there was dry land, and he never came back. Then Japheth's wife took sick and lay with her face to the wall and grieved, and Mrs. Noah muttered that the child needed air and sunshine and quiet, and Mrs. Shem took it as an insult to her son's lusty cries. There was a real family row and the menfolks went on down to sit with the animals, and Noah released the dove in hope. She came back, though, and he took her in quietly without telling what he'd done, and waited another week.

Mrs. Japheth got thinner, and paler, but the next time the dove brought in a green leaf, and Noah bent over and put it in her hand. Her thin face lighted with joy, and she put the leaf tenderly in the chubby fist of small Ham, who crawled up just then; turning, she fell

17

peacefully asleep. One more week they waited and released the dove again. She never came back, and everyone said, "When?" And Noah said, "Wait! God will say when."

The next week God *did*. He opened the ark, I guess, just as he had closed it, and animals and people, out they came. And Japheth's wife, leaning weakly on him, raised her face to the sun, and young Ham wiggled to be put down to explore. Noah got a smug look on his face and, pulling from his belt a small cutting, bent down to plant his first grapevine. The boys stood solemnly round, watching him, but Mrs. Noah, practical as always, said, "Girls, if we were to set up right over there, that flat stone would make a grand place for the cook fire. Boys, don't let those goats wander too far! I'll want some milk for the cooking! Japheth, that girl's stood long enough!" And God, looking things over, stretched his rainbow between earth and heaven, "Because," said he, "it'll remind me I never mean to treat my people so again."

# ABRAHAM STORIES

# God Calls Abram

IN THE LINE OF SHEM, the oldest son of Noah, there was a man called Terah. He lived in the city of Ur among the Chaldeans, and there he raised his family. When he was well on in years, having three grown sons, his third son died, leaving one child. Soon after, Terah decided to leave Ur and move to the land of Canaan. His second son Nahor stayed there in Ur, but Abram, his firstborn, and Lot, his grandson, he took with him.

It was a long move to Canaan for a household with all its cattle and household goods and servants, so they began it by easy stages. They moved, first, north and west to Haran to skirt the desert. When the household reached Haran it became clear that Terah's strength was failing; Abram coaxed, "Father, settle here a while and regain your strength. Canaan will be there when you are ready to travel on."

Whether Terah knew his end was near or whether he really believed he would go on, I can't say, but they buried him there in Haran, and when the household set out for Canaan Abram was its head. Abram was seventy-five years old when God spoke to him and said, "It's time to move on now! Leave your father's house and I will show you the land I am giving your descendants. I will bless anyone who helps you and curse anyone who gets in your way, so obviously that for all time to come, the name of Abram shall be used as a blessing."

Once again the household packed up all its belongings—clothes and kettles and tents and treasures. Once again the servants and cattle and sheep and goats moved in a noisy procession away from the city toward Canaan. Abram's family consisted of Lot, his young nephew, and Sarai, Abram's wife, and she was barren.

There was an ancient tree at Moreh, and as Abram traveled he reached that place, and God came to him again and said, "This is it, Abram. This whole land will belong to your descendants!" And Abram said, "That's nice, God. But if you don't mind I don't think I'll fight this many Canaanites for it!" So he set up an altar to God there, but he kept on moving.

For quite a few years, that seems to have been the story of his life. As his flocks increased, so did the need for water and pasture, and he moved to find them.

Finally there was a terrible year. Everything dried up in the Negeb where he was pasturing his flocks, and Abram determined to move down to Egypt. Before he moved into that populous and organized kingdom, Abram made one quiet arrangement.

Sarai may have been a disappointment as far as producing heirs was concerned, but she must have been incredibly lovely to look at, and Abram was no fool! A widow is fair game, and easily made if her husband is a stranger in your land. "Sarai," said he, "just do me one little favor. When anyone asks, you're my *sister*. No need to say we're married, and then when this pesky drought is over, we'll slip away and be no worse off for it."

Sarai did as she was told, and it wasn't long before the pharaoh was loading Abram with gifts. Before anything could be done to stop him, he had whisked Sarai away to his palace. God was *not* pleased!

Not only was God not pleased, but he took a swift and nasty vengeance on Pharaoh. The whole house of the Pharaoh was stricken with plague, and all females, both human and animal, were made barren. Pharaoh got the point, and he said, "Get me Abram here and get him fast!"

When the messengers brought Abram into Pharaoh's court he said, "Abram, what is this? You've played a dirty trick on me if ever I saw one. You told me Sarai was your sister and let me take her for my wife, and now God's mad at me and taking it out on my whole household!"

Abram stood on his two feet and told the truth. What else could he do? "I was scared!" said he. "I figured Sarai was too lovely to go unnoticed, and I knew you had an eye for a pretty woman and I was afraid you'd kill me to get her. Besides, it wasn't really untrue, what I said. Sarai and I did have the same father."

21

God must surely have softened Pharaoh's heart, and it just may be that Pharaoh was honest enough to admit to himself that he would have done exactly what Abram had said. Be that as it may, he gave Sarai back to Abram and told him to pack up and get out of there, and he sent some men along to see that Abram did it.

God lifted the plague from Pharaoh's house, and Abram headed north. As they reached Bethel and pitched camp, a brawl broke out between Abram's herdsmen and those of Lot (who by now had a big household of his own). Abram looked at their huge company and realized that no area would support both of them. Calling Lot to him, he said, "We are of the same blood, and it's wrong to have our households quarrel. Let's part now in peace before this gets serious."

Abram and Lot walked out together and surveyed the land, and Abram said, "You take your choice, Lot. If you go left, I'll go right. If you go right, the left is fine by me."

Lot looked down into the valley of the Jordan River. It was rich and green and fertile, and Lot said, "That's for me! I've had my fill of running from the drought!" So Lot went to settle by the wicked cities of Sodom and Gomorrah in the valley that looked like Eden. God said to Abram, "Come! I'll show you the whole of the length and breadth of the land I'm giving your descendants." So Abram packed his tents and moved family and flocks and herds once more to settle at the Oak of Mamre at Hebron, and he built God another altar there and settled, for a time, to live in peace.

# Hagar and Sarai

SARAI, AT SEVENTY, WAS a reasonably contented woman. Life was good, other than that silly affair when Abram had played the coward and told the Egyptian king she was "just" his sister (not mentioning that his half sister was also his wife). He nearly let the king take her for *his* wife (figuring he would take her anyway, by force). Well, other than that little affair, Abram had been very good to her. She was a rich woman, well fed, beautifully clothed, and waited on by a personal slave. It had been quite a while since they'd pulled up tent stakes to junket off to a new land, and with that irritating nephew, Lot, away off down in the plain, things were altogether prosperous and peaceful. There was just one fly in the ointment, and Sarai's eyes darkened with pain and the deep furrow came between them when she thought of it. Sarai was childless and beyond any hope of bearing children, and Abram, for whatever reason, had taken no other wives. He never spoke of it much to her, being a kind man, but she knew his longing for an heir.

For the hundredth time, Sarai thought again of the solution practiced by so many. It didn't seem quite right, and yet a man needed sons, and if not sons of *her* flesh, then very close to that were reckoned the sons of a slave who belonged to her mistress, body and soul. Suddenly, with a surge of real love for this husband of so many years, Sarai looked up at him and said, "Abram, you need sons!" Now this was no news to him, but for Sarai to say it certainly was news. What on earth was the woman getting at? But he hadn't lived with her this many years without knowing that when she spoke she had something to say, so he just nodded and watched her determined face. Beautiful still, he thought, with her dark eyes alight and the proud set of her head, and still slim and erect as a girl. Then, taking a deep breath and clenching her hands under the folds of her garment, she said, "Take Hagar, Abram. She's young and healthy and..."

"Do *what?*" said Abram. "Sarai, what on earth...?"

Somehow, now that it was said, it became easier to rush on.

"I never could give you a son, Abram, and I wanted to so badly, and now I'm too old, and if *you* wait too long... who knows? But if you were to lie with Hagar and beget a son, it would be a little like mine, Abram, wouldn't it?" Abram went out and thought it over and the idea grew on him. A son! An heir to his wealth! And if Sarai *really* wanted it that way... So Abram followed her suggestion and, as predicted, the healthy young Egyptian slave became pregnant almost immediately. Abram felt like he had a new lease on life, but Sarai was suddenly sick to think of it.

Now she had meant well in suggesting it, and she really wanted it for *Abram*, but that witch of a Hagar knew just how to twist the knife:

"I have to be careful how I lift that, lady, I'm *pregnant*, you know!"

"Look how *big* he grows in me, *my son*, and just last night I felt him move!"

"When *my* son is born, perhaps my Lord Abram will set me free. I might even bear him several more!"

Sarai was miserable and angry with herself for being jealous, and that only increased the problem. Perhaps Abram *would* favor Hagar now. Perhaps she, in her age, would be simply forgotten. So she got irritable and touchy and the once-proud head drooped and her eyes dulled until Abram said, "Sarai, what in tarnation ails you? Why can't you be as happy as I am?" And Sarai burst out, "I'll tell you why I'm not happy. Ever since I gave you Hagar to bear you a child and she got pregnant she's been insufferable! She despises me and gloats over me; and after I, myself, gave her to you, you've let her behave like that to me, and I'm so *mad...*" and tears spilled over from her dark eyes as she ended, "The Lord judge which is right, you or me!"

Now that last was maybe a bit dirty, because Abram was pretty sensitive to what God thought. On the other hand, the fact that he hadn't ruled his household too wisely hit home and rankled a bit, so Abram snapped, "Very well, she was your slave and yours she remains to deal with. Do what you damn please with her." And he stalked out of the tent.

Sarai knew she'd angered Abram, but she also knew that she just couldn't live with this mess any longer, and now Hagar paid twice over for every jibe and every haughty look. The hardest jobs fell to her lot, and Sarai was swift to rebuke and seemed to take pleasure in humiliating her. One day Hagar, grown clumsy in her advancing pregnancy, stumbled against her mistress's favorite piece of pottery, and Sarai's slap left her half-dizzy with its strength, and when she shrieked at Hagar, "Child of a dog, leave my sight and never return!" Hagar stumbled out of the tent and kept on walking, meaning to do *just* that.

Down the way, toward the setting sun, was the little town of Shur; Hagar, realizing that she would have to beg food and shelter soon, headed in that direction. But it was hot, and she was too heavy to walk swiftly, and so the day was nearly spent when Hagar stopped near the well on the way, to drink and rest. Bone weary, hot, no longer supported by her flash of anger at Sarai, Hagar huddled there under the couple of scraggly trees that shaded the place. She'd never been more alone in her life, and she felt like curling up and dying right there. Then, unbelievably, an angel of the Lord stood there, a messenger from Abram's God, and he said: "Hagar, slave of Sarai, where are you going?" And Hagar stammered, "I... I'm running away from my mistress because..." and the angel said, "Yes, yes, I know, but that won't do. You're bearing Abram's son, and you need to go back. You'll still have to be Sarai's slave, but I'll give you so many descendants that no one will be able to count them. By the way, when you have your son, call him Ishmael, because God has heard your cry of distress."

The angel was gone, and Hagar rose as if in a dream and headed for home. I guess by now Sarai was a little ashamed of herself, and Hagar told her tale and said, "Have I really seen God and lived to tell about it?" And she called Jehovah, ever after, "A God Who Sees," and so that particular well came to be known as "The Well of the Living One Who Sees Me." And true to God's promise, Hagar bore Abram a son, and called him Ishmael, which means "God hears."

# Isaac Promised

ABRAHAM WAS SITTING in front of his tent under the sacred trees of Mamre. It was just past lunchtime and he was digesting his noon meal and resting a little. He had closed his eyes against the shimmering heat of the day, when suddenly he heard voices. Abraham was certain there'd been no one there as far as the eye could reach just a moment ago, but there was now! There were three of them, and not his own men, but strangers dressed for traveling, just kind of standing there looking his way. Distances were long between places out here, and travelers were few; besides, Abraham was a hospitable man, so he got right to his feet and went out and bowed low and said how nice it was they'd come and they surely looked like they could use a rest and a cool drink, and maybe a little something to eat, and wouldn't they just sit right down in the shade and he'd see to it right away.

"Well," they said, "thanks a lot," that sounded great, and Abraham rushed right off to tell Sarah to bake some of her super-special cakes, and he chose a tender calf from the herd and had a servant set about dressing that for the meal. He brought out something to drink and water to wash up in and, in a shorter time than you might think, laid out quite a pleasant little feast. Those men ate with an appetite like they hadn't seen food for a week, and all the time Abraham went back and forth bringing more bread, pouring the wine, and urging another helping of meat on them. Finally, when they couldn't be persuaded to eat another thing, and the food and dishes were all cleared away, Abraham sat down again in the shade and said, "Friends, what's news in the places you come from?"

Then they asked an odd question: "Where's your wife, Sarah?" Abraham was a little puzzled, but he said, "Why, she's over there in the tent." (It was not, after all, usual or seemly for a *woman* to come out and sit with the menfolks.) One of them went on, just as if it were a usual conversation, "We'll be back this way in about a year, and Sarah will have a son by then. And your name shall no longer be called Abraham, but Abraham, because you will be the father of many nations. And your wife shall be called Sarah."

Now Sarah knew her place, and she had stayed modestly in the tent, but there was nothing that said a woman couldn't listen to anything she could lay an ear to, so she had her head right up to the door flap and was peeking through the crack and taking it all in when he said that. Sarah, mind you, was *old*. It had been a long time since she had stopped having monthly periods, and the idea that she should even take an interest in sex at *her* age struck her so funny she chuckled a little bit to herself there inside the tent. "Not only that," thought she, "but is an old man like my husband going to beget a son?" But Sarah wasn't the only one who could hear what she wasn't exactly meant to, and the Lord (because that's who one of these mysterious strangers really was) said to Abraham, "Why did Sarah laugh? Why did she say, 'Is this really possible that I should have a child at my age?' Can't God do anything?"

Sarah was scared! It was one thing to eavesdrop discreetly on the menfolks. It was another thing entirely to get caught doing so, and laughing at them in the bargain, and suddenly she was aware these were no ordinary men, so Sarah said, "Oh, no, not *me*—I didn't laugh! Surely not me!" But the Lord said, "You did too, Sarah, you laughed!" And Sarah stood there quaking, but that was all that was said. The men just got up and said they had to be on their way, and Abraham walked along with them a piece. A relieved and wondering Sarah stood at the tent door, watching.

"Are you traveling far?" said Abraham as they walked.

"No," said they, "just on over to Sodom." And Abraham said, "Oh, really? I've got a nephew down there; look him up. Lot's the name and tell him I said to take good care of you." By now they stood looking over the plain and the other two men went on, but the Lord and Abraham stopped there.

And the Lord thought, "I'd better tell Abraham what's up." So he said, "Abraham, I've heard terrible things about Sodom and

Gomorrah. The rumor of their evil deeds has reached clear up to heaven, and if things are as bad as they sound, this is no pleasure trip. I'm going to blast those people off the face of my earth."

Abraham stood there a little while in silence, remembering the young nephew who had grown up in his care. He wasn't a bad kid—a little flighty sometimes, maybe a little quick of temper, but not *bad*, not downright dirty-wicked like the Lord seemed to be talking about, and besides, Lot was still his kin. So Abraham took a deep breath and he said, "Lord, suppose—just suppose—there are, say, fifty people down there that are really good folks? You're not going to kill those fifty good, honest, decent folks just because the rest are stinkers, are you, Lord? Lord, this just isn't like you, to punish the innocent and the guilty alike. Lord, you're the judge of the earth, and you've *got* to be just, Lord. Surely, for those fifty you would save the city?"

And the Lord looked at Abraham, knowing already because he was the Lord, that the fifty weren't there, and he said, "For fifty, Abraham, I'll spare the whole city."

But even while he was saying it, Abraham began to have *his* doubts, so he said: "Lord, I know it's nervy of me to keep at you this way, but suppose only forty-five are found? Surely for that five you won't doom the rest?" And God said, "I won't destroy the city if I find forty-five." And Abraham said, "But forty? Lord, maybe there are only forty…""For only forty, Abraham, still I will spare it."

By now Abraham was beyond caution. "Thirty, Lord? Or twenty?" And to each, God replied: "For those I will hold my wrath if they be righteous."

And finally Abraham said, "Lord, I know I've been brash, and please don't be angry. Hear me just once more and I'll shut up. Suppose there are just *ten* men down there who aren't wicked. For those ten innocent men—?"

And the Lord smiled and he said, "Even for ten, Abraham, I will hold my hand." And the Lord went away, and Abraham walked slowly home with a niggling little foreboding of disaster in his mind. But *ten*! God *had* promised him, and surely in that whole city there must be ten decent men?

# Lot Entertains Angels

THE ANGELS LEFT ABRAHAM HAGGLING with God over the fate of Sodom and Gomorrah and proceeded down into the valley, and just as the long shadows of evening began to deepen and the quick desert night to draw near, they reached the gates of Sodom where Lot sat, of an evening, enjoying the coolness. They made as if to pass by, but Lot said, "Wait, there is room in my house, and welcome! You need to wash the dust from your feet and have a bite of supper and—well, to tell the truth, this isn't exactly a place that cares about strangers. You'll be much safer under my roof!"

So the angels acceded to Lot's urging, and he made them welcome. He and his family fixed a special supper, and then as they sat down to exchange news there was a sudden commotion outside, and someone began to beat on the door.

"What's that?" said the guests. "Sounds like a *riot* out there. My word, this *is* a violent city." And Lot said, "Don't worry! I'll— I'll see to it!"

But his face looked mighty grim, and the furrows of worry deepened around his eyes. Mrs. Lot looked scared to death, and she hustled the girls off into the back of the house, out of sight. (Before this tale is over, Lot comes off rather less than he might, but right at this point you have to admire the man's guts, for he stepped outside into that rowdy, drunken mob and closed the door firmly behind him.)

Lot was no innocent, and while he didn't care for his neighbors' moral code, up to now it hadn't affected him either way, and he could just kind of live and let live. But this time he found himself face-to-face with a very ugly demand. The shouts, drunken and jocular at first, became increasingly surly and threatening. This crowd proposed no less than a homosexual rape of the two strangers. Lot coaxed and pleaded. These were guests under his roof! What of the sacred duty of a host to protect them? Finally he even offered them his own daughters as a sort of ransom, but the crowd just got uglier, and that's when one of the ringleaders howled.

"This †*#& foreigner comes here among us on our turf and the S.O.B. *judges* us yet!" A second joined in:

"Let's treat the #*† worse than we do them!" And the whole male population of the town surged forward against this one lone man to tear his door down and wreak their vengeance on him and his. And Lot stood! The man *was* good. Against all possibility he was ready to die for those two strangers even if there was little hope of preserving them. But they had other ideas. They reached out and pulled him inside and slammed the door—but not before a strange thing had happened. The townsmen who had their hands almost on Lot suddenly staggered and clutched the air wildly and began to brawl and tangle with each other in utter confusion. Why, they couldn't even find the door of the place, and Lot, wiping the sweat from his face, thought he hadn't heard of such a thing since his grandfather's tale of the confusion of tongues at the tower of Babel! And he began to more than wonder who these strangers were who could rob men of their God-given faculties with a casual wave of the hand.

# Escape from Sodom

THE MEN OF SODOM HAVE GONE their way, swearing and stumbling. The silence of the night is almost eerie, and Lot's two guests reveal what he has suspected ever since they saved him from the mob. So these are angels—messengers of the Living God. His heart leaps at the knowledge that he has lived to see them, but now they begin urgently to unfold their errand. The stench of Sodom's wickedness has risen clear to heaven, and if it needed anything else, tonight really put the little tin lid on it!

"Have you other family not in the house?" they urge. "Sons-in-law? Sons? Anyone else? For your sake, we will save them too. Gather quickly all who are dear to you. At sunrise you must make haste to leave the city before we absolutely wipe out this blot on the landscape!"

"Daddy!" sobs his eldest daughter. "If we've *got* to go, how about the men you've betrothed us to?"

"Yes," chimes in his practical wife. "I don't suppose you'll find husbands for two daughters out there among the sticks and rocks of the wilderness, and they're already overly ripe for marriage."

The angels nod assent, and Lot slips out to find the two young men. By now they seem to have cooled off and sobered up some, and after all, you can hardly refuse to speak to your future father-in-law. The girls, if alien, were handsome wenches, and their dowries, it was rumored, were no mere pittance. So grudgingly, but politely, they let Lot in. They may have, by now, been feeling a little sheepish about their part in the earlier mob scene. For that matter, Lot seems to have forgotten it, because all he has to say is, "Come on! You've got to get out of this city with us. God is going to destroy it at daybreak!"

You'd think, after what had happened earlier, they might at least have listened. They were, after all, struck blind like the rest, but they

31

seem to have been struck deaf by now—or stupid. They simply look at Lot and clap each other on the shoulder and say, "This is a real *trip!* 'Get out of town,' he says! Who does he think his God is, anyhow? He isn't even one of our gods, and he's going to do us in, is he? That's a real laugh!"

And Lot, with a sinking heart, returns home with the news.

There isn't much left of that troubled night. The men talk quietly. The women scurry around packing twice what they can carry in small household treasures and then unpacking and rejecting and repacking. Finally dawn begins to show—a pale streak on the eastern horizon—and the angels say, "*Now,* Lot! Go!" But Lot hangs back and his wife wails and balks and the girls cling to their mother whimpering until finally the angels take them firmly by the hand like small children and lead them out of the city toward the desert.

"Now, run! Run for your lives to the mountains!" says the angel. "Run and *keep* running, and whatever you do, don't look back!"

But Lot, brave enough in the face of last night's hostility, feels suddenly old and bereft and *tired.* He remembers the long, hard years when he lived as a nomad in his uncle's tents. He has become used to security and a settled life in Sodom.

"I can't do it! I will simply *die* of it, and then where's the use in going at all?" he pleads. "Look, there's that little settlement out yonder! I could make that, and it's just a small place. I'd be safe there."

And the angel says "Okay, okay! I won't let the destruction come there, but hurry! *Run!* I can't do a thing until you get there."

So Lot and his household hastened off to the small town of Zoar. Just as the sun was rising they reached its refuge, and as they did, there was a rush of sound and a stench of hot sulfur behind them. Mrs. Lot turned full around to stare and was turned into a pillar of salt. Lot, bowing his head in horror, grabbed his two daughters and pulled them into shelter behind the nearest wall, and there they crouched while the whole fertile plain and the two cities on it were covered with what sounds to me like a volcanic eruption. Be that as it may, God destroyed the cities as he had promised, and when Abram, seeing the smoke and flames from a distance, came to look down on the valley, he saw only a smoking desolation where a fruitful plain had been. But Lot, according to God's promise to Abraham, lay safe in the small town which to this day is called Zoar, which sounds like the Hebrew word for *small*.

There's one more dismal detail to this story. The grieving Lot was afraid to stay even in that small city and so, taking his two marriageable daughters with him, he holed up in a cave in the mountains. As he drew more and more into himself, and the chance of ever getting out of there to civilization became more and more remote, the two girls began to become desperate. There were no homes and husbands—no children to carry on their father's name, no one to care whether they lived or died. So they agreed on a devious plan. Lot had become so depressed and careless that it was a simple matter to get him drunk of an evening, and after a few tries to make sure he really *was* stoned, they did what they knew would horrify him if he were in his right mind.

With calculated care, each lay with her father until she had conceived a child. In due time, each had a son, and that, says the story, is where the Moabites and Ammonites came from. It sounds a lot like an ethnic slur of the first water to me; nevertheless, that's how the book of Genesis records it.

# Isaac's Birth

SARAH WAS PREGNANT! No doubt of it at all! There had been the months of queasy mornings, and then she began actually to show with child, and now, at last, he had moved within her—and not just a feeble push or two, but good healthy kicks that left her gasping for breath and radiant with joy. And as Abraham watched anxiously, her body thickened and her step slowed, but her dark eyes glowed, and the lines on her face seemed like a thin disguise laid over the face of the beautiful girl he had married. Finally the day of birth came, and Abraham, like fathers since time out of mind, paced up and down and waited anxiously, with the extra weight of the knowledge that Sarah was really too old to bear a child, and yet, God had promised—yes, he *had* promised a son, but *had* he promised Sarah would be all right? And the women hurried into the tent and out again, distracted and uncommunicative, and Abraham waited. Finally there was the lusty yell of a newborn child, and Abraham was glad and scared all at once. Sarah? Then, just as the tent flap was pulled back to announce the birth of his son, Sarah's *laugh* rang out, and again, not the voice of an old woman, but the musical laughter of the girl he had married all those years ago. And he heard her gasp, "God has brought me joy and laughter! So much so that it will spill over to everyone who hears of it! They will all laugh with me and share my joy!" And she mused contentedly to her women, "Who would have said to Abraham now, 'Sarah shall nurse children,' yet *I* have borne him a son in his old age, yes, I *myself* have given Abraham a son!"

On the eighth day, when Abraham circumcised the child and gave him his name before God, remembering Sarah's joy he called his son Isaac, so that all his life he should bear the joyous name "he laughs."

For a long time things went smoothly in Abraham's tents, and Sarah's joy in her son was such that nothing troubled her. Finally the day came when Isaac was weaned; his father made a great feast in his honor, and somehow, after that, it seemed to Sarah her son wasn't quite as close to her. She began to watch jealously how things went with him, and one day the inevitable happened. Ishmael, the older half brother from Abraham's union with Sarah's slave, was playing with Isaac and, in brotherly fashion, he went too far and plagued the younger child to where he set up a howl for "Mama!" Sarah came flying to protect her treasured child, and Ishmael was cuffed soundly and sent off in disgrace. It didn't take any time at all before Sarah was after Abraham to get *rid* of that child.

"Isaac is your *real* son," she argued, "the one God promised. Ishmael is only a slave's child—almost a *mistake*, really, and he never should inherit with the true son of your marriage. Abraham, get him out of here! If you *love* me, *and* Isaac, you won't let him stay here and taunt us!"

Abraham was sick about it. Promises or no promises, Ishmael *was* his son, and as much his flesh and blood as Isaac was. He loved Sarah, but he also loved Ishmael, and the whole deal seemed shoddy! But God said, "Abraham, just do as Sarah says. She *is* right in one way. It is from Isaac I will give the descendants I promised. But I won't let harm come to Ishmael, who is also your son, and he too will be father of a great nation."

So Abraham gave Hagar food and water and put Ishmael on her back, and sent her away into the desert. Hagar walked a long way, and the days were hot and the child was heavy, and finally, somewhere into the second or third day, the water and food were gone and Hagar was hopelessly lost. There seemed no hope at all, and she laid Ishmael under the scant shade of a small bush and went off about a hundred paces and sat down. "For," she said, "I can't bear to watch him die." But she could still hear his fretful wailing, and she too began to weep. Then the angel of God spoke to her.

"Hagar, do not be discouraged, God hears you. Pick up your child and comfort him, because God means to make of him a great nation!" And as she wiped her eyes, she saw a well of water. Whether it had been there all the time and she had been too distracted to see it, or whether it was something more spectacular in the line of a miracle, I can't say, but Hagar hurried over and filled her water skin with the sweet, cool water, and they both drank and washed their faces. After that there was courage to go on, and they came to a place where there were people and food, and there we leave them, except for the fact that years later when Ishmael had grown to be a tall young man and a skillful hunter, his mother found him a wife from her own people, and they were the beginning of a great tribe of people, just as God had promised Abraham.

# Offering of Isaac

ABRAHAM, THE PATRIARCH—we look at him through the kind mists of time that obscure Abraham the shyster who billed his wife as his sister to save his skin and nearly let another man take her. They soften Abraham the bargainer who haggled with God over the righteous men in Sodom, and Abraham the skeptic who decided God "helped them that helped themselves" and took a concubine to assure his bloodline even though Sarah had been promised a son.

But one thing you have to hand the man for all his follies and foibles. When God said, "Go!" Abraham went, and when God spoke, Abraham listened with respect. So one day (when his beloved son Isaac was colt-legged tall and all noise and movement), when God came and called, Abraham said, "I'm here!" and God said, "Abraham, I want a sacrifice from you." And Abraham said, "Of course! Whatever you ask!" because he loved God, and God had been good to him beyond measure, and his eyes followed his gangling son's antics over yonder in the sun. And God said, "Take Isaac, your only son, whom you love, to Mount Moriah and sacrifice him to me."

God left and Abraham sat stricken. There was no thought of disobeying. Abraham always did God's will, and that was that. One thing his long life had taught him: When you have to do a hard thing, do it now! Three days it was to Mount Moriah, and that was time for God to change his mind, or the world to end of Abraham's grief! Methodically he made his plans and promised Isaac he could go along, and packed the needed gear for the trip to start early the next morning. No need to tell Sarah. Time enough when she *had* to know.

So next day they started early toward the distant peak, and each day Abraham's steps got heavier and Isaac got more excited, until that last morning when they left their gear and servants and took only the wood and the fire and the knife and began to climb that last fateful slope. Jehovah was stone silent, and Abraham's strong old heart pumped on even though he knew he couldn't bear this day and live.

"How far now?" said the child. "Will we go clear to the top of the mountain? Will God meet us up there? Will I be able to see the tent and mother from that height?" The older man, sunk deeply in his own troubled thoughts, seemed hardly to hear, replying in monosyllables if at all; and the excited child, permitted to go on his first grown-up jaunt to sacrifice to his father's God, had been three days pestering his father and the two servants with questions. We smile to see his eagerness, but the old man's face was grim and bleak. The child capered around the small outcropping of rocks ahead and suddenly returned to stand before the old man and demand with urgent puzzlement, "Father, *I* have the wood for the sacrifice and *you* have the fire and the knife for the kill, but Father, what are we to sacrifice? We don't have a *lamb*." The old man stopped and leaned wearily on his staff, his dark eyes raised to heaven and his face wrenched with pain. The child shifted uneasily, sensing that this question had stirred depths in his father the others had not.

He listened to a distant bird call, watched a hawk sail across the nearer ridges, felt a puff of wind on his back, and shifted the wood on his shoulder. As if returning from a long journey, his father looked at him, his face quiet now with the look of serenity that comes from somewhere beyond hopelessness. "The Lord God will provide himself a lamb," said the father gently. The child skipped on, content. His father's God, after all, does marvelous things, and while this doesn't look like sheepherding country up here, perhaps his father knows something Isaac doesn't.

As they neared the top of the mountain, the wind blew strongly and there was no breath for questions. The view was awesome suddenly, and it seemed nothing else in that whole world was stirring. *Is God in that strong wind?* wondered Isaac; *would he be able to see him as his father did and talk to him?*

Mother said she heard God's voice once, but that was ages ago, before he was born, and then she only stood behind the tent flap and eavesdropped. She *said* (how often he had coaxed the story from her) that God promised *him* to Father, and said he would be named

Isaac; that was a funny name, Isaac. It meant "he laughs." The corners of his mouth curved up to think of it, and that's not all God said. The part Isaac liked best was when Abraham would sit out in the cool of night by the door of his tent and, putting his arm around him, would say, "And God promised that *your* children would be as numberless as the stars in the sky and be princes and ... "

He came back from his daydream to find his father's hand on his shoulder, and to see tears running in the weathered furrows of his face. Swiftly, as if he raced against some power that might come to prevent him, the old man looped the coil of rope from his waist around the child's body and pulled it close, the touch gentle, as always, and he laid Isaac on the stones they had stacked for an altar as tenderly as he used to lay his little one on his pallet when he was half asleep at night. Moving with a desperate deliberateness now, Abraham raised the long knife with both hands, but Isaac's scream of terror was drowned out by a huge voice crying, "Abraham! Abraham!" so that the whole mountain seemed to shake. The knife clattered away on the stones as Abraham dropped to his knees beside the altar, his face on a level with Isaac's now. For a moment there was silence, and then, "Don't hurt the boy or do anything to him. You have obeyed God with your whole heart, and that is all that is required of you."

Abraham, like a man wakened from a dream, reached out and pulled Isaac's warm young body against him and wept. Then Isaac said, "Father, I can't hug you back until you untie the ropes!" and with a roar of laughter and a final gigantic squeeze, Abraham set his son on his feet and loosed the cords so that they slid to the ground. And looking past his irrepressible son, capering and stretching in his freedom, Abraham saw it, a ram caught in the brambles, and Isaac, at the same moment, cried, "Look, Father! Can't we give that to God? You promised I could help sacrifice. You *did*, you know!"

So together they tied the ram and laid it on Jehovah's altar. And Isaac, suddenly *still*, stood tall beside his father and handed the knife and the fire pot with careful hands, and knew for a moment, far beyond his years, what this love of his father's for God must be. He remembered that God had given *him* as a present to his parents (for so Sarah had taught him) and now, God had given him as a present to himself. Isaac, looking up into the blue of heaven, longed, himself, to know this loving God.

Picking up their things, they moved quietly away from the still smoldering altar, Abraham, like the old man that he was—wearily, but with a great serenity and joy on his face; Isaac, sedately now, as if in this one afternoon he had left childhood behind him on that altar. He matched his steps to Abraham's now, offering him a shoulder to lean on in the rough places. Now there was no need for words. Was ever such a gift offered and returned with love? And all his life long Isaac must have remembered the measure of the love between his father and God, and running beneath it must have been the knowledge that his life was God's gift twice over.

# A Wife for Isaac

SARAH, THE WIFE OF ABRAHAM, lived to be 127 years old, and when she died he mourned her deeply. In the land of Canaan, Abraham bought a field with a cave, and there he buried her, but Isaac was sadly grieved at his mother's death and would not be comforted.

The place was lonely without Sarah, and Abraham was more than ever aware what a joy she had been to him. Looking at his grieving son, he thought, "That's what he needs—a wife!" He called his trusted steward to him and said, "It's high time we married off Isaac. I'm an old man, and I want to see my grandsons before I die!"

Logically, I suppose, Isaac might have married one of the local beauties. Certainly there was cordiality between Abraham and the Canaanites, but Abraham had other ideas. In fact, he made the servant swear the most solemn and binding oath that he should go back to Upper Mesopotamia to his father's people and find Isaac a bride.

The servant balked a little. "What if the girl won't come?" said he. "Am I to drag Isaac all the way back there to marry?"

"God forbid!" said Abraham. "God called me out of that place with the assurance that this land should belong to my descendants, and Isaac is to stay right here! If the girl won't come, she won't come, and I won't blame you or hold you to this promise. God's angel will go ahead of you and show you the wife to choose. After that it's up to her."

So the servant took camels and, loading them with choice gifts from Abraham's store, set out for Nahor's city. It was nearing evening when he arrived and stopped at the common well outside the city. The time of success or failure seemed very close to him, and he prayed, "Look, Lord, God of my master, be with me and show your faithfulness to my master. When the maidens come to get the household water, I'll ask the one I choose for a drink. If she says yes and offers to water my camels as well, I'll take that for a sign."

The prayer was hardly finished before a lovely girl came out and went to draw water. As she straightened up with her pitcher on her shoulder he made his request. Looking at the dust on his clothing and the tired lines of his face, Rebekah said, "Drink my Lord," and she lowered the pitcher to her hand so he could drink from it. The water tasted wonderful on his parched throat, but even more wonderful to his ears was her soft voice, saying, "Your camels are thirsty too. I'll get them as much as they need." And without waiting for his reply, she emptied her pitcher in the trough and ran to get more.

In silence he watched her lithe body and quick step and he thought she was as generous and able as she was fair. Had God truly prospered his journey so soon? As she straightened from the well for the last time, he set a lovely gold nose ring in her nostrils and clasped two handsome bracelets of gold on her arms and said, "Child, whose daughter are you? Is there room in your father's house for a stranger to spend the night?" Looking at the richness of his gifts, Rebekah, flushing and dimpling, replied, "Lord, my father is Bethuel, son of Nahor and Milkah, and there is both room and food for your caravan in my father's house."

This, Rebekah realized, was no usual situation, and shouldering her pitcher of water, she hurried home to tell her parents. Laban, her brother, took one look at the quality of the trinkets the excited Rebekah was wearing and set off at a run for the well. The servant thanked God heartily for sending him to the house of Abraham's brother, and by the time dusk fell they were settled in Bethuel's house.

By the time the men had stabled and fed the camels and got the strangers water to wash their feet, the women had hurried around and cooked a good meal. It must have smelled delicious and looked even better to Abraham's servant, but he simply had to know before he ate whether God really had made things quite this easy.

To the eager ears of Laban and Bethuel he unfolded his tale—how Sarah, late in life, had given Abraham a son, and how his father had determined he shouldn't marry out of the tribe. He explained how he had sworn to find a wife for Isaac without knowing quite how to choose and how he had proposed the sign to God.

"And when she not only gave me a drink, but watered the beasts also, I thought, 'Here is a maid both fair and virtuous.' But when she said she was of Nahor's line then, indeed, I praised God, who had graciously led me to choose the granddaughter of my master's brother for his son. Now tell me whether you will show kindness to my master and let me take her to his son."

Bethuel and Laban listened with growing excitement as the tale unfolded. When it was over, they said, "There's only one answer possible. This is clearly the will of God. Rebekah is there before you; take her and go."

Once again, Abraham's servant praised God. Then he rose and ate his meal and, opening his packs, gave rich presents of jewels and clothes to Rebekah and to her parents and brother as well.

When morning came, the servant was all for getting an early start right then, but Rebekah's kinfolks said, "Why not wait a little? Rest up for the journey. Give us a week or ten days to get her ready." And he replied, "Don't delay me. Abraham is anxious and he is very old. Let him know as soon as may be how God has blessed this trip."

It did make some sense, and they said, "Let us call Rebekah and see how she feels about it." When Rebekah was brought in they asked her if she wanted to go, and she said "I do!" and so they blessed her and sent her on her way with joy.

The camels' feet seemed to fly on the trip back, and the hearts of the party were light with mirth. So eager were they to reach home that the last day they pushed on into late evening to reach home that night. Now Isaac had taken to walking out of an evening and looking across the fields toward the direction from which they must come. He knew it was really too soon, and yet—

This particular night he saw a dust cloud, and then a caravan, and finally, unmistakably, he recognized his father's lead camel's particular walk. As Isaac stood watching, the camels halted and a slim figure jumped from the back of one and hastily veiled her face. Many were the looks he cast her way as the servant related the tale of her choosing. At long last he was free to take her hand and lead her to his tent. So Rebekah became Isaac's wife and he loved her dearly, and was comforted for the loss of his mother.

Abraham lived to the ripe old age of 175 years. When he died, his sons Ishmael and Isaac buried him beside Sarah, and God blessed Isaac as he had blessed his father before him.

# JACOB AND JOSEPH STORIES

# Isaac and Rebekah's Sons

ISAAC REJOICED IN THE fact that Rebekah, like his mother Sarah, was a beautiful woman. In fact, it's recorded in the tales of their life that he once pulled Abraham's stunt of telling King Abimelech of the Philistines that she was his sister. In his case it was hardly warranted, but God protected him anyhow. Nobody made a grab for Rebekah, and one day when Isaac was hugging and kissing his wife with what was obviously more than brotherly affection, the king tumbled to the situation. He just fussed at Isaac a little and put out the word that the kingdom was to handle him with kid gloves.

The time came, though, when Isaac became so prosperous that Abimelech decided the land wasn't big enough for both of them and asked Isaac to move on. Being a peaceable man, Isaac did just that. The first place he settled and dug a well the local shepherds grabbed for it, and he said, "Take it!" and moved on. His servants dug a second well and the same thing happened. The third time they dug a well it went uncontested, and Isaac sighed with relief and settled down to stay. "Here," he said, "there is room."

Now, I've said that having a wife who was like his mother in beauty gave Isaac great joy, but there was another likeness he could have done without. Year after year went by and still she was childless. Isaac remembered very well his father's tale of how he had been virtually begged from God's hand, and he, like Abraham, cried out to God over Rebekah's barrenness. Like Abraham, he too got his wish.

Rebekah was delighted to be bearing Isaac a son (and who could doubt it would be a boy?), but it was a *miserable* pregnancy. The morning sickness that lasted all day she could have stood. The backaches that made sleep impossible were only a nuisance. But as the child grew within her, she swelled to fantastic proportions, and he was *never* quiet. Her whole body was bruised. God knows, she was glad enough he was lusty, but this was ridiculous! One day she wailed, "If it's going to be like this I may as well die right now and get it over with!"

Isaac comforted her as best he could, and then he had an idea. Maybe she would like to go to a holy place and consult God on her own behalf (at least it would give her something to do that would take her mind off her discomforts). Rebekah thought that wasn't a bad idea herself, and when she came back she was so pleased with herself her wails were more like bragging than complaining.

"Twins, Isaac! Think of it! Not one son, but *two* God is giving us! He said there were two nations warring in my womb. But Isaac, he said the oddest thing. He said that the older should be servant of the younger. Now, that's not right, is it, Isaac? Whatever could he *mean*?"

For his part, Isaac couldn't have cared less. "*Two* sons," he thought, "after all these years, two sons!" The generosity of God was surely great! And he went off to arrange a little thank offering and to pray for Rebekah's safe delivery.

When the time for Rebekah's confinement came, she gave birth to twin boys, just as God had promised. The firstborn was covered over much of his body with a fine red hair, and they named him Esau, but before she so much as had time to catch her breath, the second was born. So close on his brother's heels did he come, by the way, (the midwife told her with glee) that he was actually holding on to one of his heels as if he meant to pull his brother back and take first place himself. He was a smooth, comely child, and they called him Jacob. All their lives it was to be so, for as they grew up Esau was a man's man and spent his time out in the wilds hunting game. He was a crack shot with his bow and a tireless hunter, and Isaac favored his firstborn, who brought him the game he enjoyed so much.

Jacob wasn't exactly a mama's boy, but he stayed quietly at home among the tents. He couldn't see for the life of him why the son of a man as rich as Isaac should go out and get tired and filthy and work up a sweat over a chunk of stringy game meat while there were fat kids in his father's flocks. So Jacob stayed around home, and when Rebekah wanted help with something, or just someone to talk to, it was Jacob who was always there, and I suppose it was just natural that she came to feel much closer to her younger son than to Esau.

A strange thing happened as a result of the two men's diverse life-styles. One day Jacob decided what was wanted above all else was a good pot of lentil soup. I don't know if you've ever cooked with dried lentils, but if you have, you know two things. One is that their preparation is pretty much an all-day affair. The other is that between the smell of onions fried in olive oil that go with them, and the pungent odor of the stewed vegetable, they are enough to drive a hungry man to great lengths.

On the particular day Jacob got in the mood for stew, Esau had gone out early to hunt. As a matter of fact, I'm not sure he hadn't been out for several days, as he often was. If hunting was good, he could always start a small fire and roast some of the day's game for supper and figure on getting back with as much meat as he could carry after a couple of days. This time, though, it hadn't worked. I mean to tell you, Esau hadn't shot a *thing*, and finally he had had to return home empty-handed and *ravenous*.

As Esau approached home, his nostrils were assailed by the marvelous aforementioned scent of lentils and oil-fried onions. His stomach took another gnaw at his backbone. The water gathered in his mouth, his head turned giddy with hunger, and he broke into a ragged lope in spite of his weariness.

Jacob was leaning over the pot, giving a few last stirs to be sure his culinary masterpiece was precisely the right thickness, and slurping a little off the spoon when Esau burst in. Tact wasn't Esau's strong point, and besides, he half believed by now he was starving.

"Gimmee!" said Esau. "I'm exhausted and starving, and that smells like heaven! Give me some!" Jacob knew his brother's almost childish humors and he thought fast. "Sure," he said, "you can have all you want, but you'll have to pay me with your birthright."

Esau was a man of one passion at a time, and just now that passion was hunger. Maybe he didn't really believe Jacob would do it, but more likely he just didn't think. Anyhow, he said, "Yeah, sure, okay! Just give me the soup. What good is a birthright when I'm dead of starvation anyway?" And he reached for the soup.

Jacob pressed home his advantage. He dished out a bowl of the fragrant stuff and held it just out of Esau's reach. "Swear!" he said.

"Swear that the birthright is mine, Esau!" and Esau swore, almost carelessly. The elated Jacob handed him a huge bowl of the stuff and brought him bread—the good, tough, flat bread of the valley, crusty and resistant to the teeth and vastly comfortable to the stomach. Last of all, he fetched a skin of wine to wash the meal down with. Esau ate ravenously, and finally, with his belly full, made sleepy by the wine, he cast himself on his bed and fell asleep with never a thought for what he had done.

# The Birthright

WITH THE SAME UNCOMPLICATED hunger he had for the lentil stew, Esau decided to get himself a wife. Just as he appeased his hunger with the lentils because they were handy, he satisfied this need with a local girl because she was handy, and he brought home Judith, the daughter of a Hittite who lived nearby. After he got her nicely settled in, he brought home Basemath, the daughter of another Hittite. It all went so fast that Isaac and Rebekah didn't have much say in the matter, but they were bitterly disappointed in Esau's choice of girls from outside family and tradition.

Isaac kind of got over the whole affair of Esau's marriages—especially when the grandsons began to arrive. Esau was still, after all, his favorite; and besides, Isaac was nearly blind now, and he mostly stayed quietly in his own tent away from the womenfolks. Rebekah, on the other hand, had to live with them, and they had such strange ways—not like her own people at all, she mused sadly. She thought about it a lot, and it rankled, which may be part of the reason she behaved as she did. I suspect she had also heard the story of the lentil affair from Jacob at the time, and it must have worried her that the son destined to head the family at his father's death should take it so lightly.

One day when Isaac was feeling a little low, what with his failing sight and all, he took it into his head that he was dying. So Isaac called Esau to him and said, "Who knows how long I have to live? I could be gone tomorrow, and it's time we set things in order. Go out with your bow and shoot some game to make me that savory stew that tastes so good to me, and when I have eaten it I will give you my blessing."

Rebekah waited just long enough to see Esau out of sight and she sent for Jacob. "Look," said she. "Remember that birthright bit you told me about? Now's your chance to collect—and if you miss this one there may not be another. Run out and fetch a couple of fat kids from the flock and I'll fix the savory he asked Esau for. By the time the spices are in he won't know the difference, and you'll get the blessing that's rightfully yours anyway!"

Jacob wasn't averse to a little double dealing, but he just couldn't see how it was going to work out. "I know he can't see," he protested, "but Mother, he's no fool, and when he embraces me to bless me he'll know my skin is too smooth to be Esau's. I'll get a curse yet for my pains!" "We've got to risk it," said Rebekah. "Look, if he curses you, let the curse be on me! Now *run!* We haven't all that much time."

So Jacob did as he was told, and while the meat was cooking, Rebekah fastened the skins of the kids on Jacob's arms and neck and put Esau's good clothes on him. "Now talk *low,*" she said, "and don't say any more than you have to." Then she gave him the savory and some bread she had made and pushed him off toward his father's tent.

Isaac was quite surprised when Jacob said, "Father, I am here." And he asked uneasily, "Who are you, my son?" Jacob took a deep breath and replied, "I'm Esau, your firstborn. Rise, Father, and eat." "But," protested Isaac, "you are back so soon." Jacob was too far in to back out now, so he replied glibly, "Your God put game in my path." Isaac was still uneasy and he said, "Come here and let me touch you so I'll be sure it's Esau." And Jacob had no choice but to move closer to his father. Isaac really was blind by now, and Jacob made sure his hand went to the hairy covering on Jacob's arm. Finally Isaac sighed and said, "All right. I'd have sworn that the voice was Jacob's, but I'd know the hairy feel of Esau's arm anywhere. Bring me the meal you've brought so I may eat it and bless you."

Isaac ate in silence, and since Esau was not a talkative man, Jacob had the sense to keep still, and at last Isaac pushed away his meal and said, "Come closer and embrace me, Esau. I'm still not quite sure..." And he smelled Esau's clothes (which had been a clever touch of Rebekah's) and sighed with contentment. "Yes, you smell like a fertile field that God has blessed." And he went on to invoke for him all good things and made him master of his brothers, finishing, "May he who blesses you be blessed and he who curses you cursed."

51

It was with a mixture of relief and triumph that Jacob slipped out of his father's tent just in time to see Esau returning with his game. Guessing rightly that he would dress it before he cleaned up, Jacob gave Esau's clothes back to Rebekah and made himself scarce. By the time Esau took his savory in to Isaac, Jacob was nowhere around.

"Rise, Father, and eat the game your son has prepared," said Esau. And Isaac, who had been in an old man's doze, said, "Hmmf? What? Who are you?" Esau replied, "I am your firstborn son, Esau." Isaac was wide awake now, and he shook like a leaf. "Who was it, then, that brought me food before you came? And I ate it unsuspecting and blessed him, and blessed he will remain!"

Suddenly, the birthright that had seemed not worth worrying about was infinitely dear, and Esau cried out, "Father, bless me too. Surely you have kept a blessing for me?" But Isaac said, "Son, I have already made him your master, and that I cannot change." "Father, was that your only blessing? Give me one too!" Isaac was silent a long time and then he said, "You will live in poor and undesirable places. You will live by your sword and serve your brother, but eventually you will shake off his yoke and win your freedom."

Esau went out hating Jacob, and he made no bones about it. "Soon the time will come to mourn my father," said he, "and then I'll *murder* the sneaking bastard!" When Rebekah heard this she moved fast. "Go to my brother Laban," she told Jacob. "You know how Esau is. He'll forget it all in a couple of months. Let's don't have a repeat of Cain and Abel!" And to Isaac she said, "You know, what's done can't be helped, Isaac, and we might as well see to it that Jacob doesn't marry another of these foreign hussies. Why don't we send him on back to Laban's place to look for a wife. That will give Esau time to cool off as *well* as get us a good daughter-in-law."

So Isaac sent Jacob away as Rebekah had suggested, and Esau, finally tumbling to the fact that his wives didn't please his parents, went out and tried again. This time he chose one of the daughters of Ishmael and took her as a third wife. Whether Isaac and Rebekah approved I can't say, but with Jacob's departure the household settled down a lot.

# Jacob Seeks a Wife

WHEN ABRAHAM'S SERVANT WENT to Haran seeking a wife for Isaac, there was an impressive caravan, but Jacob seems to have set out like a fugitive—by himself, and probably on foot. Jacob was no outdoorsman. That was Esau's bag, and at the end of that first day he was weary and footsore. As twilight fell, he sought a sheltered hollow there in the open country and, having eaten a little of the food Rebekah sent with him, he braced a convenient rock under his aching neck for a pillow and fell into an uneasy sleep.

As Jacob slept, he dreamed a marvelous dream. A ladder stood by his head and, as he watched, it stretched from earth to heaven and angels of God came and went between the two. Finally, God himself came and stood by Jacob and said, "As I have been Abraham's God, so will I be yours. The blessings I promised your father, Isaac, I will indeed fulfill through you. You shall own the ground you stand on and your descendants will spread in all directions until they can no more be counted than the bits of dust in the earth under your feet. I will make you a blessing to all people and bring you back safe where you stand."

When Jacob woke from his dream he said, "God is here, and I never knew this was a holy place! It is the gate of heaven!" Then he rose and set up the stone he had slept on and poured oil on it for an offering. This was the first time Jacob had talked with God for himself, and he made a vow. "Lord God, if you do as you say— keep me safe and fed and clothed—if you bring me back safely to my father's house, this monument shall be recognized as a holy place, and a tenth of everything I have shall be yours."

As Jacob traveled he began to harden and his muscles ached less. By the time he reached the fields near Haran, he was a different man from the soft youth who bid Rebekah farewell weeks ago.

One afternoon Jacob saw a well in the distance, and around it, flocks of sheep with their shepherds. Being both thirsty and eager for news, he bent his steps in that direction. When he arrived he found the well covered with a heavy stone and the shepherds just standing around. Politely he inquired of them where they hailed from. "From the city of Haran," they replied.

Jacob was very pleased at the idea of being so near his destination, and he inquired whether they knew of his Uncle Laban, and how things were with him. The shepherds agreed that they certainly knew Laban and indeed, there was his daughter Rachel coming yonder with her father's flock.

Jacob would have liked very much to have this meeting in private, so he urged the shepherds, "Come on! Get your flocks watered and get back to pasture. You're wasting good daylight when they could be eating!"

"Oh," said the shepherds, "we can't *do* that. It takes all of us to lift the heavy covering off the well. When we are all gathered, *then* we will water."

So Jacob waited and watched while Rachel came up with Laban's sheep. Mind, I'm not saying he was showing off or anything, but casting a sidelong glance or two at the beauteous Rachel, Jacob braced a shoulder under the well cover and heaved it off and watered Laban's flocks for her. The other shepherds, meanwhile, were explaining to Rachel about the questions the young stranger had been asking.

When all the flock was watered, Jacob turned to his lovely cousin and kissed her, and in joy at his coming finally to Laban's country he burst into tears. He explained he was Rebekah's son, and the excited Rachel ran ahead to tell her father while Jacob came at a slower pace with the sheep. When Laban saw his sister's son, he ran and embraced him and said, "You truly are flesh of my flesh—and bone of my bone! Come in, son, and welcome. Tell us all about the folks at home, and how was the journey?"

It felt mighty good to eat a full meal and sleep under a roof again, and of course there were feasts for the visiting cousin, and before it seemed possible, a whole month had passed. I'm not sure how much Jacob told Laban about his reasons for leaving home in a hurry, but he certainly made himself useful about the place. He was especially helpful around the flocks where Rachel was to be found. Finally Laban said, "Kinsman or no, if you're going to work this hard for me, you surely deserve some pay." Jacob replied, "I will trade you seven years' work for your daughter Rachel, for I love her!" What else *could* he offer? He had no dowry. Laban agreed that he'd rather marry his daughter to Jacob than to a stranger, and so they struck the bargain. The eager Jacob worked for seven years, and counted the days until Rachel should be his.

The next part of the story is the greatest irony of the whole tale, for the clever Jacob who had taken Esau's blessing by a trick of false identity got "taken" himself just as cleverly. We've said before, Rachel was beautiful—all curves and dimples and dancing dark eyes. Then there was the plain older sister. Leah was her name, and she was *drab*—dull-witted, plain-faced, clumsy—altogether unmarriageable while her vivacious younger sister was in the picture. Laban saw his chance! They made a handsome wedding feast and called in all the neighbors, and Laban saw to it the bridegroom's cup was filled and refilled. That night, as the feast quieted down, he brought Jacob his bride, heavily veiled, as was the local custom. By this time Jacob was in no shape to be too sharp-eyed anyway, and it was only when he woke with a real hangover and looked down at his new wife that he realized what had happened. It was Leah who lay beside him!

Jacob stomped out of his tent, leaving a trembling and tearful Leah to await the outcome, and sought out his uncle. "I've been robbed!" he stormed. "Seven years I've slaved for you so I could marry Rachel, and now you've given me that—!" But Laban raised his hand. "Just a minute! Custom is custom, and among our people, the youngest may not marry before the eldest. I'll tell you what, though. Finish out the usual wedding week, and I don't see why you can't have Rachel too! It's only another seven years' work, and I'll even let you have her to enjoy while you are working it off!"

What could Jacob *do*? He loved Rachel dearly and wanted her, but like it or not, he was not only married to Leah, but dependent on her father for his very food. For that week, at least, Leah had him to herself, and I hope he was kind to her, because from then on she was to play second fiddle, and she knew it.

What Rachel thought of the whole affair is not recorded, but the next week she, too, became Jacob's wife, and he openly favored her over Leah and for seven more years he labored for his Uncle Laban to earn her. Now I call that poetic justice.

# Jacob and Laban

JACOB, AS WE HAVE said, favored Rachel, and he made no secret of it. God looked at the unhappy Leah and he thought "I'll fix that!" and he gave her a beautiful son.

"Now," thought Leah, "surely he will love me!" and before Reuben could toddle steadily, she had another son. In quick succession there were a third and a fourth. Jacob was certainly pleased, and if he still looked at Rachel with his heart in his eyes, he was mighty taken with his handsome little boys, and Leah took comfort in her children.

The barren Rachel was frantic! If Leah could have sons so easily, why should she, her husband's avowed favorite, go childless? One day, in a fit of discouragement, she wailed at him, "Give me sons or I'll *die!*" and he scowled blackly at her and roared, "Am I God almighty that I can lift the curse of barrenness?" and he stalked out of her tent.

Rachel realized she had angered her husband, but her desire was a gnawing, corroding thing, and she finally settled on the same solution as had Sarai before her. She gave Jacob her slave Bilhah. Jacob was quite willing to please Rachel, and besides, a man could never have too many sons. Sure enough, Bilhah conceived right away and when she was delivered, bore a fine baby boy, and Rachel said, "God has heard my prayer and given me a son!" Bilhah bore Jacob a second son and Rachel said smugly, "I have fought God's fight with Leah and won!"

Leah, seeing that she did not conceive again, began to worry and gave her slave Zilpah to Jacob. She too had two sons for him, and both Rachel and Leah seemed ready to call it a draw until one day when Reuben, Leah's eldest, found some mandrakes. He remembered they were supposed to be a potent aphrodisiac, and he brought them to his mother.

Reuben had no more than left the tent when in came Rachel. "Please, Leah," she said. "Please let me have some too! You have so many sons, and I—!" Seeing the tears in Rachel's eyes, Leah remembered the little sister of her childhood and was moved, but she remembered also the years of being "second-best wife," so she replied sourly, "It's not enough you should steal my husband's affections! Now you want to take my son's mandrakes too!"

"Please," Rachel begged. "Please, Leah! You can have him all to yourself tonight! Promise!" So Leah relented, and when Jacob came home she went out to meet him, dressed and perfumed and as seductive as she knew how to be. She told him of the bargain. Well, Jacob didn't mind—anything to keep peace in the household. So once again she conceived and gave Jacob another son, and another, and finally a daughter was born, and Leah said "Surely, now that I've borne him six children Jacob will honor me!"

Finally God took pity on Rachel, and she too conceived. Her joy in that one son, Joseph, came near to being as great as Leah's for all six. "If only," she said, "God would give me another!" But Jacob had other worries. It seemed as if the birth of Rachel's child tipped some fine balance, and he longed to provide for his household and move out on his own. In Laban's house he was, after all, only a son-in-law, and at Laban's death, the sons would inherit. Jacob opened his trouble to Laban. Laban replied that it seemed fair enough and asked, a little cautiously, what Jacob had in mind. Neither man trusted the other in the least (would you have?), so after a bit of sparring, they struck the agreement that Jacob should go on keeping flocks and that every black sheep that was born would be his, and every speckled goat.

The tale runs that Jacob put peeled and speckled twigs before the breeding stock at the watering tanks where they mated. I suspect his selective breeding was a bit more sophisticated than that. However it was done, it all comes to the same thing in the end: "God blessed Jacob's flocks with increase." I'm sure he did. I'm equally sure that, in this case, "The Lord helped them that helped themselves." Laban's sons evidently thought so too, because they began to murmur that Jacob was stealing their father *blind* and maybe they had better look into it. Certainly Jacob had prospered marvelously, between God's blessings and his own efforts at increasing them. He owned not only flocks, but slaves and camels and donkeys and tents.

Jacob realized when he gave his yearly accounting to Laban that things were pretty tense. He wasn't surprised when, a bit later that day, God said, "It's time to go home, Jacob. You've got plenty to go on, and I'd not dally if I were you."

Jacob didn't even go back into Haran. He had Rachel and Leah brought out to the sheep pastures, and when they got there, he sat down and let them in on his plans. "I've worked like a horse," said he, "and Laban has changed my wages and gone back on his bargain ten times over. But God, the God I worshipped at Bethel, has cared for me, and now he has sent his angel to me in a dream and bid me return to the land of my father."

Rachel and Leah were realists. They had no illusions about their place in their father's house; what's more, they agreed, it served him right. Hadn't he sold them for a price, and spent it as he saw fit without thought of provision for them and their children? "Surely," they said, "whatever you've gained from Laban is fairly ours!"

Laban, as Jacob well knew, was out at sheep shearing in one of his other flocks. That afternoon they gathered all the belongings they valued in Haran, Jacob set his wives and children on camels, and they headed south toward Mount Gilead.

Leah and Rachel had little doubt where their future lay, and they went, for the most part, gladly. Still, they had lived all their lives in Haran, and the future held so much strangeness. Perhaps that's why Rachel did the odd thing that caused such uproar later. Just as they were leaving Laban's house she ran back and snatched the teraphim—his household gods—and hid them in the loose folds of her clothing.

# Meeting at Mizpah

JACOB'S SHREWD RECKONING proved correct. It was three days before Laban found out he had left. By the time Laban decided what to do and got enough folks together to suit him for a support party, it took him seven days to catch up with Jacob, and every day he got angrier.

Jacob, by this time, had reached the foothills beyond Mount Gilead, and there he was camped for the night. Laban came almost up with him, and he camped on the mountain itself. That last night while Laban slept and chewed over exactly what he was going to do to that young jackass of a Jacob, the Lord God came to him and said, "Ah—ah—hh! Hands *off* the boy, Laban!"

Laban, for all his choler, was no man to gainsay God, so when he came up with Jacob the next morning, his tone was more aggrieved than angry. "Jacob, that was a mean trick, driving my own girls off like war hostages. I would have given you a big farewell feast with music and dancing and all. Even if you didn't want to wait that long, you could have let me kiss my children and grandchildren good-bye! You've really acted the fool, and I could make it mighty rough for you. You're luckier than you deserve that God told me 'hands off'!"

"Another thing," continued Laban. "I guess I could understand that a sudden longing for your father's house had prompted your rash departure. That I could forgive, but what really sticks in my craw is your making off with my household gods. That's about as low as you can get!"

Jacob, to give him his due, was innocent for once. He really didn't know Rachel had the things, so he replied with the vehemence of wronged virtue, "I left because I was afraid you would grab your daughters back if I proposed it, but I'm damned if I've got anything that's rightfully yours. You just go right ahead and search with our companies as witnesses, and if you find those teraphim, whoever has them is as good as dead!" Foolhardy words, if he only knew, but at that point he didn't, and I'm not sure he ever found out.

Laban set right out looking in Jacob's tent—nothing. Next he tried Leah's tent and that of the two slave girls, with the same results. Finally only Rachel's tent remained, and she, of course, had the darned things, but she also had a quick wit and a poker face. By the time Laban came to the door, she had hidden those idols in the camel's litter and she was half reclining on it looking pale and drooping. Before Laban took one step inside, she started in on him.

"Daddy, I'm terribly sorry I can't stand up in proper respect for you, but I've got a terrible case of monthly cramps with all this camel riding and all, and I'm simply too ill to *move*!" Laban looked at the lovely Rachel (who always *had* been his favorite) and he said, "There, there," not to worry, and he rummaged around her tent a little bit, and just as he began to look around the covers on that litter she moaned a little bit, and, well, Laban backed off, feeling almost guilty by now, and gave up the search.

Now Jacob's righteous indignation knew no bounds and he really let Laban have it with both barrels. "What crime have I committed? What single crime, to make you come after me as if I were a thief and rifle my belongings? See? You didn't find one single thing from your house." And while he was at it, Jacob unloaded all the bitterness of the twenty years he had been with Laban. "And," he concluded, "if the God of my fathers hadn't been with me, you'd have sent me away empty-handed. You heard his judgment last night, and it's in *my* favor!"

I won't say Laban was a sore loser, but by custom, he had a certain amount of right on his side, and no one could accuse Jacob of having been overly gracious. "Look," said Laban, "the girls are still my daughters and their sons my progeny. The sheep are by rights mine, and the camels and the slaves and the whole layout really belongs to me, but what can I do? I can't fight God, but let's make sure, in his sight, that we understand each other in this matter. Let's make a solemn covenant, you and I, that neither will feel free to break for fear of God's wrath."

Jacob agreed with Laban, and together they piled up a cairn of rocks, with the help of all their people. "Now," said Laban, "when you leave my sight, God will watch you for me. If you mistreat my daughters or take other wives to displace them, he will see it and be angry. This cairn is monument and witness that we are to be at peace. I will not cross past it to fight you, and you must, for your part, not pass it to attack me. May the God of Abraham and Nahor judge between us!"

Jacob must have been feeling mighty relieved by now. The whole thing had gone his way, and after an uneasy fashion he could still count his father-in-law as a friend—at least he wasn't a potential enemy anymore. So Jacob agreed to all that Laban said, and swore by his grandfather Abraham that it should be so; then Jacob offered sacrifice there on the mountain, and they shared a ritual meal and passed the night there together in peace.

Next morning they rose early and Laban took loving leave of his daughters and grandchildren, and he and his party turned back toward Haran, while Jacob's household set off again on the journey home to Beersheba.

There's a marvelous irony about this tale. We saw them there, two angry, scheming men, shaking their fists at each other, and finally leaving a pile of rocks to witness what God thought of any one who broke his promise. The place came to be called Mizpah (meaning "witness"), and was a landmark to all their descendants. Laban's words, "May the Lord watch between you and me when we are absent from each other," came to be a benediction, and lost all memory of the uneasy anger that prompted them. Indeed, it can now be found printed on a bit of popular jewelry designed to be split in two halves so the buyer can keep one, bestowing the other on his or her own true love!

# Jacob and Esau Reconciled

NOW THAT LABAN WAS no longer a threat, Jacob turned his thoughts to Esau. It had been twenty years since Esau had shouted that threat to kill him, but still, it wouldn't hurt to use a little caution. He dispatched some messengers to tell Esau, "I'm on my way home, and I'm really loaded. I've got all kinds of slaves and cattle, and I've got no designs on the inheritance at all." Then, as an afterthought, he added, "All I really want is to find favor with my lord, Esau."

They camped for the night, and as they moved slowly on, the next day, or maybe several days later, the messengers returned with their beasts all in a lather to report, "We told him what you said and he's on his way to meet you—with four hundred men."

Jacob was upset, to say the least. With his huge cumbersome household and all its goods, he was a sitting duck, and four hundred men didn't sound like a few friends brought along for company. Four hundred men sounded like a fighting force. Actually, Jacob wronged Esau there. It wasn't that he was hostile. He simply came prepared for anything because he didn't trust his brother. Can you blame him?

Jacob prayed: "Lord, look! You brought me on this jaunt and you've given me all these riches and wives and children. I'm terrified of Esau! Yet it was you who promised to make my descendants a great nation!"

After they had camped for the night, Jacob did the practical thing. He did, indeed, have plenty, and it occurred to him Esau might be placated by a gift. He chose 220 goats, as many sheep, and 30 milk camels with their calves, 50 head of cattle, and 30 donkeys. These he divided into groups and set servants over each. "Now," he said, "leave a good space between—half a mile or so—and head for Esau. When he asks whose stock it is, you are to reply, 'Your servant Jacob sends them as a gift to my lord Esau.'"

To the last group he gave the further instruction, "When you have said that to him, say also, 'And your servant Jacob follows soon after us.' For if I can conciliate him with gifts, he may look on my face with favor."

The gift for Esau was sent off then and there, but Jacob and his household pitched camp for the night. All the household was sent across the ford of the Jabok for the night, but Jacob remained alone. As he lay there, someone came and wrestled with him, and whether in dream or in fact, he seemed to wrestle all night. The match was so even that neither could prevail. Jacob's hip was dislocated, but still he held his opponent fast. "Let me go!" cried the unseen one. "It's nearly daylight!" "I will not," panted Jacob, "unless you bless me." "What is your name?" asked his adversary. "Jacob." And his adversary replied, "No more 'Jacob,' but 'Israel,' because you have prevailed with God and will prevail with men." Jacob said, "Tell me who you are!" but the adversary said, "Why should you ask?" and he blessed him and left. And Jacob marveled, "I have seen God face to face and lived!" He called the place Peniel, and went back across the river limping because of his hip.

The sun was no more than well up when Jacob looked into the distance and saw Esau approaching with his four hundred horses. He divided his household—first the slave girls with their children, then Leah with hers, and finally Rachel with Joseph. That's really all there was time for before Esau rode up.

Jacob strode forward to face him, knowing that the next few minutes were crucial, and as he moved, he bowed ceremonially seven times, as for a very great man. But Esau wasn't inclined to stand on ceremony. He dropped from his horse and ran to meet Jacob with arms outstretched. As Jacob straightened from that seventh bow, Esau seized him in a bear hug that almost made his ribs match his hip, and wept for joy!

When Esau finally dropped his arms, he looked past Jacob to the women and children. "My goodness, Jacob! Who are all these folks?" he said, and Jacob, just barely keeping the pride from his voice, replied, "These are the children God has given me!" Each small group came up in turn. First Bilhah with her two sons, and then

Zilpah with hers stepped forward and bowed deeply. Then Leah and her six stepped forward and bowed. At the last, the lovely Rachel came, holding Joseph by the hand. They too bowed low.

Esau watched it all, and then he said, "What was the meaning of those companies of servants I met coming here?" Jacob replied, "Just a little present, my lord Esau. I really do want your good will!" and Esau replied, "I've got plenty, Jacob. I don't need yours." But Jacob urged Esau (was he maybe feeling the least bit guilty now for having stolen Esau's birthright?), so Esau agreed to take Jacob's present. "Because," said Jacob, "I've got all I need, and I'd *like* you to have those presents, brother."

When these formalities were concluded, Esau clapped Jacob on the shoulder and said, "This is great! What are we waiting for? You get your folks together and strike camp, and I'll lead you on home. I know all the good watering places and—" But Jacob broke in, "Thanks anyway, Esau, but with four hundred horsemen, you'll be wanting to move right along. I've cattle with young, and my wives and small children need to move slowly. We'll just come on at our own pace, now that we know things are all right between us."

Esau was all for leaving at least a small escort of men to see Jacob home safely, but Jacob turned that down too. As a matter of fact, welcome or not, Jacob didn't exactly intend to live right on Esau's doorstep, and after Esau and his troop had galloped off to Seir, Jacob turned aside. He lived for a time at Succoth, but presently he moved on into Canaanite territory.

Jacob set his tents down near the town of Shechem, and here he paid a hundred pieces of silver for the land where his tents stood. There he built an altar to God, who had brought him safely back to his own country.

# The Rape of Dinah

JACOB SETTLED CONTENTEDLY in Shechem, and there he lived in peace for some years. Remember Leah's sixth child? The little girl, Dinah? By the time of this story she had grown to young womanhood. While she was Leah's child, she had her Aunt Rachel's sparkling eye and was a very pretty girl indeed. One day Dinah went out by herself to visit some of her friends among the women of the town.

No sooner was Dinah out of her father's land and among the dwellings of the town than Shechem, son of Hamor, who ruled the place, seized her. He carried her off to his tent and raped her. It's a pity he couldn't have controlled his passion a day or two. The story might have been quite different, because in the end, he decided he genuinely loved Dinah, and he succeeded in comforting her.

Jacob heard of the affair, but he felt he was scarcely in a position to make a move without the strength of his sons, who were out with the flocks. Shechem, in the meantime, had gone to his father, Hamor the Hivite (who ruled the whole region), and said, "Get that girl for me, Father. Please do! I'll simply die if I can't have her for my wife! Pay whatever they ask because I've got to have her!"

Hamor was an indulgent father, and besides, it may have looked like a simple way out of a very sticky situation. By the time they reached Jacob's place, all the boys were home, and Hamor opened negotiations. "Look here," he said, "Shechem really has his heart set on marrying your girl. We're good buddies, and what could be more sensible than you letting us take wives from your people and you taking wives from our people? You can live where you like and we will all live peacefully together."

There Shechem broke in. He wasn't interested in all this pleasant, general negotiation. "Give me the girl!" he said. "Name your price for

66

her. I don't care how much it is, I've got to have her. Only let me marry the girl!"

Dinah's brothers were furious! Their sister had been dishonored, and now the man who had done it stood there babbling about marrying her. If they just sent him off, it was no solution; still, it seemed scarcely right he should have his way, either, so they answered craftily.

"Ever since our ancestor Abraham, the men of our family have been circumcised. It simply wouldn't do for us to mingle with the uncircumcised."

Hamor, as we've noted, was indulgent. Shechem was blinded by his desire. "Besides," Hamor reasoned with his tribesmen, "if we intermarry with them and let them stay here, we will just sort of absorb them with all their wealth, and that will be our gain!" So all the men of Shechem agreed to the bargain, and all were circumcised that day. Simeon and Levi, Dinah's brothers, were crafty men, and they bided their time until the third day after the circumcision, when everyone would be stiff and sore from the wound, and then they went for their revenge.

Every male in the town was killed, and last of all, Hamor and Shechem. They took their sister, Dinah, away and they pillaged and plundered the entire town. Not only did Hamor's craftiness not get him Jacob's wealth, it lost him his own, and his life as well.

When the boys had finished the job, they went home to their father, taking their sister with them, back to her mother's care. Jacob was horrified. "What have you done?" he said. "You've made my name stink through the whole countryside! It's one thing to lay waste to Shechem when the men are already disabled, but we are a small tribe, and when they hear of this the Canaanites and Perizzites will gang up on us and slay us."

Simeon and Levi were signally unrepentant. They felt they had defended the family honor. All they had to say was, "Is our sister to be treated like a whore?"

# Jacob's Return

ONCE AGAIN GOD SAID to Jacob, "Move on. I want you to go down to Bethel and make your home there. I want you to build me an altar at Bethel in memory of my coming to you as you fled from Esau."

Once again, Jacob packed up his household, gathered his flocks and droves and herds together, and prepared to move back a little closer to the land of his fathers—the land that God had promised him would belong to his descendants.

Remember those household gods Rachel had swiped from Laban? She evidently still had them around the place. Evidently she was not the only one who kept a few of the foreign deities, because Jacob felt it necessary to call the household together and lay down the law on it.

"Those foreign gods," said Jacob, "have got to go. The Lord God who brought me safely to Haran is leading us back to the land of my fathers. He asks for an altar and a sacrifice, and before we go, it's high time we got rid of those!" So all the household brought their foreign gods and their earrings to Jacob and he buried them beneath the oak tree at Shechem.

If ever a man needed God's help, it was Jacob as he set out for Luz. The affair of the Shechem massacre was still very much in people's minds. The story records simply that "a divine terror" fell on all the towns and prevented them from hindering Jacob. I can't imagine anything less would have done it!

After all these years, Jacob returned to Luz in Canaan, where he had promised God his allegiance if God prospered his journey, and set up an altar. He renamed the place Beth-El. God repeated his promise to prosper Jacob and again named him Israel.

As the slow caravan headed on for Ephrath, Rachel went into labor with her second child. The labor was a very difficult one, and Rachel was no longer a young woman. The midwife spoke encouragement to her: "Don't be afraid, all's well! You're having a fine baby boy!" But Rachel was dying, and she knew it, and with her last breath she called the child Ben-oni, which means "son of my sorrow." But Jacob, looking on the son of the wife he loved so dearly, said, "Not so! But Benjamin" (that is, "son of my right hand"). And so he was called.

Rachel was buried there at Bethlehem, and Jacob raised her a monument which became a landmark to all their people to come. The small Benjamin made the twelfth and last son born to Israel.

There is an odd little irony recorded here. Remember the zeal of Dinah's two older brothers that helped to drive Jacob from Shechem? They figured the family honor shouldn't be sullied. Well, the oldest of her brothers, Reuben, really mucked that up. It is tersely recorded that he went and slept with his father's concubine Bilhah, and that Israel knew of it.

At last Jacob, now Israel, returned home to Isaac's dwelling. I find it a bit ironic here, too, that the whole ugly mess over the blessing occurred because Isaac thought he was dying. Here he is, at least thirty years later, still alive.

Isaac died at the ripe old age of 180, and Esau and Jacob buried him. After the burial was over, Esau quietly picked up his household and moved over into the mountainous region of Seir. There simply wasn't enough room for both big households to live on Isaac's land, and Jacob, after all, had the birthright.

Israel's line was to be the chosen people, and from their bloodline the Messiah was to come. Esau, however, was not forgotten. God gave him five sons, and from them the Edomites are descended. And the brothers lived out their lives at peace with each other.

# Joseph Sold

JOSEPH WAS RATHER A pain in the neck as kid brothers go. At seventeen he was helping shepherd his father's extensive flocks. Bilhah and Zilpah's sons were doing the same work, and Joseph was in the habit of coming to his father and retailing the local gossip and complaints about them—scarcely an endearing habit!

Jacob really didn't help the family situation much either. He openly favored this boy, who was born to him late in life and was the son of his beloved Rachel. He not only listened indulgently to Joseph's tales about the older boys, but he had a handsome gift made for him. Nobody in Jacob's household went ragged, but Joseph was elegant!

That handsome coat—made with long, full sleeves, and decorated—was the last straw! Joseph had been hard to take before, but now they could hardly speak a civil word to him. It was about this time Joseph had the first of his dreams, and he didn't mind telling those, either.

"Listen, my brothers, to this dream I had!" said Joseph one day as they watched the flocks. Dreams were taken seriously as portents, and they all turned to listen.

"We were out binding sheaves for the harvest, and each one of us bound one and set it down. Now *my* sheaf stood right straight up where I set it, but all your sheaves gathered around and bowed to it." I don't doubt the kid had the dream, but telling it really didn't help family relations much either. "So," sneered his brothers, "you want to lord it over us." And they hated him even more.

Finally even Jacob had enough. The next time Joseph dreamed, he saw "the sun and moon and eleven stars bowing down to me." This time his father was there too, and for once took his favorite to task. "Is the whole family going to bow down to you, a younger son? What sort of a dream is *that* to have?" And the older brothers sulked with anger, but Jacob just sort of kept it in mind.

Evidently Jacob paid some attention to the enmity among his sons. For a while Joseph seems not to have gone out with the flocks. One wonders, in fact, whether Jacob had uneasy memories of how it was between him and Esau (and he a younger son, grabbing for the birthright). Eventually, though, the day came when he wanted to check on things.

"Joseph," said Jacob, "the boys have the flocks up at Shechem, and I need to be sure things are going well with them. I'm going to send you on up there."

"Sure!" said Joseph. "Why not?" It was, after all, a little boring around home. You know how your feet itched at seventeen? *Anything* for a change! So Joseph set off for Shechem. The trip was easy, and the feeling of freedom great, but when he reached Shechem the boys didn't seem to be there. He wandered around the countryside a little bit and finally found someone who had seen them and said they had moved on to Dothan, so he headed off that way.

Sure enough, as Joseph got over near Dothan, there were his father's flocks, and he could recognize his brothers some distance off. Unfortunately, they could recognize him too, and they used the fact to good advantage. By the time Joseph got to where they were, they had their plot laid.

It isn't exactly clear how many of the older boys were with that flock, but certainly there were three or four, and Joseph really had no idea of needing to protect himself. The first man's embrace turned into an imprisoning hold, and in a very few minutes Joseph had been stripped of that irritating coat and dumped into a dry well close by. There seems to have been some quarrel as to what his ultimate end should be. Some were for killing him outright, and others just wanted to abandon him and leave him to die.

Reuben has gotten some pretty bad press in these stories. He was the one, remember, who lay with his father's concubine. At this point, you could really admire the man. Reuben had heard their plans and said, "Look, murder is pretty nasty stuff, especially when it's your own brother. You know how it was with Cain. Let's just throw him in and leave him." He really intended to slip back and effect a rescue after the others had left, and he drifted off after the flocks, figuring they would follow. The trouble is, they didn't.

A little later, Judah saw an Ishmaelite traders' caravan approach, and it seemed to him he had the perfect solution—just as final as murder, but no bloodshed, and it would put money in their pockets as well. Joseph was hauled up and out of the well, protesting angrily. The traders couldn't have cared less. His brothers were scornful. Silver changed hands, and the caravan moved on toward Egypt with another slave.

When Reuben came back to see what they were dawdling about, he went right into the well, and finding it empty, tore his clothes in mourning and said, "What am I going to do? Our father will *kill* me!"

The answer they came up with was expedient, and either they didn't tell Reuben what had happened, or he didn't see much he could do about it. They killed a kid from the flock and smeared that spectacular coat with its blood, and they sent it to their father. Oh, they sent a message with it. They were innocent and solicitous about it.

"Could this be Joseph's coat? It surely does look like it, and we found it just lying there by itself, and all bloody."

Jacob had no doubt at all. That was Joseph's coat, and his son was dead. It was obvious that he had been attacked by a wild beast. Jacob must have blamed himself for sending Joseph off alone, and he grieved inordinately. All his other sons and daughters tried to comfort him, but he turned from them and wept bitterly, vowing he would go down to the land of the dead with Joseph in his grief.

As for Joseph, if he longed for a change of scenery, he was certainly getting it. The young dreamer was taken down to Egypt, and there he was sold into the household of Potiphar, commander of the pharaoh's guard.

# Joseph as a Slave

JOSEPH WAS A REALIST, in his own way. By the time he reached Egypt, he realized he'd better make the best of the situation as it was. When the traders began bargaining with people, he let it be known that he was articulate and clever. He was probably an attractive young man as well. Remember—Rachel, whose beauty captivated Jacob, was his mother. Potiphar was pleased with the boy, and he thought he would make a handsome house slave.

Joseph was rather relieved to be sold into a position that was fairly soft. He may well have lived better in that rich man's house than he had when he was tending sheep. He took pride in his work, and Potiphar praised his clever young slave and gave him both more freedom and more responsibility.

Joseph, who had a good deal of executive ability, had chafed in the role of youngest son. Here was a situation with scope for his talents. Joseph worked hard, but above and beyond that, Jahweh blessed him. Everything he put his hand to prospered, and the whole household of Potiphar was blessed for his sake. Potiphar, seeing that Jahweh blessed Joseph, and watching his affairs prosper in Joseph's hands, made a decision. He'd never really liked fooling around in the affairs of household and estate. He was a soldier at heart and found all that business tedious. He handed the whole affair over to Joseph, and as long as Potiphar got his meals on time, he was more than content.

There was one fly in the ointment—one cloud in Joseph's sky. Potiphar's wife was a real floozy, and besides, she was bored! Potiphar, who never had been a red-hot lover, had deteriorated into paunchy, middle-aged indifference, and she wanted some action. At first she was just making eyes at the handsome young slave her husband had bought. It didn't work. "Maybe," she thought, "he's so inexperienced he doesn't *understand.*" Well, *that* could be mended pretty easily.

One day Potiphar's wife came right out and said, "Come lie with me, you gorgeous man, you!"

Joseph knew a sticky situation when he saw it, and he said, "No, thanks. Not only," he said, "is it a sin in Jahweh's eyes, but your husband trusts me. There's nothing in this house I can't do as I like with, because he has put it all in my care. Only you, who are his wife, has he withheld from me, and we're going to leave it that way."

Day after day she coaxed and teased, and Joseph continued to refuse. One day Joseph came into the house on an errand and there wasn't a servant in sight. "This time," she thought, "I really have him." She grabbed him by his tunic and refused to let go. "Come on! Sleep with me!" she coaxed.

Joseph panicked. Not only was the woman shameless, but she really had him in a suspicious-looking situation. He slipped out of his loose tunic, leaving it in her hand, and ran out of the house. Hell hath no fury like a woman scorned, as the old saying goes. Potiphar's wife was no exception.

As soon as Joseph left the room she set up an awful caterwauling. It brought the servants running, just as she had intended. Putting on her most aggrieved air, she held out Joseph's tunic. Her hair and clothes, disordered by her struggle to *keep* him there, seemed an eloquent proof of the exact opposite. "Look!" said she. "He has brought a Hebrew slave here to insult us! That wretched man actually tried to force me to sleep with him, and when I screamed for help he ran away so fast he left his tunic here!"

If the other servants knew the woman was a liar, and they probably did, they weren't about to say so to her face. Besides, once again, Joseph had been favored above those who had been there longer than he. Quite possibly there was more than a little rancor toward him, and they were secretly pleased to see him in trouble. So they all murmured, "Yes, ma'am!" and "It certainly is beyond bearing." And if there was anyone who could have helped, they didn't step forward.

That night, when Potiphar came home, she was all ready for him with her tale of woe. After all, she had the tunic as proof, and she really played it to the hilt—how this foreign slave had actually tried to rape her, and only her screams saved her.

Potiphar, according to the Bible text, was furious and had Joseph thrown in prison. I wonder—it seems almost a slap on the wrist for a slave who had assaulted the master's wife. I've always wondered whether Potiphar didn't have a fair idea of what really had happened, and simply got Joseph out of the way and then forgot him.

Whatever Potiphar knew or didn't know, Joseph was in trouble again. The other, with his brothers, he rather brought on himself, but this time it really did seem unfair that he should be jailed. However, as we've said before, he was a realist, and he set out to make himself indispensable to the jailer. Jahweh did his part, blessing all Joseph's efforts, and as time wore on, the jailer gave the young Hebrew more and more responsibility.

One day two men who stood near the pharaoh, his cupbearer and his baker, were brought in to the prison keeper's house. True, they had displeased the pharaoh enough to be taken into custody, but they were no ordinary prisoners, and Joseph was sent to wait on them. One morning when he went in they were long-faced. To his queries they replied that both had dreamed. In the pharaoh's court were men who would interpret dreams—magicians and wise men—but here in prison, what could they do?

"Cheer up," said Joseph. "Surely dreams belong to Jahweh, and he will tell us what they mean! Come, tell me what you dreamed."

They felt they had nothing to lose, so the cupbearer told his dream of a vine that grew and blossomed and fruited with grapes on three branches, and how he had plucked the grapes and pressed them into the pharaoh's cup and put it in his hand as he used to do.

"That's simple," said Joseph. "In three days Pharaoh will release you and restore you to your former position. When he does, remember me and ask for my freedom. Not only was I stolen and enslaved, but I'm in here for something I didn't do."

The chief baker decided maybe he'd risk asking about his dream too. He'd had three baskets of Pharaoh's favorite cakes on his head in his dream, but birds swooped down and ate them all. Joseph gave a straight answer, but not a very comforting one. "You too," he said, "will be released in three days, but you will be hanged on a gallows and your corpse left for carrion birds to devour."

Three days later Pharaoh celebrated his birthday. During the festivities he sent for his cupbearer and baker. The former he restored to favor, but the baker was hanged, just as Joseph had foretold. Joseph waited hopefully for word from the cupbearer, but as day followed day into weeks and months the hope faded, and he settled down to make the best of his situation, trusting that Jahweh was with him. The cupbearer, of course, had forgotten.

# Joseph Freed

JOSEPH HAD BEEN IN PRISON for two years since the Pharaoh's cupbearer left and had long since given up any hope of help from that direction when something happened to remind that rather careless man of Joseph. Indeed, it became to his advantage to get Joseph out of prison. Pharaoh began having nightmares. Twice he dreamed. Once there were fat cows coming up out of the Nile—seven of them, but as they approached him, seven of the skinniest beasts you ever saw came up and devoured them. The second night there was a beautiful stalk of grain with seven fat ears on it, but just as he was admiring it, another grew beside it with seven ears of shriveled, burnt, thin grain and simply swallowed it up.

When he woke from the second dream, Pharaoh was in a sweat. This had to be more than just something he had eaten. Clearly, these were omens, and he sent for his wise men and magicians from all over the kingdom. They whispered and shuffled and looked wise. They discussed the details and pondered and consulted, but nobody came up with an answer. Pharaoh wasn't renowned for his patience in the first place, and he had begun to suspect his wise men were a pack of pompous fools. In fact, he showed every sign of becoming more than a trifle peeved. "Just as he did that time," thought his cupbearer, "when he clapped the two of us in prison!" Then, of course, he remembered.

The cupbearer wasn't a *bad* man. He hadn't deliberately abandoned Joseph. He just forgot, and now he said to Pharaoh, "I've done something careless! I totally forgot a man I promised to help, and now I believe he could help you! Remember a couple of years ago when you were displeased with me and your head baker? You had us confined in the jailer's house?"

Pharaoh remembered it vaguely, but he couldn't see what that had to do with his dreams. "Only listen," said his cupbearer, "and I may have help for you. We, too, dreamed. Each one of us dreamed of our future, but could not perceive what the dreams meant until this young Hebrew (I guess he was the slave of the captain of the guard) came to our aid. He told me I would be restored to your gracious favor, and he predicted the baker's execution. It was surely just as he said!"

Joseph was going quietly about his usual duties at the prison when he was called in haste to his master's house. He was shaved and bathed and dressed in clean clothes and new sandals. Before he quite realized what was happening, he was being hurried off in the care of Pharaoh's guard because "Pharaoh wants to talk to you." There was hardly time for a quick prayer to Jahweh before he was in Pharaoh's presence.

"Look here," said Pharaoh. "I've had these puzzling dreams, and all the wise men in Egypt are at a loss to tell me their meaning, but I've heard it said of you that you have particular powers at reading dreams." The brash youngster who came to Egypt thirteen years ago might simply have replied that it was so, but at this point in his life, we begin to see a man whose experience has matured and perhaps humbled him, and he replied, "It's not my power, my lord, but Jahweh will surely give you an answer for good."

Pharaoh launched forth: "There were these lovely fat cows—splendid beasts. Seven of them came up from the Nile. The seven that came after were pathetic! I don't suppose there are seven such thin, miserable, bony creatures in all Egypt, yet when they had de-voured the seven fat cows, they looked not a bit better off for it. It was the same with the grain in my second dream—the fat devoured by the poor and blighted—and *seven*, always *seven*."

"My magicians," said he, casting a sour glance in their direction, "can't tell me a thing. What could it mean?" Joseph listened quietly, and Jahweh answered as he had before. "Yes," said Joseph, "Jahweh has a message for you. He is telling you his plans for the land so that you can be prepared when he does what he intends."

"The dreams are one and the same," Joseph continued. "The seven fat cows and ears of grain are seven years of such plenty for the whole land as you can hardly *imagine*. That's the *good* news. The *bad* news is, the seven lean ones are seven years of famine. It will be a famine so bad that people won't even remember there was ever such a thing as plenty. The reason the dream came twice is because Jahweh is impatient to begin what he plans."

Pharaoh and his counselors sat stunned. What was to be done about this information, or were they simply helpless before this grim prediction? But Joseph, with his quick mind, moved right on. "What you need to *do* is set up a system to store the grain in all your major cities. Don't leave it to chance, but collect a percentage of it in Pharaoh's name. When the lean years come, there will be enough to save Egypt from being wiped out. Oh yes, you'll need an overseer to mastermind the project. Someone with executive ability who can govern the land wisely during this time."

Pharaoh looked at his counselors and asked, "Do *you* know anyone else possessed of Jahweh's wisdom in the matter? Who could be more apt than this man?" And they nodded agreement. Pharaoh turned to Joseph and said, "You're *it*! You be my chancellor and rule the land as you say. You are my second in command." In proof of it, he slipped off the signet ring with which official documents were sealed and put it on Joseph's finger.

Before that day was out, Joseph, who had begun it an imprisoned slave, was clothed in fine linen with a gold chain around his neck. He was given a chariot nearly as fine as Pharaoh's and runners to cry "Make way" before him. Before the month was out, he was given Asenath, the priest's daughter, for a wife. Once again Joseph, being a realist, set out to do a really good job of what was at hand, only this time it was ruling Egypt. And once more, Jahweh was with him and blessed his efforts.

# Joseph's Brothers Come

WHEN JOSEPH WAS CALLED before Pharaoh he was thirty years old. He had spent thirteen years as a slave, and I must say, he soon made up for lost time. He hurried from one end of Egypt to the other supervising the collection of food and keeping track of how much was stored in each city, until finally Jahweh had sent grain in such plenty they lost track of how much there was.

Joseph didn't spend *all* his time on the run, though. By the time the years of plenty were over, Asenath had borne him two sons, and he treasured them as only a man who has been denied home and children until his thirties can. The first he called Manasseh, "because," he said, "God has made me forget all my suffering and my exile in his birth." The second he named Ephraim "because God has made me fruitful in the country where I was miserable."

By the time the seven years of famine came, Joseph was an established and honored man in the land.

At first the people ate what they themselves had put by. Finally, as the drought continued, their private stores were gone, and they said to Pharaoh, "You've got all that grain stored up! Feed us or we will starve to death!" Pharaoh replied, "Go talk to Joseph. He's in charge of all that." So the people went and asked Joseph for food and he said, "Certainly you shall have it—for a price." And he collected money and possessions for Pharaoh in return for the grain.

Not only was Egypt stricken by this seemingly endless drought, but so were all the lands around it, and Joseph sold grain to them too. Up in Canaan, Jacob's sons watched the grazing lands burn out and the streams slow to a trickle. They saw the crops wither before they came to harvest, and they knew that without help they couldn't live much longer.

One day Jacob called in his sons and said, "Egypt is selling grain. Take some money and go down and get us enough to tide us over or we will all perish of hunger before the rains come!" So the ten sons of Jacob started off—the ten older ones, that is, for since Joseph's disappearance, Jacob hardly let Benjamin, the last of his beloved Rachel's sons, out of his sight.

A man may get a good bit older-looking in thirteen years, but when he's the brother you grew up with, and still herding sheep as he was, he's recognizable, and Joseph, seeing the ten sons of Israel, knew them at once. For them it was different. They had no idea whether their brother was alive or dead. They certainly wouldn't have expected him to be a prince of Egypt, and his clothing, his hair, his language, even his name were Egyptian.

The brothers bowed to the ground and begged to buy food, but Joseph frowned and insisted they were spies. "You've come to find our weak points while famine is on us!" he accused. They protested their innocence, and as men will who would prove themselves honest, they told him intimate details. "We are twelve brothers," they said. (Even now they thought in terms of being twelve!) "How twelve?" said Joseph. "I only see ten of you!" "Well, you see, our father kept the youngest with him. He's only a child, really. The twelfth—he is no more. He's... dead."

Joseph insisted stubbornly that they were spies. "The only way to prove your story," he said, "is to fetch that younger brother here. One of you may go get him, but the others are under arrest, and if he doesn't come back, they die as spies!"

For three days Joseph detained his brothers. They were terrified, but what could they do? Finally, on the fourth day, Joseph said, "I'll tell you what. I'm a man who fears God, and I'll be easy on you. I'll keep *one* of you in prison. The rest can take back the needed food and bring me the boy."

It must have seemed a strange whim to these men, that this Egyptian prince should insist on seeing Benjamin, but he held their lives in his hand at this instant, and if they did not return with food soon, their families would starve. They had no choice, they agreed, but to do as he said. One thing they thought they saw very clearly. "It's a judgment on us," they said. "We are being called to account for Joseph's death. He pleaded with us to release him, and we were hardhearted." Can you blame Reuben if he said, "I told you so?"

Joseph, of course, understood every word they said, but since he was using an interpreter, they couldn't know this. When it really got to him he left the room and wept, but he returned when he regained self-possession and spoke to them. In their sight he had Simeon bound and led off to prison.

Now the sacks were filled with corn, and, at Joseph's command, each man's money was put in his sack. A full day's journey out they opened a bag to feed the beasts and found one man's money had been put in the sack. They were heartsick. "What has Jahweh done to us?" they said, and they hurried on to their father uneasily. They told him of their strange meeting and that Benjamin must return to free Simeon, and then they emptied their sacks and found that each had his silver back. Israel and his sons were seized with great fear.

"You are robbing me of my sons!" cried Jacob. "Joseph is dead and gone. Simeon is held in Egypt, and I don't suppose I'll ever see him again. I can't do a thing to protect myself from that. I must simply bear the grief. But Benjamin," he said, tightening his arm around his youngest, "Benjamin shall surely not go! If harm should come to him, who is all I have left of Rachel, I would *die* of grief! No!"

Reuben coaxed, "But Father, if we take him to Egypt we can free Simeon, and the prince said that this would prove our honesty and we could trade in the land. We could buy food enough to keep ourselves alive. Look, Father, I give you my own two sons as surety. If I do not bring Benjamin back to you unharmed, you may kill them. That's how carefully I will watch over him."

But Jacob raised his voice in the helpless anger of a very old man who, seeing himself powerless in so many things, clings to what little power he has. "Out!" he roared. "Out of my sight. Benjamin shall not go!" The brothers looked at each other grimly and left. Perhaps in a day or two the old man could be coaxed to reason. For now, at least, there was food, and Simeon must simply fend for himself unless they could find a way to change things.

# Return to Egypt

THE LAST OF THE FOOD bought in Egypt was used up, and still the rains didn't come. Jacob called his sons and said (as if the matter had never been discussed), "Go back to Egypt and buy us a little food." Reuben just shut his mouth and looked grim, and this time Judah took up the conversation.

"Father, we *can't* go without Benjamin. The man specifically told us that we wouldn't even be admitted at his gates unless we brought him. If you are ready to send Benjamin, we will start off this very day, but until you make up your mind he's got to go, we won't stir a step. That man wasn't fooling. We would not only get no food, we might easily lose our lives as well!" Jacob looked all around at his nine sons' faces. Not one held out any hope to him.

"Why did you do this to me," he wailed. "If you hadn't opened your big mouths and blabbed about having another brother, he'd never have *known* it! If only you'd have shut up, Benjamin wouldn't have to leave me!"

Judah replied, "Father, we couldn't help it. He seemed interested in all sorts of personal details about us. He asked the most uncanny questions, like 'Have you another brother?' and 'What about your father? Does he still live?' He simply would not even *talk* about selling us food until we had told him everything."

Come to think of it, the whole affair *had* seemed eerie. Why on earth would an Egyptian prince care whether their father lived or was dead, and who would have supposed he would demand to see that one brother left home when the other *ten* had stood before him?

Jacob began to droop, and the tears came to his eyes. He was beaten, and he knew it. There was no chance for any of them if the boys didn't go, and there was no point in seeing Benjamin starve to death. Judah, seeing his father weaken, urged gently, "Come, Father, trust him to me so you and we and our families may not starve. Look, if we hadn't dallied about it, we could have been there and back by now."

Then Jacob said to them, "If it's got to be done, do it right. Don't go empty-handed like beggars. Take double the money so you can return what was in your sacks, and take the man some gifts. Carry him some of the local products—some balsam and honey, some resin and tragacanth. He might be pleased by some pistachio nuts and almonds. Let's assume that the money in your sacks was an honest mistake. Take Benjamin, since you must, and may Jahweh move the man to be kind to you and return me both my sons."

As quickly as they could, the brothers packed the gifts and set out. Not only did they want to leave before Jacob changed his mind about Benjamin, but they also realized that food was dangerously short. As for Benjamin, while he hated to see his father grieve, he couldn't remember when anything had been so exciting! Imagine a trip to Egypt with the other men—he who was always kept home! And a chance to see the court and meet a real prince and—!

Once the trip was begun, they pushed hard to get to Egypt in haste. They lost no time in going directly to the public warehouse where Joseph arranged the sale of grain. Joseph looked up from his work and saw them there—ten dusty, travel-stained men with their beasts. *Ten*, his quick eyes confirmed, and his heart leaped with joy, but Joseph hadn't got where he was by being impulsive. He turned an impassive face to his chamberlain and said, "Those ten Hebrews—take them to my house, and prepare a good meal. They'll be my dinner guests this noon." And he turned back, outwardly calm, to the business at hand.

The chamberlain led the brothers away, and they talked softly among themselves. "They mean to enslave us and take our donkeys. They blame us for having taken back our money," they said. When they arrived in the courtyard, they decided they could at least try to explain, so one went up and bowed to the chamberlain and said, "Sir, we want to explain to you that we came to buy before. When we got home, our money was in our sacks. We don't know how it got there, but we've brought it back, and more to buy with this time. Believe us, we're honest men!"

The chamberlain listened politely to these obviously uneasy strangers, and then he said, "Peace to you. There's nothing to worry about!" He either had some grasp of what Joseph had done, or he had his orders, and he continued, "Your God and the God of your father has put treasure in your sacks. I certainly received the money you owed for that grain!" Then he went in the house and returned with Simeon, no longer bound, but free to stay with them.

It was all a little like a dream. They were invited into the house like honored guests—that lovely airy house of an Egyptian prince. The servants brought water for them to wash, and the chamberlain bid them make themselves comfortable while he went to see to the meal they were to share with his master. With great joy they opened their packs and arranged the gifts they had brought for this peculiar prince. They swapped stories with Simeon and wondered at their good fortune.

At noon Joseph came, and bowing humbly, they gave him their gifts. He spoke kindly to them and again asked the *oddest* questions. "That old man—your father—is he still alive? How is he? Is he well?" They replied that he was well, and again they bowed low.

Now Joseph turned his eyes at last directly to Benjamin, his mother's son. "Is this your younger brother?" he asked, fighting for composure, and knowing well that this tall young man was the little brother he had left behind. "God be good to you, my son," he said. Then, suddenly, it was more than he could bear, and he turned and strode swiftly to his private chamber and wept.

Presently, Joseph returned. He was composed now, and all traces of tears were washed away. "Serve the meal," he ordered, and he courteously saw to the seating arrangements. He, himself, sat alone. There was a second table for the Egyptians present, and at a third, directly opposite his, he had his brothers seated in strict order of their age. They looked at one another in awe. How could he have known?

As the meal progressed, he proved a charming host. They drank with him and were relaxed and happy. As a special honor, he sent them portions of food from the dishes at his own table, and they couldn't help but notice that Benjamin's portions were by far the largest, and his eyes returned often to the young man's face.

# Joseph Unmasks

MOST OF US HAVE, at some time, brooded over what we'd like to do to a brother or sister or friend to "get even" for something. If ever there was a man who must have done a lot of this kind of brooding, Joseph was that man. Thirteen years he'd spent in slavery, and now he was Pharaoh's right-hand man, with power to kill or save, and his brothers—all of them—were unprotected strangers in his house.

Still, there was the father he had loved. To kill his sons was to kill Jacob. There may have been some memory of better times before that day they seized him. He may even have come to understand a little of how insufferable he had been. Then there was Benjamin— the loved little brother grown to young manhood. Joseph decided on mercy, but not without a little more cat-and-mouse. The brothers seemed truly to regret the evil they had done him, but he wanted to test them a little more.

The morning after his banquet, their sacks, loaded with as much grain as they would hold, were put on their donkeys and the brothers made an early and joyous start toward home. Their joy was soon ended. They were hardly out of the city when an armed party galloped up behind them, led by Joseph's chamberlain, who made a terrible accusation.

"You've done an evil thing in exchange for my master's kindness! You've stolen his silver cup—the one he uses for reading omens!" said the chamberlain.

"No way!" said the brothers. "We even brought back the money we found in our sacks, remember? Are we likely, then, to have pilfered the treasure of a man who was so kind to us? See here, if you find that cup on us, the one who has it shall be killed, and the rest of us be your slaves. We're that sure of our innocence."

This scene is almost funny. They *were* sure of their innocence—and with good reason. The chamberlain was equally sure the cup was there. He had put it in the sack himself. I must say, he played his part to the hilt.

All the sacks came down from the beasts' backs and each man opened his own. The chamberlain started with Reuben's. There was the silver he'd paid, back in the bag, but no cup. By strict order of age, the chamberlain checked them, sifting the grain at the bags' tops through his fingers and showing up the silver. It was no surprise when Benjamin's silver showed up, but then the chamberlain plunged his hand in deeper.

"Aha! What's this?" he said, and before their horrified eyes he held aloft the silver cup. It glowed in the morning sun as he flourished it in their faces, and they knew they had been framed. Not a man of them believed Benjamin *had* taken the cup, but neither did they believe it would do a bit of good to say so.

They tore their clothes in grief and, reloading their donkeys, returned sadly to Joseph's house. It was mid-morning by now, but strangely, he was still there in his courtyard. The chamberlain's story was soon told (the more so, since Joseph already knew it) and Joseph turned on the eleven brothers.

"What is this you have done?" said Joseph. "Surely you must know I'm a reader of omens and would find you out!"

"What can we say to clear ourselves? Jahweh himself has exposed our guilt!" said Judah. "Let us all be reckoned your slaves!"

"I couldn't think of such a thing," replied Joseph. "Only the one who had the cup is guilty. *Him* I keep, but the rest of you are free to go in peace. You may return safe and sound to your father." How easy he made it for them. I wonder, were they the least bit tempted? If they were, it was short-lived, for almost at once Judah stepped closer to Joseph and said, "Please, my lord, let me speak with you privately."

Joseph nodded curtly and led Judah a bit aside. "My lord," began Judah, "you are like the pharaoh. Let your mercy be as great as your power! Remember how you asked of our father? How we told you he is old and frail? Remember also that you told us we must not come without his youngest son—the very one accused."

"My lord, the child is the last son of his favorite wife, who is dead. She bore him only two. Years ago the older one disappeared." (Had Judah been in any shape to watch he would have seen the muscles tighten around the prince's mouth, but that was all.) "Our father's whole life is tied up in this child of his old age. If he sees he is gone, he will die before we can even explain. My lord, do not bring his white head in sorrow to the grave!"

Joseph was *almost* satisfied. Here was a genuine caring for his father, and he knew it. Once more he turned his head to master his emotions: Judah, reading it for rejection, fell on his knees and pleaded, "My lord! My lord! What can it matter to you which of us stays? I promised my father by my own life no harm should come to Benjamin! Of your great mercy, do whatever you like with me. I don't care what happens to me as long as my father need not bear the death of his favorite son. I tell you, their lives are as one, and the loss would kill him! My lord, he has borne enough grief in the loss of the other one. I beg you!"

Joseph turned sharply and barked an order that the servants were to leave them alone. At the harshness in his voice they scurried, and as the doors closed behind them, he raised the startled Judah to his feet and wept unashamedly.

"My brothers!" he cried in their own Hebrew tongue (and speaking it like a native!). "My brothers, don't you *know* me? I am Joseph!" And then he added through the tears, "Is my father *truly* still alive?"

They were dumbfounded, and possibly more frightened than they had been before. This powerful prince, the brother they had treated so cruelly? Surely their lives were forfeit, and they would be lucky if it was a quick death. That, alone, would be more mercy than they could expect!

Now Joseph, drying his tears, began to see in their faces not the joy and wonder he felt, but the naked fear of his power, and so he coaxed gently. "Come closer to me, my brothers. Come here." And as they did he said, "Don't grieve any more, and don't be afraid of me, but share my joy. Look, Jahweh has done a wonderful thing for us out of your evil deed."

So Joseph went on to tell them of the dream of Pharaoh and the seven years of famine. "And only two are past," he said. And they remembered the brother whose dreams had, suddenly, the credence of current reality. "Jahweh sent me here to preserve your lives," said Joseph, "and the lives of many on the earth, for so he made me Pharaoh's right-hand man."

Now at last the fear began to thaw in their hearts. This was no pagan Egyptian ruler, but a worshipper of Jahweh, their father's God, and strangest of all, one of *them* by blood. With that marvelous administrative faculty we have seen in him before, Joseph pulled himself together and began to plan.

"We've got to get you down here where I can see that you're fed," he decided. "The trip to where you are now simply isn't practical for five more years! There's no reason at all why you shouldn't live over in Goshen. It's a good land and there's plenty of space, and it's *near* me."

The eleven brothers still stood silent with their mouths hanging open. This switch from disaster to joy to disaster and back again was a little unnerving, to say the least. Joseph knew that—he'd been there, remember! So he started again, patiently, as to a child.

"Go to my father quickly! Tell him, 'Your son Joseph says Jahweh has made me lord of all Egypt.'" That was clever of him. Jahweh alone could have made such fortunes believable. "Tell him to bring his household—children, grandchildren, servants, cattle—where I can provide for them. Look! It's my own mouth speaking! Surely you can tell him that, and Benjamin, my brother, surely you know me? And hurry! Oh, *hurry* and bring my father where I may see him again!"

At this, Joseph burst into tears once again and threw his arms around Benjamin's neck; Benjamin, embracing him in return, dropped his head on Joseph's shoulder, and he too cried. Those tears seemed to thaw the last of the fear and anguish and mistrust, and all the brothers embraced Joseph. Finally, calming themselves, they sat down to catch up on the years past and to make plans for the immediate future.

# Israel Comes to Egypt

WHILE JOSEPH AND HIS BROTHERS sat talking, his puzzled household had sent word to Pharaoh. Not only had Joseph received these strangers in strict privacy, but his uncontrolled sobs had been heard at some distance. This was so unlike the self-possessed Joseph that it really concerned them.

Presently someone—perhaps Joseph's chamberlain, who seems to have been in his confidence on much of the affair—volunteered that these men were Joseph's long-lost family. It was no news to Pharaoh that Joseph was a Hebrew, and there was also no question in his mind that this particular Hebrew had saved Egypt from disaster. Pharaoh did the handsome thing. Joseph was a popular man around the palace, and everyone agreed it was just lovely to think he'd found his family.

Pharaoh sent a message over to Joseph's house right away: "I'm delighted to hear your brothers have come! Surely you want to keep them with you, and to bring your father and all the rest of the family too. Tell them to go right home and bring the rest of the folks down here. Tell them nothing is too good for Joseph's folks, and they can command the best Egypt has to offer."

Somebody happened to think that for women with little folks, and an old man, that was a grueling trip, and Pharaoh, who didn't do things by halves, said, "You know, you're right!" So he sent a further message to Joseph. "Send the wagons down to Canaan so your father and the little ones can ride up here in ease and not have difficulties on the way! Send plenty of food for the journey, and tell them never mind about their possessions—just bring themselves. We've got plenty for them here!"

Once again, Israel's sons started home for Canaan, but this time with wagons and extra food and gifts. For each brother there was a handsome suit of clothes, and for Benjamin, the beloved younger brother, three hundred shekels of silver and *five* suits of clothes. For his father there were ten donkeys loaded with the best gifts Egypt could offer and ten donkeys loaded with food enough to make the journey easy. I guess Joseph would have packed the whole land of Egypt for a present in the exuberance of his joy if he hadn't seen the practical impossibility of it. Besides, they were returning so soon! And his last words to his brothers as they set off were, "Don't worry any more. Don't be upset on the journey. Just hurry back!"

When the boys had been gone that long, Jacob had begun to worry. The day he thought they should have been back he strained his eyes toward Egypt and fretted. The next day he openly lamented his foolishness in letting them go. By the third morning he was a basket case. In vain did the women try to persuade him that maybe one of the beasts was lamed and caused a layover or perhaps the prince was busy and couldn't get to them right away. Jacob's sons had been swallowed up—devoured by the same evil that had dogged them these two years—and he *knew* it.

When they saw the dust in the distance, they didn't even tell him about it. "Let's wait," they said. "Don't let's get his hopes up until we're sure." Then, as the group got closer, Reuben's wife swore she could recognize his lope by the lead donkey, but Dan's wife protested there was all that other stuff with them, and it couldn't be *their* menfolks, and with one thing and another, nobody told Jacob the boys were home until they walked in on him themselves.

He looked at them as if they were ghosts, and when Judah blurted, "Father, we've got news you won't believe!" it was sheer redundancy. He didn't believe *them* yet. "It's Joseph," said Judah. "We found Joseph, Father. He's alive, and ruler of Egypt, and he's sent you all these presents, and you're to come down to him."

At first Jacob was like a somnambulist. He had gone from the certainty that *all* his sons were dead to hearing that even the one he'd known to be dead for over twenty years was alive. Finally, after they had repeated all that Joseph had said to him and showed him some of the gifts, he began to grasp it a little, and Benjamin said,

"And the *wagons*, Father! Joseph sent wagons so you and the family could ride back to him in ease! Come on out and see. They're really grand!"

So Jacob, leaning on his youngest son's arm, went out to see those marvelous Egyptian wagons. When he had seen and comprehended the reality of these luxurious gifts, his spirit revived. "It is enough! Joseph, my son Joseph, is alive! I'll see Joseph again before I die!"

It was all they could do to keep Jacob from starting off then and there, he was that excited, but in spite of Pharaoh's hyperbole, they knew very well they needed to pack up their possessions and move their herds and flocks along, and that took time to organize.

At last the unwieldy caravan got under way—wagons and flocks and people, on foot and on beast, heading off toward Egypt. At Beersheba, Jacob halted and offered sacrifices to Jahweh, and once again Jahweh spoke encouraging words. "I will go with you to Egypt, and make you a great nation there, and I will bring you back to Canaan when it is time. And Joseph's own hand shall close your eyes."

So Israel's household moved on to Egypt, and when they arrived, Joseph presented them to Pharaoh. Coached ahead of time, they asked for the grazing lands of Goshen. Pharaoh acceded graciously, and suggested to Joseph that some of them might be willing to oversee the pharaoh's flocks too, since herding wasn't exactly the Egyptians' thing.

The seventy people who had come to Goshen settled and prospered and grew to be a large tribe. Thirteen more years had passed when it became clear that Jacob was near death. Joseph went to him, taking his two sons. First the two men spoke alone, and Jacob asked his son to vow that he should not be buried in Egypt, but in the burial place of his people in Canaan. Then Joseph brought his sons in.

Jacob adopted Joseph's two sons on the spot, and they have been counted ever since among the tribes of Israel, but when he blessed them he did a strange thing. He crossed his hands so that the youngest was at his right hand. Joseph protested, but Israel insisted he knew what was right. Did he remember himself and Esau, that old, old man?

Israel blessed all his sons then, one by one, and prophesied their futures. Having done this, he lay back on his bed and died. Joseph and his brothers mourned their father, and when they went up to

Canaan to bury him, much of the royal household went along to do him honor. So Israel was laid to rest in the tomb of his fathers.

When Israel's sons returned to Egypt, the old unease revived. What if Joseph had only waited for their father's death to take his revenge on his brothers? They sent him a message: "Forgive us and spare us for your father's sake." Joseph wept, and calling them to him, he said, "I'm not God to judge other men. You meant evil, but God has made it good for us all. I will provide for you and your families and keep you safe."

Joseph lived to see grandchildren and great-grandchildren—to the third generation. When he was dying, he called his brothers and said, "I know I'm dying, but God, who brought us here, will remember his oath to return you to Canaan. When he does, *then* take my bones with you and lay them with my ancestors." Then he died, and they embalmed Joseph's body and laid it in a coffin there in Egypt in keeping for the day of their return to the Promised Land.

# MOSES, JOSHUA, AND THE EXODUS

# Moses' Early Life

AFTER THE GOLDEN AGE when Joseph was a prince in Egypt and kept his family there in Goshen in great honor, a new line of pharaohs came to the throne. As Israel multiplied, Egypt became wary of them, and bit by bit the laws became more restrictive on them until finally they were out-and-out slaves of the dynasty. But Israel was a hardy people, and even in this plight they increased, and their sons were sturdy and bright-eyed, and Pharaoh said, "That's got to stop!" So he told the midwives in Goshen, "If a boy is born, *kill* him!" But they were not willing to do this, and so they lied to the king and said, "They have their babies so easily it's all over before we get there!" So Pharaoh got mad, and he set his own people on them. By royal decree, all the Hebrew boys born were to be thrown in the Nile and drowned.

There was one family that managed to conceal a small son, though. For three months they hid him in their house, but then his robust cries began to be just too noisy. So they themselves put him in the Nile— irony of ironies—but in a small reed basket, waterproofed with pitch, and right where one of the princesses came down to bathe. Remember how a healthy three-month-old baby looks, his fat wrists and chubby hands and feet waving? The bright eyes? The crows of delight and the way he grabs for your face or earrings when you bend over him? The way those small hands feel on your face?

Pharaoh's daughter had never held a baby before, and when she got the warmth of him in her arms and heard his crow of delight, a piece of her heart she didn't even know about moved, and when an enchanting little dark-eyed Hebrew maiden slipped up and said, "My, what a cute baby! Are you going to keep him?" she found herself suddenly sure that she was, and when the maiden said guilelessly, "You'll need a wet nurse. Shall I get you one?" she just hugged him closer and nodded assent.

So Miriam, Moses' sister, ran to fetch his mother to suckle him; the princess, if she guessed, pretended not to, and so this mother kept her son until he was weaned, and got paid for it as well.

So a Hebrew came to live as a prince of Egypt again, and as Moses grew in the palace he learned the ways of Egypt and its language and policies. When he was a tall young man he went out one day to watch the work on a new project, and suddenly, seeing an overseer beating an Israelite, he saw red, and he struck the Egyptian dead and buried him on the spot.

The next day Moses went out again, and seeing two Hebrews fighting, he tried to intervene in the quarrel, and one turned on him in anger and snapped, "Are you going to kill *me* like you did the Egyptian?" Moses was nobody's fool. If this man knew, so would Pharaoh, and if that was the case, Moses' life in Egypt wasn't worth a puff of wind. Moses left right then! And Pharaoh's wrath pursued him, but not fast enough!

Moses settled in Midian and there he met the daughters of Jethro the priest. Jethro had no sons, and his daughters cared for his flocks. They managed pretty well except that the bullies at the waterhole gave them a bad time. Moses stepped in one day and when the girls came home twittering, Jethro saw a good thing and he said, "Idiots! Don't leave him standing there! Go ask him if he'll come for supper!" So they did—and he did. Jethro and Moses took each other's measure and were satisfied and Jethro said, "Stay here with us! You can have Zipporah here for a wife. I'm getting on a bit and the girls need to settle and marry." So Moses settled as a herdsman in Midian, and if it was pretty different from the life of an Egyptian prince, it was also a good bit quieter. Zipporah bore him sons and he was a respected man in the area; life was good.

Then God stepped in. Well, yes, he'd been there all the time, but he hadn't said much and nobody really expected him to until that day Moses stood on the mountain and saw a bush light up with fire and just continue to burn without burning up. Moses went over to look and a voice said, "Take your sandals off! The very ground you are on is holy!" And God said, "I'm Jehovah! Your people's God. Go on back to Egypt, and tell them I've heard their cries and I'm going to rescue them and you're going to lead them to the land I promised Abraham they should have. Now's the time, and you're my man!"

Moses argued. How was he to tell the people God's name? How would they believe it was really God who sent him? "And besides," he finished a bit lamely, "you know what a poor speaker I am. Lord, I stutter, and who's going to listen to that?"

God was a bit annoyed with Moses. Here he'd taken the care to save him from death as an infant, placed him in the palace to learn Egyptian politics, saved him from Pharaoh's wrath for murder of an officer, and given him the long years of training and growth in the house of Jethro, a priest of God, and now the darned fool stood here shifting from one foot to another, making excuses!

Nevertheless, God was patient. "My name," he said, "is holy! Just tell them I'm the God of Abraham and Isaac and Jacob and Joseph—*and their God*. They will believe because, well, what's that in your hand?" "Why, er—it's a staff," said Moses. "No, it's not," said God. "Drop it!" Moses did and found himself leaping back from a poisonous snake where his staff had been. "Relax," said God. "Just grab its tail." And Moses did, a bit gingerly, and there was his staff again. God pulled two more small miracles, and then he said, "Convinced?" Moses said indeed he was, and God said, "Good! So will *they* be! Hang onto that staff, we're going to be using it."

"Now, as to your speech—don't be silly. Who gives speech in the first place? Who makes men see and hear and talk? If I want you a silver-tongued orator, don't you think I can manage it? But I'll tell you what, let's divide the weight of the job a little. You head back for Egypt. The old Pharaoh is dead and it's safe now, and your brother Aaron is already preparing to come meet you. You be the brains of the operation and let him do the talking. Does that make you feel better?"

Evidently it did, because that night Moses said to Jethro, "I'd like to go back to Egypt and see how it is with my family. I hear the old pharaoh's gone and I should be safe." Jethro looked at him a long time and he said, "You do that, son. Take Zipporah and the boys with you too. Your folks will want to see their grandchildren, and I have a hunch this may take a while."

So Moses loaded his wife and sons on a donkey, along with what they needed for the trip, and started back to Egypt, a quiet Midianite shepherd with a heavy wood staff going to start an Exodus, because God told him so, leaving behind the peaceful hills of Midian's grazing country to become a wanderer all his life so that in God's good time Israel might come home as God had promised Abraham those many years before.

# Exodus

ALL THE OLDER FOLKS in the Israelite community remembered Moses—a handsome lad, and a sort of tribal triumph in that all the other boys his age were murdered at birth, and he not only lived, but did it in that very heart of Pharaoh's realm, the palace. The young princess was a willful girl, and after all, what harm, thought indulgent Pharaoh, could one little Israelite do—especially such a cute one. Besides, he was to be brought up as an Egyptian—no problem! That bothered some of the Israelites too, and somehow they managed, I don't know how, to do something about it. Moses knew he was no Egyptian, and he had a pretty good grasp of what that meant. And that had been his downfall, for he had fled the results of having murdered in his anger for his people.

Now it was rumored Moses was back. His family was pretty closemouthed about it, but everyone knew he was up at court—he and his older brother Aaron—talking to Pharaoh. Some said he was trying to get things a little better for the young folks; some scowled and muttered he'd a darn sight better lie low and let them be forgotten before things got worse than they already were. Turned out they were right, too. Pharaoh acted like a nest of hornets and redoubled the cruelty of the guards. Why didn't that darned fool come away from there before he got them all killed, and why didn't Jehovah help them?

And Moses, twiddling his thumbs there in the royal city, prayed, "Jehovah, look what's happening—it's just making things worse!" And God said, "Tell old Pharaoh I'll send a plague!" Pretty soon the Israelites had something more to do than worry, because they were watching the Egyptians fight frogs and flies and locusts, and every time Pharaoh would decide he couldn't stand any more he'd say "Okay—let them go." Then Moses would ask God to remove the plague, and God would do so; then Pharaoh would forget how bad it had been—or maybe figure God was about out of ideas—and he'd take back his promise.

Finally the day came when God said, "This is *it!* Tell all the Israelites to pack up, Moses, and get together all the riches they can collect from the Egyptians and prepare this special meal. Tell them to put the blood from the lamb on their doorposts and tell them to *stay inside!* For as I am God, I will slay every firstborn male, both man and beast, that isn't behind one of those blood-marked doors this night." Well, there was some grumbling, but the people had seen enough of the other plagues to figure it might be a good idea to stay under cover. Old Pharaoh just laughed—there wasn't any power on earth that could do such a thing— and he redoubled the crack palace guard and set two extras indoors at the crown prince's door and called his slaves to entertain him. The night wore on, and in spite of everything he could do, Pharaoh got a little uneasy. He told himself it was silly. He reminded himself that his magicians had duplicated Moses' tricks a couple of times and, with a little more practice, would copy the rest. He had himself almost convinced when his cupbearer—a towering young noble who stood always at his uncle's right hand (for he was the pharaoh's younger brother's first-born, and a great favorite)—gave one terrified scream and crashed to the floor at his feet, unmarked by any wound or sign of ill, but dead. Unmistakably dead. And as screams and wails spread through the palace and the streets below, Pharaoh strode in haste to the room of the prince. One of his guards lay dead, the other crouched over him in disbelief, and inside the chamber the crown prince lay lifeless. Pharaoh stood as if turned to stone.

Across the land the picture repeated itself over and over except in Goshen, where Israel lived, and there the word went urgently from door to door. The angel of death has passed over. Arise! Bring your things. We're going *right now.* And they scooped up their sleeping babies and their troughs of dough for the morning's bread, and they rounded up their cattle. Like a strong river let free of its restraining locks at flood time, they poured out of the land of Egypt, and Pharaoh let them go—nay, on the crest of his grief he *urged* Moses and Aaron to get them out to their sacrifice. "And," he added forlornly, as if it could help anything now, "pray to your God for me as well."

But as grief wore on, Pharaoh's thoughts turned to anger and a desire for revenge, and he ordered out his terrible war chariots in pursuit of Israel—Israel on foot and with cattle and small children and aged folks in their slow, unwieldy march, and the Red Sea dead ahead, barring their escape. But over them hung a pillar of cloud, and God's angel in it. The night they camped by the sea they saw Egypt's chariots come in a cloud of dust, and they wailed to Moses, "Were there no graves in Egypt that you brought us here to be slaughtered? We should have stayed slaves and kept our lives at least!" And God said, "Hush! This is my victory, and it's going to be spectacular if you just do as you're told. Moses! Cleave the sea with your rod!" Well, Moses stretched out his rod, and a howling east wind blew a highway through that sea, and it was bounded with tall green walls of water that looked as if they were made of cut glass, and Israel streamed through, with shouts of joy, to freedom. But as the final stragglers came up the bank, those shouts turned to terror and dismay, for down the far bank and onto their road thundered Pharaoh's war chariots—six hundred of his elite troops and thousands more behind—and Israel cringed wailing on the shore. But as the pharaoh's men passed into that awesome cut, the horses reared and plunged in terror, and the east wind screamed, and the chariots mired and slewed in the wet sand, and in the dark of the night men cursed and stumbled and finally they cried, "Turn back, for Israel's God fights for them against us!" And God said to Moses, "Stretch out your hand." Just as dawn broke, Moses stretched out his hand, and that howling east wind gave a sort of sigh and ceased to blow, and with a mighty crash those green walls of water tumbled down, entombing the fighting host of Egypt.

Israel woke as from a bad dream and, like children at an unexpected summer holiday, they shouted and sang and clapped each other on the back, and Miriam the Prophetess took her tambourine, and all the women danced after her as she sang,

*Sing to the Lord for he has risen in triumph!*
*The horse and his rider he has hurled into the sea.*

So, after four hundred years, Abraham's seed started back to the land God had promised him so long ago.

# Israel and the Golden Calf

THE EXCITEMENT OF THE Red Sea crossing and the taste of freedom buoyed Israel for a while, and so they came to Mount Sinai and there they camped, and Moses went up to talk with God. For a while it was just fine. It was nice to settle down and live in peace for a few days, but Moses didn't come back, and the mountain smoked and grumbled, and the people began to get uneasy. Aaron tried to hush them, but he wasn't the leader Moses was, and besides, he wasn't too sure himself where this strange, dark brother of his had got to.

Finally the people were muttering right out loud, "We've been deserted! For all we know God's tired of us and gone off somewhere and Moses is dead. How long are we going to sit here in this desert and have no leader? Make us a God so we can worship—one we can see, not clouds of fire and wind, but something solid we can touch."

So Aaron gathered up all the gold earrings and cast a gold calf, just like in Egypt, and all the people brought animals to sacrifice, and food and drink, and they had a feast. It was such a relief to have a controllable, visible god that they let go of everything they'd ever promised or learned, and the feast became a drunken sexual orgy.

God said to Moses, high on the mountain, "Here, take these tablets I've written my laws on and get down there. You wouldn't believe what things those people are doing! I'll destroy them! Every one! And I'll make a nation of your children only!"

But Moses reminded God of his friendship with Abraham and Isaac and Jacob and Joseph and his promise that their children should have the land of their fathers. God said he wouldn't destroy them this time, but Moses, when he got in sight of the golden calf and the debauchery of the feast, was so furious that he threw down God's tablets of law so violently they shattered, and Moses stormed into camp. Well, with Moses back, people began to see what they'd done, and they sneaked off, leaving Aaron to face his furious brother. Moses demanded, "Why? Did they threaten you with torture? Did they bribe you? Why have you done this sinful thing?"

Aaron shuffled his feet a bit and alibied, "Well, you know how stubborn they are, and when you didn't come back I sort of, kind of, well…gave in, and took all their earrings and melted them and—do you know what? They turned into this gold bull calf right there in the fire."

Moses wasn't impressed! And as the story goes, he ground up the gold calf into a powder and dumped it in their drinking water. And he stood at the camp gate and said, "All who are faithful to Jahweh come here to me." And many did—the men of the tribe of Levi in particular—and he ordered them to take their swords and kill the unfaithful, and they did—around three thousand of them. And Moses said, "This day you have consecrated yourselves priests to the Lord!" Moses went slowly back up the mountain and he said, "God, I know that was a terrible sin. Forgive them, please, but if they must be destroyed, neither do I want my name in your book of life!" And God said, "I will lead them as I have before. I won't wipe them out utterly, but the time will come when those who have done this must suffer," and a great illness fell on the camp because of their unfaithfulness. But still God led them on toward the land of promise by Moses' hand, kept them safe in their journeyings, and took no more vengeance for their sin, but forgave it.

# Miracles in the Desert

AFTER THE ELATION over the destruction of Egypt's war party, Israel turned its face from the Red Sea and toward the desert of Shur. Their fathers had been wanderers, a free and hardy folk, but these people had lived in the Egyptian civilization all their lives, and these barren reaches were terrifying. Not only were they unprotected save for their flimsy tents, but the food they had brought was beginning to look scanty already.

One thing bothered them worse than shortage of food. There had been no water for three days. There was real excitement when they came to Marah and saw the stream there, but the excitement turned to consternation when they found the stream so bitter it was simply unfit to drink. Through cracked lips and parched throats they grumbled, "What are we to drink, Moses, now that you've got us here?"

Moses appealed to Jahweh, who said, "Why, drink this water. Those branches will sweeten it." And when Moses threw them in the water, the branches made it good, and the thirsty people drank their fill. Jahweh said to the people there, "Listen to me and keep my laws and I will heal you as I have healed these waters, and not harm you as I did the Egyptians."

Once again Israel moved on. First they camped at Elim, where there were trees and springs, but Moses urged them on their way into the desert of Sin between Elim and Sinai. Now there was no food left. They were about a month and a half's time from the excitement of leaving Egypt. The novelty was worn thin.

"Why didn't Jahweh just kill us off in Egypt where we could have died with a full belly?" they whined. "Why did he haul us clear out here to starve to death?" And they cast black looks at Aaron and Moses.

Jahweh spoke to Moses. "I have heard the people's complaints, and I will answer. I will send them food raining down from heaven.

Each day they must gather what they need. No more. On the sixth day they shall gather for sabbath also. I will test and see if they keep my rulings for them."

Jahweh also promised meat to the people, and when they were gathered at Moses' command he showed his glory over the wilderness in a cloud. Moses told the men of Israel that Jahweh would give them meat that evening and bread in the morning so that they should know he was God. "For," said Moses, "who are we? But it is not against us you have complained, but against God."

Sure enough, just at dusk, an incredibly large flock of quail hovered and settled on the camp. The hungry people killed and ate to their hearts' content. The next morning there was a heavy dew on the camp. When it dried in the sun it left a strange white residue on the grass, almost like frost. It tasted like coriander (that lovely, slightly peppery, bread spice) and was plentiful enough to feed everyone.

Each household was to pick up as much of the manna as it required for *one* day, remember? You know how people are. Maybe they thought they'd better get plenty while it was here (who knew whether it would come tomorrow?). Maybe they thought if they got enough today, they could relax tomorrow. Whatever they thought, God wasn't impressed. Next morning, when those smug housewives went to get out their stash of manna, it smelled to high heaven! Not only that, but it was alive with maggots!

After that nasty little mess, nobody tried to horde manna, and when the sun got high the extra manna seemed to melt. The sixth day, when Moses said, "Gather double," they listened and did just that. This time it remained sweet and usable for two days.

Did I say they listened? Well, *most* of them did, but there are always a few who can't *believe*...Those few took their baskets and trotted out on the morning of the seventh day to gather manna. Were they surprised! It simply wasn't there. God said to Moses, "How long will these people act that way! This is my sabbath. That's why I gave them enough for two days. They are to rest on the sabbath as I told them!" And after that, they did. For forty years the Lord Jahweh fed his people in this way.

Once again Israel moved on toward Canaan, and once again there was no water and the people grumbled. "Why did you bring us out of Egypt? Did you think it would be fine if we died of thirst—we and our children and cattle? Is that it?"

Moses said, "God, what am I to do? How do I deal with these people? They're within a hairbreadth of stoning me!" And Jahweh answered, "Take your rod, that rod with which you divided the sea, and strike that rock. I will be standing before you on it and water will flow for the people in their sight."

Gathering the elders together, Moses went to the rock of Horeb, and as he struck the rock, sweet, clear water gushed out, and the people drank and were satisfied. But as people will, they saw only Moses' "miraculous staff" and not Jahweh there on the rock.

As Israel approached Rephidim, King Amalek gathered troops against them, and Moses sent Joshua out to lead the men in their first battle. "I will stand on the hilltop," promised Moses, "with the staff of God in my hand invoking Jahweh."

Joshua led the troops down into the plain. The battle was hard fought, but each time the Israelites looked up and saw Moses there, they knew that God fought for them and were strengthened. Finally Moses wearied, but as soon as he dropped his hands the Israelites wavered and panicked. Quickly Aaron and Hur brought a stone where he could sit, and on either side they stood to hold up his hands. All that long day the battle raged, and as the sun crept across the sky, Moses sat praying to God with Aaron and Hur supporting him. Israel fought bravely, and as the sun set, the last of the Amalekites were slain.

In the name of Jahweh, Israel had won its first battle; when it was over, Moses built an altar to Jahweh in celebration of the victory God had won for Israel.

# Land of Promise

THE PROMISED LAND WAS almost in reach, and Israel made camp near the edge of the desert, while Moses spoke with God. Jahweh said, "Choose from among the men of Israel a group of men to look over the land for you, so that you can know what I'm giving you, and plan how you shall enter it."

Moses gathered all the men of Israel above twenty years of age together and took a census—a sort of informal draft, if you will, to assess the strength of his available fighting force. From each tribe he chose a leader to go in the scouting party.

"Find out," Moses said to these men, "what the land is like. See if they live in open fields or walled cities. Find out whether they are well armed, and whether they are warlike or peaceful. While you're there, bring us back some of the fruits of the soil so that we may know if it produces well."

The agreed time for this exploration was forty days, and while the people settled in to await its results, the dozen men slipped away into the land in twos and threes to avoid the obvious. The produce was impressive, and grapes were just beginning to ripen. Did you ever smell an arbor full of ripe grapes under the summer sun? Heaven . must smell like that—especially if you've been months and months in the desert.

The longer those spies stayed in the land of Canaan, the better it looked. Manna, after all, *is* food, but here were the lush fruits they recalled from Egypt. They cut a branch of grapes to take back. They got some pomegranates and figs too. It was wonderful to taste these things again.

The riches of the land were obvious, but when they returned to camp to make their report to Moses and the people, they had a different effect on different people. Everyone agreed it was a "land of milk and honey." "But," said some worriedly, "it's not going to be a pushover! We saw walled cities and armed men, and what's more, we saw some of the sons of the giants down there!"

Caleb, of the tribe of Judah, and Joshua, representing Ephraim, spoke right up. "It's as rich as they say, and there certainly are some things to be overcome, but what does that matter? Jahweh promised us the land, didn't he? Why should we fear them?"

The other ten men all lined up and took turns panicking! "Oh my, that was a terrible land!"

"That was a land that devours its people."

"There are walled towns!"

"Armies—like you wouldn't believe!"

"I saw giants!"

"Yes, indeed! We saw giants so big that we looked like—like *grasshoppers* to them. They acted as if they'd squash us with a casual stamp of their foot!"

Then the other Israelite men took up the refrain they seem to have been best at. "Oh no! We've simply come out here to be slaughtered! We'll be cut down and our women and children made slaves! God could just as well have starved us to death in the desert as to let us come here to get hacked up with swords."

Joshua and Caleb and Moses harangued and remonstrated. They tore their clothes and prostrated themselves before Jahweh. "Look," reasoned Caleb, "their gods have been made useless. Their power deserts them because Jahweh leads us."

All they got for their pains was mutiny. I don't know who started it, but someone mumbled they'd be better off in Egypt, then someone else said, "There's talk of returning to Egypt," and someone else began organizing an informal caucus so they could choose a leader to take them back to Egypt. While they were at it, a few fatheads got the idea going that they should stone this Moses who got them into such a predicament, and those other three fanatics with him!

Things were getting mighty nasty when those four men prostrated themselves to Jahweh before the Tent of the Presence. It was, after all, *his* party, and they appealed to him for his will. Then, in sight of all the people, the glory of God appeared in a cloud over his tent, and he spoke to Moses.

God was furious! How often was he to hear this people whine that they should have stayed slaves? What sort of an army would *this* make? "I'll blast them," he said to Moses. "They aren't fit to bother with. I'll make a nation of you—start over like I did with Abram!"

And Moses said, "Begging your pardon, Lord. I know they're a stubborn and obstreperous people. I know they've provoked you beyond all reason, but Lord, think of your loving kindness! Think of your mercy! Think also, Lord, of the *looks* of the thing. If you wipe the people out, all the lands will say, 'Aha! Their God couldn't keep his promise. He brought them out of Egypt, but hadn't the power to establish them as a nation elsewhere!' Lord, we surely don't want that, with all due respect!"

Well, God was merciful, but even Moses had to admit that bunch of whiners was no crack fighting force, and God changed the plan. "For forty days," he said, "I showed those spies the wonders of the land. Now, for every day of that, the people that rejected me shall wander a year in the wilderness until all the adults who turned me down are dead. Joshua and Caleb, only, shall come into that land!" And the other ten scouts died then and there.

As is often the case with mob psychology, the people, seeing what had happened, veered from one extreme to the other. Jahweh was *mad* at them! There were ten leaders *dead*, and they'd better do what he wanted in the first place before more of them were struck down. Now the same ones who had been organizing to go back to Egypt turned their attention to organizing to fight Canaan.

Moses held his head! "No! No! No!" he said. "It's too late now! You rejected Jahweh, and you're fortunate to have come off with your lives, but you certainly can't expect him to support you in battle *now* after you've played the coward and rejected him!"

The leaders, as usual, couldn't hear the sense in Moses' commands. They did arm and organize and mount a hasty and disastrous attack on the peoples of the highlands. When the troops went out, neither

Moses nor the Ark of the Covenant went with them. They remained in the camp. The attack was a disaster—the slaughter was frightful, and those warriors who escaped were chased and harried all the way to Hormah. So, with the Promised Land to their backs, the people of Israel turned once again to wander in the desert.

# Rebellion and Jealousy

YOU AND I, WITH twenty-twenty hindsight, see Moses as a leader inspired by the God who called him. For the people he led, he was a man, and fallible, and—nobody's perfect, and leaders in particular can seem like a pain in the neck. I guess that's how the affair with Korah got going.

Korah was no upstart kid, but a respected man in the community. He, and Dathan and Abiram who joined him, were among the Levites who served in the Tent of the Presence before the Lord. Korah came to Moses and said, "You act as if God was your personal property! Aren't we *all* the chosen people? Didn't Jahweh call all of us out of Egypt? You and Aaron make all the decisions and do all the talking, and it's getting too thick for a lot of us." (There were 250 men, to be exact, for whom Korah spoke.)

Moses saw it as jealousy against Aaron, under whom the Levites served, and he warned, "It's not against Aaron you speak, but against God himself who chose us to our tasks!" And he called Dathan and Abiram to appear before him. They flatly refused to come. "Who are you," they said, "to lord it over us? Where is that land flowing with milk and honey you promised us when you led us here? *This* sure as hell isn't it!"

Moses was livid! And he turned to Jahweh and said, "I pray you, don't receive their offering! I've done them no injustice. I've never even received so much as a donkey from them." Then Moses summoned Korah and said, "Tomorrow we will have a trial. Bring your censer, and let each of your followers do the same."

The next day an assembly was proclaimed, and all those in rebellion brought their censers with coals and incense and stood at the Tent of the Presence. God said to Moses and Aaron, "Just get out of the way! I'm going to *destroy* this faithless mob! This time

I've really *had* it with them!" Moses and Aaron fell on their faces and begged, "Surely, God, for only one man's sin, not all should die!" and Jahweh agreed. "But," he said, "stand clear of the dwellings of Korah!"

Moses moved all the people back so that Korah and Dathan and Abiram and their households stood alone at their tent doors. "Don't go near them," Moses said, "nor touch anything that is theirs lest you be caught in the perversity, and you too perish for their sin."

The people moved back, leaving these households at their doors and the 250 men who followed them standing before the Tent of the Presence. "Now," said Moses, "as the Lord God is judge, if these men die a natural death, the kind of death we all expect eventually to die, then I'm discredited. I'm a fake and a fraud and God never sent me. If, on the other hand, Jahweh does something violent and unforeseen, so that these go down alive into the land of the dead, then they are punished and I am vindicated."

There was a moment of unreal silence, as if the earth and all in it held its breath, and then there was a muttering rumble that sounded like it came from the depths of the earth. The ground under their feet shifted and shook, and the people clutched each other in terror. The Lord God opened a fissure right at the feet of those three doomed households, and they and all their possessions were hurled headlong into its depths. One awful moment their screams were heard, and then the earth closed over them.

All the rest of the people of Israel turned and ran for their lives. "For," they said, "the earth must not devour us and our children." All, that is, except the 250 men who had supported Korah's rebellion. Jahweh sent a great flash of living flame that consumed them on the spot.

When things had settled down a bit, God said to Moses, "Have the unholy flame from those censers removed from my sight, but the censers themselves have been consecrated at the price of those men's lives. They are to be beaten out into flat sheets and used as a covering for my altar. They will serve to remind men that only those properly consecrated shall come to serve at my altar lest I release the power of my wrath on them."

That should have been the end of the affair. Looking back on it, as we are able to do, one would have supposed Israel had been frightened enough by God's power to stay mighty quiet for a long time to come. But that's looking back through the eyes of many God-fearing tellers of the original tale.

What Israel saw, on the spot, was not so much the power of Jahweh in protecting his chosen leaders and keeping his people pure as the fact that Moses had done it *again*. He, and he alone, had called that assembly and appealed to God. Three whole families had been wiped out as a result of God's wrath, and 250 fighting men had perished in the flames. And they cried out against Moses as a murderer.

God roared out his wrath and his intent to wipe them out once more, and Moses once again pleaded for the people's lives. But God had begun a terrible plague already, so Moses told Aaron, "Quick! Take your censer and go through the camp performing the rites of atonement before they all die of God's wrath!"

Aaron took his censer and went among the people, and he stood between the living and the dead and swung the censer and the fragrant smoke rose between them, and the remaining living remained alive. Even so, there was a toll of 14,700 dead from the plague. And that's not to mention those who died because of Korah's rebellion.

# Moses' Last Days

REMEMBER THE CHILD FISHED from the bulrushes who was raised by one of the princesses in Egypt? Remember the swift-tempered young prince who struck an overseer dead and had to flee the country? Remember the quiet shepherd of Midian whom God sent back to Egypt to free his people? And the brother God called to help him do the talking? To Moses and Aaron they seemed a far-off dream, for now they were old, old men, and the last forty years of their lives had been spent as nomads.

Almost all the people of their own age were dead. Some had perished of Jahweh's wrath, but many simply died of old age and lay buried in the wilderness where Israel had wandered. And now it was Aaron's turn. Few men are given to know the hour of their death if it is to be a peaceful one, but the Lord Jahweh said to Moses, "It's time Aaron should be gathered to his people. Remember that I said at Meribah that he should not see the Promised Land. Take Aaron and Eleazer his son up on Mount Hor. Take the priestly clothing from Aaron, and put it on his son Eleazer before Aaron's death, for there on the mountain he will be gathered to his fathers."

Moses called all Israel together, and in their sight took Aaron and Eleazer up the mountain. Slowly they climbed—two old, old men, and the young one with them—quietly, because it was a sad moment, but peaceably too. Aaron's life had been long, and he had served Jahweh well, and in that there was great contentment.

When the priestly robes were laid on Eleazer's shoulders, Aaron reached out and touched his strong son's hand, and then, lying down quietly as if to a well-earned rest, he let go of life.

As the people watched at the bottom of Mount Hor, they could see two figures coming down the path. Moses, bent and slow with age, and beside him Eleazer in the priestly garments, slowing his steps to those of his uncle. And as they watched, they set up a wail of mourning for Aaron who was no more. Thirty days they camped at the foot of the mountain and mourned Aaron's death before they moved on.

Once again, Israel skirted the land of Edom, keeping always to the desert, and once again the people rebelled. Funny, but it seems to have become almost a refrain with them. "Why did you bring us out of Egypt to starve and go thirsty? Why did you drag us into this stinking place?" Now, most of them couldn't even *remember* Egypt, and they certainly had no grasp of the hardships of the slavery there.

God's response to the refrain looks pretty predictable to us at this distance, too. He was somewhat less than enchanted. After he had gone to the care of bringing them out of bondage and forming Israel into a nation, he expected respect and obedience.

This particular time, God didn't even warn Moses. He sent a plague of stinging serpents, and their sting was deadly. At least the people perceived it as God's wrath, and they said, "Moses, *do* something! We didn't mean any harm!" So once again Moses appealed to Jahweh: "Lord, do you intend to destroy this people you've brought so *far*?"

God said to Moses, "Well, no, I'll spare them, but they've got to understand I'm doing just that. Make a fiery serpent, Moses, that looks like the real ones, and set it up on a pole, and tell those who are stung to look up at it as a sign of my mercy."

Moses took bronze and cast a serpent and set it in the center of the camp, and as word spread, people brought out their sick and dying to look at the sign of God's mercy. The deaths stopped and the people rejoiced. They did something else, too. They told and retold the story of God's mercy, shown by that brass model of a serpent, so vividly that many generations later a Jewish man recalled it from the memories of his childhood to explain how when he, Messiah, was "lifted up" on the cross it would provide the means of God's mercy to all the people who looked to him.

Moses was a very old man now, and the last of his generation. At 120 years, he was still clear of eye and firm of voice, but Jahweh came to him and said, "All right, Moses! This is it! It's almost time for Israel to enter the land I promised them. I myself will go before the people into the land, which you may not enter. Come up to the top of the mountain, and I will show you all the land before you die."

When you've led a people as long as Moses had, it sort of runs in your very blood, and Moses said, "All right, Lord. I'm ready and all, but Lord, what about my people? They'll be like a bunch of silly sheep milling around without a shepherd unless you choose someone to succeed me before I go. Let me see that, Lord."

And God said, "Good idea, Moses! We'll see to that right now. Call Joshua, whose reports on the land showed faith in me. He shall lead the people and possess the land in honor." So Moses called Joshua and gave him authority in sight of all the people so that they would revere him as leader.

When Joshua had been duly confirmed, Moses stood by the Tent of the Presence to bid the people good-bye. It wasn't a very kindly speech, by the way. Jahweh had told him the people would return to their apostasies and that they would be punished for it so that they wondered if he had given up on them. Moses made a song to teach the people to recall his warning by when he was gone. Then he blessed the people, tribe by tribe.

At last God said, "Come on, Moses. That's it! It's time for you to lay it down!" So Moses turned and walked up the mountain—this time by himself, but perhaps remembering the time he made the walk with Aaron on Mount Hor. Slowly he climbed to the summit of the mountain and God said, "Look, Moses! Isn't it beautiful?" And he let Moses see the whole length and breadth of it, and Moses lay down one last time with his face toward the Promised Land and so he died. Jahweh, himself, buried Moses in one of the mountain valleys, but no one ever knew exactly where. And Israel mourned Moses' death for thirty days, saying, "There was never a man like Moses, nor ever will be again, who spoke to Jahweh face-to-face!" Joshua, son of Nun, became leader of Israel, and when the prescribed days of mourning were past, he turned their feet toward the Promised Land in hope.

# Balaam and the Ass

AMONG THE MOST DELIGHTFUL of the tales of Jahweh's dealings with Israel is that of Balaam and the ass. Perhaps that's because Israel doesn't really do anything except sit there and look impressive. And there's the crux of the matter! Israel looked *darned* impressive and Balak, king of the Moabites, was scared. He had heard of the Amorites' rout, and he looked at the size of that mob of people, desert-hardened now, and he called in his elders. "Look," said Balak, "they are like an ox cropping grass, and it's moving this way. In a few more mouthfuls they'll be *on* us, and I don't think we've got the strength to defend ourselves."

After careful counsel everyone agreed that this called for more than ordinary measures. Balak commissioned a few of the elders—a suitably impressive group—to travel over to Balaam's place. He gave them a generous purse of silver to pay for the divination that was wanted and instructed them, "Tell Balaam to come over here and curse that mob for me so we have some defense against them."

When the elders of Moab and Midian came to Balaam's house, he invited them in hospitably and made them welcome.

"Now," said he, "what can I do for you gentlemen?"

"Well, actually," said the chief of them, "we've come with a message from Balak, king of Moab. He sends you word that he knows that what you bless stays blessed, and what you curse is doomed. He wants you to come over and curse that mob that has come up out of Egypt so we have a fighting chance against them."

Balaam was an honest man, and he said, "It's Jahweh who curses or blesses, not me; but stay the night with me, and I'll be glad to see what he has to say for you." That seemed fair enough—at least until the next morning when Balaam came in. "I'm sorry," he said, "but God says those are his people and they are blessed. I can't touch them!"

The elders trailed back to Balak with the message. "Damn!" said Balak. "Does that pipsqueak think I didn't offer him enough or what?" So he sent a larger and even more impressive group of men, and he sent a higher price for the divination and probably a few handsome gifts. Balaam met the delegation courteously, as before, and again he repeated that God did the cursing when any was done, but he'd be glad to check with him about it. The elders pressed him a little. "Did he understand," they asked, "that Balak was prepared to make him a rich man?"

That really irritated Balaam. It sounded awfully close to bribery. "Look here," said Balaam, "I told you before I can only do what God tells me should be done, and if Balak turned his whole house into one solid stack of silver and gold, I couldn't do what Jahweh forbids!" But he invited them to stay the night while he consulted Jahweh to see if there was any further word.

I'm not entirely sure what happened. Balaam seems to have believed that God said he could go. Next morning he told the elders, "I'll come along, all right, but remember—it's God who does the cursing, and he's been mighty quiet about that, all told!"

The elders weren't too worried. Once they got Balaam over to Moab, they'd done what they were sent for, and Balak could handle it from there.

There they were, trudging along the road with Balaam in the lead. He rode a gentle little donkey he'd had for years. She was a real gem for a man who often got lost in his own thoughts and forgot to pay attention to the road. That's why it really surprised him when she suddenly veered off the road and started across country. He gave the reins a jerk to bring her back, and beat her a couple of times. She just rolled her eyes and laid her ears back and trotted on, because now the angel of the Lord who had barred her way with drawn sword was gone.

The next time the angel barred the path it was between walls. When he appeared suddenly she shied to one side and Balaam's foot got scraped against the wall. "Stupid beast! What ails you?" he roared, and this time he really beat her. It was irritating enough to be going off on this chase with no clear idea of what might be permitted, but this was infuriating!

119

The third time the angel barred the path, it was in a place so narrow there was no way of avoidance. The ass simply refused to move, and when Balaam beat her she lay down under him. The enraged Balaam took his stick to her angrily, but God gave her a peculiar defense. "I've been your donkey since we were both youngsters," said she, in a human voice, "and have I ever before refused to serve you faithfully?"

"Well, no," said Balaam sort of automatically, without quite realizing that she'd never chatted with him before either. Then God opened Balaam's eyes to see the angel with the sword.

"You're a mighty lucky man, Balaam, to have such a faithful beast! Why did you beat her three times when each time she saved your life? I'd have killed *you* if you'd come closer—but not her!" This was a *strange* day, to say the least, but Balaam, who was perhaps more used to such things than you and I, said, "I've sinned! I didn't know. If you want me to go back, I'll go back!"

The angel said, "Well, no, now that you're on the way, go on ahead, but Balaam, don't say anything unless God tells you what to say. I'm warning you!"

So Balaam jogged on toward Moab. When he met Balak, the king said, "What was the problem? Why didn't you come when I first sent for you? Did you maybe think I couldn't make it worth your while?" Balaam replied, "All right, all right, I'm here, but let's get one thing straight. I can't say anything except what God tells me."

At Balaam's instructions Balak built seven altars and offered seven sacrifices. Balaam stood aside to listen to God. When he came back he said to Balak, "How can I curse those whom God doesn't curse? I see Israel from the crag—a people apart and numerous as the dust of the earth. May I die the death of the just and my end be one with theirs."

Balak was understandably irritated. "I bring you up here to curse this mob, and you *bless* them. What kind of talk is that?"

"I can only say what Jahweh tells me," said Balaam. "We could try again. Maybe this time he'll be favorable to you." So they set up seven more altars in another place and offered seven more sacrifices. Once again, Balaam went apart, and when he came back he said, "Jahweh says when he's made up his mind, it's made up! He's brought Israel out of Egypt and he intends a royal place for them. They are like a lion who will surely devour his prey!"

Balak was considerably upset. "Look, I brought you here to *curse* these people. If you can't curse them, at least don't *bless*." He could hardly believe his ill fortune, so he said, "Come over to the far hill where you can get a good look at them. Maybe from there you can curse them." Once again the sacrifice was made, and once more Balaam prophesied for Israel.

That was more than enough for Balak. "Three times you've blessed those I hired you to curse," he said. "You certainly can't expect me to pay you for *that*. It's all your Jahweh's fault you get no fee too!" Balaam replied, "I've said what I had to say, and as long as I'm here, you may as well have the rest of it." So he blessed Israel once more and predicted the final doom of Moab, Amalek, Bashan, and Midian. Then, mounting his gentle donkey, he jogged off toward home. This time the journey proved uneventful and the beast silent. But Balak, with a sinking heart, turned home to prepare for battle with Israel.

# Joshua and the Walls of Jericho

JOSHUA, FOR MOST OF his long life, is the "also ran"—the errand boy, the man who trails the great Moses around camp. Three times we see him briefly before Moses' death. Moses, it is recounted, made the sun stand still by sitting on the hill holding (or having held) up his hands. Joshua, in the valley below, had the dirty work—the blood and dust and heat of battle. Moses went into the Tent of the Presence and talked with God and came out with a shining face. Joshua, we learn almost as an afterthought, "stayed there in the tent." Why? Doing what? We don't know.

His one big chance as a hero was to spy out the Promised Land. He did, and he and Caleb did their best to convince the people that God had it in the bag for them. No one believed them. On the very eve of what should have been their first victory, Israel refused to hear and turned tail and ran. And Joshua, quietly obdurate, followed along after Moses. Then one day there was no Moses to stand behind, and God said, "You, Joshua." Joshua—quiet, obdurate, obedient as always—stepped into Moses' shoes, and Israel, instead of falling apart at Moses' death, recognized the man who had always stood in Moses' shadow and accepted his authority.

And now those waiting years were over both for Joshua and his people, and God said, "Let's go take the land! Jericho first!" And if there were any doubts, God took care of those lavishly. Remember the Red Sea and that dry path across it? So did Israel! They told it with awe to all the children as they grew—how God let Moses hold back the sea.

In the path to Jericho raged the Jordan River at its flood stage, and Joshua ordered the priests who carried God's covenant box, "Wade in and stand in the middle." They did, and the last bit of water flowed past their feet, and Jordan piled up as if a hand held it a ways upstream, and Israel walked dry shod into the Promised Land—like a page of history torn out of the past and set into the day where you live. Danger lay ahead this time instead of behind, and the box came up out of the stream and the restrained waters, unleashed again to their usual bed, and twice as strong, rolled down the valley and overflowed their banks and drove Israel even closer to the formidable walled city of Jericho. But the people of Jericho didn't do a thing—just sat there, smug and safe from this horde of nomads, behind their thick walls. They closed their gates and got set to repel the siege.

But God said, "Don't fight! Walk! Blow your ram's horns—seven of you priests—and the rest of you walk behind the ark around the city and be silent in my presence." And they did, and Jericho peered through the crannies and was amused and a little puzzled. The second day they came again, and Jericho heard them and watched and wondered. And the third and the fourth. The silence was eerie, broken only by the mournful wail of the horns, and they began to worry what sort of God was in that box that none dared approach except his chosen priests. For six days this went on, and it got scarier and scarier—those grim, close-mouthed faces and the utter silence of all save the horns and the steady thud of their marching feet. On the seventh day they watched again, and it was a sort of relief when that round was finished and they could be expected to go back to camp. But they didn't. They swung that corner where they'd begun, and it seemed as if their tempo increased ever so slightly and the horns wailed and the faces hardened with a sort of fierce joy and they went on and on and on until it seemed as if that steady tramp! tramp! tramp! tramp! would split your head open. On and on and on they went for hours, "and this will be eight ..." There was a deadly silence, waiting, every foot still, every hand on a sword, while the world seemed to hold its breath, waiting. Then, slowly, ceremoniously, seven of the chosen around the box raised the ram's horns to their lips and blew a mighty wail. Then, like the Jordan freed from its fetters, those hosts of warriors opened their mouths in a mighty shout of such strength it seemed the stones themselves must be shouting instead of just echoing the roar. "Hallel lu Jah!" they cried, and those ancient and unbreakable walls simply crumbled like dry earth, and Israel poured over them, roaring and swinging their swords.

A recent archeological find on the site of ancient Jericho tells us that the walls fell, all right—outward, as if they might have been pushed in panic. Be that as it may, whatever agent Jehovah used, the day was his and Jericho was totally destroyed.

# The Ban

THE AMOUNT OF WHOLESALE slaughter in the Old Testament battles always has a strange ring to the modern ear. That fighting men should be put to the sword is logical. That cities should be burned and looted is, unfortunately, a very human trait. What really sounds strangest to me, though, is that God should have been understood as commanding the wholesale slaughter of all living things—animals as well as people—after the city was taken. This practice was known as the ban. Any man who kept any of the things from a city under ban was to be destroyed himself, for he had offended God by so doing and brought the ban on himself.

Jericho was one of those cities under ban, except for one odd little side agreement, which Jahweh was understood to accept, possibly because it had been sworn to before the ban was pronounced. Joshua had sent a pair of spies into the city a few weeks before the Israelites advanced on it. They were to slip into the city sometime during a busy day and obtain whatever information they could about fortifications and the location of things in general.

One thing that's more than obvious about a stranger in town is that he doesn't know what is where or indeed, where he wants to go. Being well aware of that factor in their situation, these two canny Israelites checked in at a local house of prostitution. Not only was it likely to be a very unsuspicious place to stay—that particular desire knows no national boundaries—but there seemed a good chance they could pick up local news and gossip.

The plan to blend with local scenery was fine except for one thing. Jericho had evidently some spies of its own, and they had picked out those two as foreigners as soon as they saw them. Or maybe it was just some busybody. Whatever it was, before they had been there very long, there came a banging on Rahab's door in the name of the king of Jericho.

Rahab thought fast. "Just a minute!" she called. "Be there as soon as I … uh … get decent." The soldiers of the guard lounged at their ease on the doorstep and snickered. What Rahab was really doing, of course, was hurrying the Israelites up to the housetop. She hid them under some flax stalks she had up there, and then she went to the door.

"Oh yes!" said Rahab. "I did let them in for a minute. Israelites, were they? Fancy! They actually thought they could spy us out, did they? Such brass! But they didn't stay long. They seemed in quite a hurry to leave. I guess they wanted to be out of town before nightfall, because they made a point of asking me when the gate closed. Maybe if you hurry you can catch them. I shouldn't think they'd have gotten very far, though I've not the least idea which way they were heading."

The soldiers hurried off to get the gates opened to let them out, and they chased off into the twilight searching for the two men. Rahab, being a practical woman, returned to the housetop to strike a bargain with her guests.

"I've saved your lives, I think, and I'd like to ask a favor in return," she said. They had heard the whole affair, and believe me, they knew what they owed her. It might also have occurred to them that one shout from her would bring half the city down on them even now. When Rahab asked for her own life and the lives of her family to be spared, it seemed a reasonable bargain. She also gave them what may have been the most valuable bit of information they had gathered. Jericho, she told them, was terrified. They had heard of the Red Sea crossing and Israel's current military victories, and they saw clearly that Israel's God was a mighty leader.

Rahab also gave them some practical advice. "You can't outrun the guards, so hide out where they've already looked. Then when they give up you can slip out of hiding and get away safely." They told her to gather all her people into her house and keep them there. If anyone went out, his life wasn't protected, but all within would be spared. They gave her a scarlet cord to mark the house with, so no one would mistake it when they returned, and she got a rope and let them down from a window outside the wall of the city. (Her house was built into the thickness of the wall.)

After three days of pursuit, the soldiers of the king came to the Jordan, and there they concluded that the men had given them the slip and outrun them. When they returned to Jericho, the spies went back to camp; there Joshua confirmed their bargain with Rahab because she had saved their lives. In fact, when the city fell, he sent them to bring out Rahab and her family before the ban was enforced, and they were permitted to live with the Israelites after that.

There was one other exception to the ban to which Jahweh didn't take so kindly. Soon after Jericho fell, Joshua sent a scouting party up to Ai, and they returned with the word that, compared to Jericho, it should be a pushover. Instead of moving the whole tribe up to besiege Ai, they sent a fighting force of three thousand men. It seemed plenty under the circumstances, but something went terribly wrong! Ai rushed out to defend itself with a surprising fierceness, and Israel broke before they ever reached the town gate. Thirty-six men were killed right there, and the rest turned tail and ran.

Ai chased the fighting force Israel had sent all the way to Shebarim, where they cornered them and made a shambles of what was left of the force. This time they didn't even retreat. They scattered, every man for himself, and they slunk back to camp in twos and threes.

Joshua prostrated himself before Jahweh's ark. The elders of Israel did the same, and they mourned bitterly all that day. Joshua prayed, "Lord, Jahweh, why have you deserted us? This is terrible public relations. All of Canaan is going to hear of it, and if they all get organized and come after us at once, *then* what will you do for the honor of your name?"

God said, "Joshua, stop that groveling and stand up here and listen to me. I *told* you that if Israel broke the ban on Jericho it would fall on their own heads. There's a man in your midst who brought the ban on Israel. Find him and get *rid* of him!"

So Joshua called the people all together, and before God they cast lots. The lot fell on the tribe of Judah. They cast again, and of the clans of the tribe it fell on Zerah, and all the rest of Judah fell back with the other tribes to watch. The third time the lots were cast, the family of Zabdi was singled out. They stood there before Joshua, a small knot of men shifting uneasily and avoiding each other's eyes. As the men came forward, one after another, each was declared free of guilt, until Achan, who was Carmi's son and Zabdi's grandson, was singled out.

Joshua looked at Achan and said, "My son, give God glory. Pay him homage and tell me what you've done!"

You could've heard a pin drop when Joshua finished speaking, and Achan gasped, "Yes, sir. I did it. There was this one house where they had such lovely things, and before I set it on fire, I picked up a cloak of the weaving of Babylon. It seemed a waste that such a lovely thing should be destroyed, and I coveted it and took it. There was silver with it too, and a brick of pure gold. They're under the earth in my tent. I was frightened of what I had done, and I hid them there." Joshua sent men to search, and there lay the small heap of spoil.

With a sad heart, Joshua pronounced the ban on Achan, and he and all his household were killed, and they and all his possessions buried under a cairn of stones to mark the grave of an outlaw.

When Achan had been destroyed, Israel marched again on Ai. This time the destruction of the town was complete. All of its people were destroyed and the town burned to the ground, and Israel rejoiced that once again Jahweh went with them into battle.

# JUDGES AND OTHER TRIBAL TALES

# Othniel, Ehud, and Deborah

THE MOVE OF ISRAEL into the Promised Land, while it started with the spectacular defeats of Jericho and Ai, was not a clean sweep. It was a long series of battles, and even when most of the twelve tribes had laid claim to an inheritance in the land, there were other peoples around them and rulers left who were a threat to their possession. As long as Joshua lived, they kept the memory of God's leading them, but when he had lived to be 110, Joshua died. He was buried with honor on his own land in the highlands of Ephraim.

After Joshua's death, the memory of Israel's deliverance was kept alive for a time by the elders who had entered the land with him, but one after another they died, and a new era began. As people settled down in permanent homes, they began to neighbor with the folks around them. There was some intermarriage, and the customs of the country rubbed off on them. They began to worship the Baals as their neighbors did, and God was angry. He let the king of Edom conquer his people. For eight years they were slaves to him, then some of them began to remember that Jahweh had delivered their parents, and it wouldn't hurt to *ask*. As soon as they truly turned to him, God sent help. Caleb, who had entered the Promised Land with Joshua on that first mission before the years in the wilderness, was dead now, but he had a younger brother, Othniel.

God said, "There's a man of a family that's been faithful to me before." And he sent Othniel to lead Israel. He became the first of Israel's judges. He led them to victory, and for forty years kept them faithful to God and at peace.

No sooner had Othniel died than the people slipped back to their old ways. This time the king of Moab took over. For eighteen years he enslaved them. Once again, they thought of God's power and, like children in trouble, cried for help. God sent them Ehud from the tribe of Benjamin.

Ehud was a southpaw, and a mighty clever one. He made himself a sharp dagger, and he hid it under his clothes when he took the tribute money up to the king. When the money had been paid, he and the other Israelites left the throne room. When they had gone a little way, Ehud turned back. He persuaded the door guards that he had a message, and when they let him in he said, "King Eglon, God means this message for your ear alone!" The king sent all his servants out, and Ehud said, "Just to be sure we aren't interrupted, I'll just bar the door."

When Ehud told Eglon the message was from God, he stood up from his throne. He was an obese man, and slow-moving. Besides, it was obvious to him the man wore no weapon on his left thigh, and his right hand hung casually at his side as he approached. He hardly saw the swift move of the *left* hand that drew the dagger from under his clothing and thrust it home, in Eglon's stomach. Eglon fell without even a cry, and Ehud vaulted over the window sill and ran for his life.

Because the door was locked, the servants figured Eglon wanted privacy. It took quite a while before anyone had the nerve to force it open. By the time they found their dead ruler, Ehud was urging his hurrying companions to help him rouse the fighting forces of Israel. They did just that and threw off Moab's yoke. This time God kept his people in peace for eighty years under the leadership of Ehud. There was another judge following him who routed 600 Philistines with an ox goad. That's really all we know about Shamgar, but *that's* pretty impressive.

It didn't take long after Shamgar's death for the people to slip into their old ways. This time Jabin of Canaan, with his 900 iron-plated chariots, took over, and the people howled to God for deliverance, for Jabin oppressed them cruelly.

The judges up to this time were warriors and rose to power by their strength in battle for Jahweh. Deborah, however, seems to have risen to prominence as a prophet and settler of disputes. She used to sit under a particular palm tree in the highlands of Ephraim, and the people came from all over to ask for her judgments.

Israel had been under Jabin's thumb for around twenty years when Deborah sent for Barak of the tribe of Naphthali. It's a mark of the honor in which she was held that he came right away.

"Barak," she said, "it's time we threw off Canaan's yoke, and Jahweh says to gather the tribes and start the attack."

Barak was no coward, but he thought of those ironclad chariots and the reputation for downright brutality that Sisera, Jabin's commander, had, and he said, "No way! I'm not going out there by myself. I'm just a plain fighting man, and I might get the signals all mixed up and do the right thing at the wrong time, and Jahweh wouldn't be with us, and we'd be wiped out. Either *you* come or I don't stir a step!"

"All right, I'll go," said Deborah, "but the way you're doing this will rob you of all the glory. Because you haven't trusted God enough to go on your own we will still win, but the glory of destroying Sisera will go to a woman instead of to you and your fighting men."

Deborah got up from her tree, and she and Barak together led the forces out to Mount Tabor. When Sisera heard of it, he assembled his forces and ordered out the iron chariots. He'd teach that ragtag bunch of slaves a lesson they wouldn't soon forget! And he mustered all his troops at Kishon.

There lay Sisera's forces in the valley, and before they were quite prepared to attack (for Sisera presumed, in his arrogance, that he could choose his own time), Deborah said to Barak, "Now! This is the day when Jahweh marches at your head."

Barak and his ten thousand men came whooping down off that mountain as if they'd been ten times ten thousand, and they caught Sisera entirely off guard. His troops scattered like leaves in a wind. The rout was so complete that Sisera himself could only flee on foot to look for a place to hide.

Sisera was exhausted and hard-pressed, so when he came upon the tent of Heber the Kenite he took his chances and asked for shelter. Jael, Heber's wife, came out to meet him. She spoke sweetly to him and hid him under a rug in the tent. "You keep watch," he said, "and if they come looking for me, tell them there's no one here."

Sisera had run a long way and was dreadfully thirsty. He asked for water, and Jael gave him some milk to drink and hid him again under the rug. The exhausted Sisera fell asleep. I've often wondered why Jael did what she did. Perhaps she owed some personal grudge if not against Sisera, against Jabin, who had a reputation for cruelty. Perhaps she felt that if Israel had the power now she'd better ingratiate herself and her family with them.

Whatever her reasons, as soon as Sisera was asleep, Jael took up one of the sharp pegs the tent was anchored with and a mallet that lay there in the tent. With a steady hand she drove that stake clean through Sisera's temples and into the earth beneath his head. When she was sure Sisera was dead, Jael walked out to meet Barak, who was coming in pursuit of him. "Come, and I'll show you the man you want," she said. Barak followed her into the tent with drawn sword, and there lay Sisera—dead. Talk about anticlimax!

Barak doesn't seem to have been too upset. What he said to Jael on the moment isn't recorded, but there *is* a song he and Deborah sang in celebration of the event. It begins, quite properly, with praise of God for his blessing. It describes the fighting hosts of Israel in glowing terms and indicates that even the stars in heaven fought against Canaan.

There is special praise in this warlike canticle for Deborah, who "like a mother in Israel, woke the dead villages." There is a blessing, too, for Jael, and a blow-by-blow account of her heroic deed. Barak gets only a passing mention, just as Deborah prophesied. The whole thing ends with an appeal to Jahweh for a blessing on those who love him. I can't say they lived happily ever after, but for forty years there was peace in the land.

# Gideon

THE FIFTH OF ISRAEL'S judges was Gideon, whom Jahweh called to deliver Israel from Midian. The troops of Midian carried on their warfare by destroying the food supply. If a crop was planted they ruined it. If they missed and it came to harvest, they stole it. They harried flocks and herds until there was hardly anything left. That's why Gideon was hiding in the winepress, grinding the bit of wheat they had managed to hide, when the angel of God came to him and said, "God is with you, valiant warrior."

You simply don't laugh in the face of a heavenly messenger, but Gideon must have been tempted. Instead he said, "Pardon my bluntness. I know all about the rescue from Egypt and all that, but if God is with us, why are we in the mess we're in now with Midian making our lives miserable?" And the angel of God said, "Go in the strength in which I send you and destroy Midian. I promise!" "Lord, don't be angry," said Gideon, "but I'm from the weakest clan in the tribe of Manasseh, and the least important of my family. Why me?" The angel of God said, "Never mind who *you* are. It's *I* that will win the victory; just go!" "If you are really you," said Gideon, "and if you mean to favor me, let me run and fix an offering and bring it to you as a sort of proof."

"I'll wait!" said the angel. So Gideon ran and fixed meat and broth and cakes of bread, and when he laid it on the rock, the angel of Jahweh reached out his staff, and the rock itself burst into flames and consumed the whole offering with a brilliant flash that blinded Gideon. When he could see again, the angel was gone, and Gideon wailed, "I'll die! I've seen God face to face!" But God said, "Peace! Have no fear, you will not die."

That night God said to Gideon, "Pull down the altar to Baal that belongs to your father. Chop the sacred post beside it into kindling wood. Build me an altar there on the hill, and use that kindling to sacrifice your father's fattened calf!"

Gideon figured he'd never get away with all that in daylight, so in the dark of the night he hastily finished the job, and next morning when people discovered it, Gideon was conspicuously absent. The townspeople came to Joash, Gideon's father, and said, "Bring your son out. He has destroyed Baal's altar and sacred post, and he must die!"

Joash was evidently not too convinced that Baal really meant anything, and faced them down. "What are you bawling about? If Baal can't protect himself, why should you protect him? Let anyone who pleads for Baal be put to death now that Gideon has destroyed his altar." When he put it that way, people sort of drifted off, and Gideon was rather more admired than blamed.

Once more Gideon asked Jahweh for a sign. "If you really mean I'm to lead Israel to victory," he said, "let this fleece I lay on the threshing floor be wet with dew in the morning, but all around it be dry." In the morning the ground was dry, but Gideon wrung a cupful of water from the fleece. Again he requested the same thing, but in reverse. Sure enough, the next morning's dew was heavy, but the fleece was bone dry.

Having proved Jahweh's favor to his own satisfaction, Gideon began amassing troops. Presently he had quite a mob of fighting men. He was feeling pretty pleased with their strength when God intervened. "Gideon," he said, "that's too many people. Already you're thinking about *your* strength instead of mine. Next thing people will be thinking *they* did it all instead of giving me glory. Send home everyone that has any doubt at all."

Gideon put his forces to the test, as God had told him to, and 22,000 went home, leaving not quite half that many there, and Gideon said, "Yes, I see, Lord. These few troops who really have their hearts in it will be easier to manage and we can—" "That's still too many! Take them down to the water to drink, and I'll separate them for you."

At God's command, Gideon set apart those who had lapped water with their tongues rather than kneeling to drink. There were just 300. They kept all the weapons and supplies, but sent the other men back to their tents. Before they left, he had them leave all their pitchers and horns, and these he shared among the force of three hundred. They stayed there on the hill overlooking the forces of Midian camped in the valley.

God sent Gideon on a little spy trip. He didn't really get much practical military information, but he heard a soldier tell of the dream of Midian's destruction. He slipped quietly back to his men, and when the night was darkest, God said, "Now!"

Gideon split his men into three groups of a hundred each. They quietly made a circle around the Midianite camp. Each man held a horn and each had a pitcher in which a lighted torch was concealed. "Now watch me," said Gideon, "and do what I do." For a while everything was very quiet, then they could hear the change of the guard in the camp below. Presently Gideon gave the signal. Every man blew a blast on his horn, shattered his pitcher, and began shouting, "For Jahweh and Gideon!" To the terrified Midianites the night seemed suddenly alive with torches and noise. They never doubted that each of those torches had a thousand men behind it, and they panicked and ran and, in the confusion, fought each other. They were sure there were enemy troops among them—hadn't they heard them blow the charge? Meanwhile, Gideon and his men simply stood their ground and made noise.

With Midian in flight, all the fighting men of Naphtali, Asher, and Manasseh gave chase, and while they harried them from the rear, Gideon sent word ahead to Ephraim. "Midian is in flight. Seize the water crossings so they can't get away." They did just that and brought Gideon the heads of the two slain Midianite war leaders. At first they were more than a little upset that Gideon hadn't called them to the first muster. Gideon reasoned with them. "Look, all I've done is scare them a little bit. You've had the *real* glory. God delivered their princes into the hands of Ephraim!" At that they began to see themselves as real heroes, and somehow it was hard to do that and keep up their gripe. Gideon was nobody's fool!

Gideon and his men pursued the kings of Midian toward Jordan until he ran out of provisions. Both in Succoth and in Penuel he tried to get food. Neither place really believed these 300 men were going to defeat Midian, and they refused them help with some rather cynical comments about counting your victories before they are won. Gideon was furious, and he said, "When they *are* won, I'll be back to deal with you!" He was, too, and destroyed both towns after Midian was conquered. He killed the two kings and took their riches.

Israel was impressed with Gideon, to say the least. "Rule over us," they said, "you and your sons and grandsons." But Gideon said no, he really had no mind to be a king at all. The only reward he asked was that each man give him one gold ring. There were many of these among the spoil, and they gladly complied. Gideon took them all home and had an ephod made of them for the glory of his own city, and it became a temptation to all the people. They came to worship Gideon's ephod, but the land lay in peace for the forty years until Gideon's death.

The country really went to pieces then. By complicity, his concubine's son got power, murdered his seventy half brothers (all but the youngest), and ruled as king over Israel. He ruled for only three years before he was killed trying to quell a rebellion. Ironically, a woman dropped a millstone on his head and caused his inglorious end.

# Samson's Early Life

AFTER THE DEATH OF ABIMELECH, there were seven judges whose leadership covered a period of about seventy-six years. About most of them we know little except their names and lineage.

One of the last judges of Israel was surely one of the most colorful, if not the most successful. His life story begins with the familiar refrain that Israel, again, did what wasn't pleasing to God. This time the Philistines were allowed to rule over them. They had been under Philistine rule for forty years when a woman of the tribe of Dan was visited by the angel of God.

"You are barren and have no child," he said, "but all that is going to change. Be very careful not to eat anything unclean or drink wine or strong drink. When the boy is born, don't cut his hair. He is to be dedicated to God from his birth, and he will begin to rescue Israel from the Philistines."

The woman ran and told her husband, "Look, this marvelous person came to me. He was like an angel of God, and I really think he was! He said we were to have a son, and a very special one at that!"

Manoah, her husband, didn't doubt her experience exactly, but he *did* feel he would like to know a bit more about it, so he prayed to God, "Let the angel come again and tell us what's to be done with the boy when we get him!" Jahweh heard him and again the angel came, and his wife called Manoah to hear the instructions repeated.

Manoah was absolutely delighted. "Stay and let us fix food for you in thanks for your wonderful news!" he said. But the angel replied, "I could not eat your food. Offer it to God if you like."

"Well then," said Manoah, "at least tell us your name so we can honor you when the child is born." And the angel replied, "Don't ask my name. It's a mystery."

They prepared a kid for sacrifice and offered it on a rock, and the angel ascended in the flame from it and Manoah said, "We have seen God! We will die!" But his wife said, "Nonsense! If God meant to kill us he'd never have accepted your offering. Besides, he was really quite friendly to us and told us all the things we asked!" She was proved right, too, because in due time they had a son and named him Samson, and God blessed him.

Samson grew up all too fast, it seemed. As he was their only son, I'm not saying but what he was more than a little spoiled. One day he saw one of the Philistine girls down at Timnah who really turned him on. Home went Samson and said to his father, "I've got to have that woman for my wife. Get her for me!"

Samson's parents were appalled. It was not allowable to marry outside your *tribe*, let alone outside your people, and they were God-fearing folk. "Aren't there any good Jewish girls," said Manoah, "that you have to go chasing after a Philistine?" Samson was unmoved. "I want *her*!" he said. "I don't *want* anybody else, so just get her for me!"

Samson was a pretty regular caller at Timnah now, and once when he was going down to see his own true love, a lion attacked him. God's spirit seized Samson, and with his bare hands he killed the beast and went on his way. He told no one about it. On another of his trips he discovered a swarm of bees settled in the carcass. He got himself some of their honey, and then he bethought himself his folks might enjoy it too, so he took some home, just saying he'd "found it."

Finally he went down to marry the girl, and they had a feast for seven days. They didn't exactly trust Samson, so they chose thirty young men of the region to stay with him. The first day Samson was feeling pretty pleased with himself, and he said to the other young blades, "I've got a riddle! Guess it during the feast and I'll give the lot of you thirty festal robes and thirty pieces of linen. Of course, if you can't guess, you owe as much to me." "Fair enough," said they (figuring thirty should be a match for one). "Ask away!"

*Out of the eater came what is eaten;*
*Out of the strong came what is sweet,*
said Samson.

139

The young men searched and puzzled for three days and they were still drawing a complete blank, so the fourth day a couple of them got Samson's bride off by herself and said, "You can coax this answer out of him. You'd better do it, too, or we will set fire to the place and you'll have only yourself to blame. Did you ask us here to rob us?"

The lady saw the lay of the land and decided she'd better do what they asked, so she wrapped her arms around the neck of the infatuated Samson and pouted, "You can't *really* love me or you'd tell me the answer to that riddle." He held out against her for three days, but the last day of the feast she burst into tears and wailed, "You hate me! You don't love me at all, you hate me, and I'll never speak to you again, and, and,—!"

Samson was foolishly infatuated with her, to tell the truth, and she got her way. She, of course, went right out and blabbed to them, as soon as his back was turned, that the answer was "lion," and that day before he went into the bridal room they told him the answer. Samson was furious. "You've been plowing with my heifer," he stormed, "or you'd never have gotten it!" Then with that same strange power that had destroyed the lion, he killed thirty men of Askelon, dumped their clothes at the feet of the thirty companions, and went home to his father's house in a rage.

After Samson got over his anger a little, he began to remember the charms of his wife, and he figured, after all, women will be women, and she really was an enticing beauty. Back he went, taking her a present of a kid. "I've come to my wife," he said. "Come on, where is she?"

Her father hemmed and hawed and said he couldn't go to her right then, and Samson began to get riled. Finally her father admitted, "Well, you went off so angry I figured you hated her, and I gave her to your best man. But it's no big deal, Samson. Look, she has a perfectly ravishing younger sister. Just take her instead. I'm sure she'll be more to your taste!"

Samson evidently didn't agree. "Boy," said he, "am I ever going to get even with *that* bunch!" So he caught 300 foxes and tied torches to their tails and set them free in the Philistine cornfields and destroyed their crops. The fire even spread to the vineyards and olive groves.

The Philistines asked, "Who has done this to us?" And the whole story came out, of Samson's father-in-law playing false and giving his wife away. Oddly enough, they didn't turn on Samson, but on the man who had angered him. They went to Timnah and set the house on fire, destroying the household with it. You almost feel sorry for that girl. It was a real "damned if you do, damned if you don't" situation.

Samson? He got so angry at the destruction of the girl he wanted that he went down and took revenge on the men who had done the burning and caused real havoc among them. This time he didn't go back to his father's house. He went off to the cave of Etam to do his sulking, and there he stayed by himself.

# Samson's Betrayal and Death

THE FEUD OVER SAMSON'S wife escalated into a real brawl. The people he had roughed up got together a fighting force and went down to attack Judah. When the men of Judah asked why, they replied, "We came to get Samson and serve him the same as he served us."

The men of Judah said, "We'll get him!" and sent a force of 3,000 down to Etam where Samson was. "You darned fool," they said, "you know the Philistines have us in their power. What have you done to us?" "Well," said Samson, "I didn't do a bit more to them than they did to me. If you promise not to kill me yourselves you can bind me and take me on back to get yourselves off the hook."

"We don't want to kill *you*," they said. "We have no gripe against you. We just want them off *our* backs!" So they bound Samson with two new ropes and started back. When the Philistines saw them coming they ran toward Samson, shouting with vindictive triumph at seeing their enemy being delivered bound into their hands. When he saw that, he stopped dead in his tracks and just kind of shook off the men of Judah guarding him like a dog shakes off water. He snapped those new ropes they'd bound him with like burned flax. Shaking the bonds off his hands, he looked around for a weapon.

There was the skeleton of a donkey lying there, and Samson, snatching up the jawbone, began flaying around him with it in one of those towering rages of strength. He felled a thousand men before the affair ended, and the rest didn't stay around to argue. Then he went on down to Gaza, to a prostitute's house. The men of the town surrounded the place, meaning to close in at first light. Samson slipped out at midnight, and taking the town's gates, posts and all, he carried them to the top of the hill above Hebron and dumped them. Then he went on his way.

It's no use playing "iffys," but it's hard not to wonder how different things might have been if Samson could have left the women alone. His affairs with them seem to have brought him a lot of trouble, and the one with Delilah was no exception. As usual, when he fell for Delilah, Samson left his good sense outside the door. That woman was a trap if ever you saw one, and he had no more than left her house before the Philistine elders were there.

"Get Samson to tell you why he is so strong," they said. "You can coax anything out of him!" Delilah fluttered her eyelashes and said "S'posing I do. What's in it for me?" That was talking their language, and they promised, "When we take Samson you get eleven hundred silver shekels." That was a mighty handsome bit of money, but then, Samson had been a real pain, and he was not only strong, he was tricky.

Next time Samson came, Delilah cozied up to him. She felt his biceps and she wound his male ego around her little finger some, and then she said, "Samson, I declare I never knew a man like you before! However do you *do* it? What would it take to make you as weak as other men?" Samson still had a little wit about him, so he lied. "If you bound me with seven new bowstrings, not yet dried, I'd be weak as a kitten."

Of course, Delilah went right to the Philistines. They got her the bowstrings and she hid some of their men in the house, and when Samson came in, she coaxed him into a good mood and wrapped those bowstrings around him. When he was all trussed up she yelled, "Samson! The Philistines are here!" He broke those strings like rotten thread, and they ran for their lives. Then he laughed at her.

The next night Delilah said, "That was *mean*, Samson, lying to me and laughing at me. Now *really*, Samson, what would bind you?" She really was cute when she coaxed that way, so he said "New ropes. That will do it. New ropes that have never been used!" So she tried it, of course, with the Philistines hiding out, and just as she had before, she yelled, "Look out, Samson! Philistines!" and he popped those ropes, and they took to their heels. Samson roared with laughter and Delilah pouted.

It wasn't long before Delilah was at Samson again. "You're *mean*! You really are, laughing at me and teasing me that way. I really want to know how to bind you, Samson. Come on! Tell me!" Samson looked down into her lovely face and said, "Well-ll," then something tugged uneasily in the back of his mind and he said, "Weave my seven locks of hair and peg them in the loom. That's it." With careful patience, Delilah lulled Samson to sleep and gently wove his hair into the loom and pegged it tight. Then she shouted the usual warning, with the same results as before.

At last Delilah cast caution to the winds. She no longer kept any semblance of playfulness. She *nagged*. "How can you say you love me when you don't trust me? Three times you've lied and laughed at me!" (Doesn't that line sound familiar?) Day after day she kept at him. The poor man couldn't even sleep at night. That woman was persistent as a gnat, and about as annoying.

Finally she wore him down, and Samson said, "All right! All right! My strength is in my hair. If it were cut, Jahweh's strength would desert me and I'd be like other men."

Delilah sent word to the Philistine chiefs. "This time I've *got* it. Come quick!" and they came with the money in hand. Now that she'd got her way, Delilah was sweet as honey and she put Samson's head in her lap and stroked his forehead and sang him to sleep. One of the men cut off his long locks of hair, and when it was done Delilah shouted, "Philistines, Samson! Look out!"

Samson leaped to his feet, expecting to rout them as before, but Jahweh's strength had deserted him. The Philistines bound Samson and put his eyes out, and they imprisoned him in Gaza. While he was in prison, his hair began to grow back and his strength with it. The Philistines made a huge festival to their God, Dagon, to celebrate Samson's capture.

Presently it occurred to someone that it would be amusing to bring Samson out and have him perform feats of strength for them. Not only was he blind, but he was bound with a double chain of bronze, which he wore while turning the prison mill.

Samson was led out and performed feats of strength to the delight of the crowd, and they stood him between the pillars that held up the

144

roof of Dagon's temple. All the chief Philistines were there, and Samson said to the boy leading him, "Put my hands on the pillars so I can lean against them and rest after my hard work."

So Samson's hands were laid on the pillars, and he sent up a silent prayer: "Lord Jahweh, remember me this once more and give me my old strength so that I can avenge myself." And Jahweh did.

Samson put his arms around the two main pillars and roared, "May I die with the Philistines!" And before that horrified crowd could move to stop him or to escape, Samson strained those famous arms with the incredible strength of his youth. The pillars moved and creaked and then broke in the center where he strained at them, and the whole huge temple thundered down in a mass of dust and rubble and crashing stone, and with it came all the people sitting on its roof. They, and all those on the main floor, died in the wreckage.

Samson, too, was killed by the disaster he had caused, just as he had predicted. His father's family came, and in the confusion, they gently carried off his battered body and buried him in the tomb of his father, Manoah, with great honor, for Samson had been, for twenty years, a judge in Israel.

# Samuel's Youth

TO WANT CHILDREN and not be able to have them has always been a heartbreak, but for Hannah it was heart scald as well. Like Rachel before her, she was "favorite wife," but also like Rachel, she had a rival who bore her husband sons.

Each year when Elkanah took his household up to the temple for the yearly sacrifices, he would give Hannah her portion of the fellowship offering and then he would give Penninah hers. Of course, hers was much bigger because it was to include her sons and daughters. Maybe she realized Elkanah favored Hannah, or perhaps she was just a little callous, but whatever her reasons, Penninah openly gloated over Hannah and taunted her with her childlessness.

One particular year when this happened, Hannah burst into tears and simply refused her share altogether. "I'm not hungry," she wailed. "I don't want any at all, for God doesn't favor me!" Elkanah tried to comfort her. "Don't cry, Hannah," he said. "I love you, and am I not more than ten sons to you? Come, cheer up and eat!" Hannah nibbled a bit at her food to please him, but as soon as she could decently leave the feast she went back into the temple where Eli the priest sat by the doorpost. It seemed to Hannah her bitterness was more than she could bear, and she wept openly and begged God, "Give me a child, Lord, and don't forget me utterly. If you give me a boy, I'll not even keep him for myself. Only let me bear my husband a son to remove the reproach of my barrenness. If you do that, I'll give him to you to serve you all his life!"

Eli watched for a while and then he intervened. Hannah, in her distress, had been moving her lips and gesticulating. With the tears rolling down her cheeks, she looked to him as if she were drunk, so he rebuked her. "You've had too much wine at the feast! Go sleep it off privately, and don't come making a spectacle of yourself before Jehovah!"

Hannah looked at the old priest with shock. She really hadn't been thinking of appearances. "Oh, no sir, you mistake me entirely!" she gasped, wiping away the tears with a corner of her veil. "I'm not one of those worthless women, but a true daughter of Israel. You see I have a great grief, and I thought if I begged Jehovah for help he might relieve my sorrow. I forgot myself in my resentment and unhappiness!"

Eli smiled at her then and replied, "Then God grant your request and give what you ask so earnestly. Go in peace, daughter." And with a strangely light heart, Hannah returned to the feast. Suddenly the food tasted *good*. She had hope again, and when Elkanah spoke to her she smiled the old warm smile he loved. The next morning they got up early, worshipped God, and headed for home, and before long Hannah had much to smile about. She was pregnant! When it was time for the child's birth, Hannah had a son. She knew she was the happiest woman alive. Remembering her vow, she said to Elkanah, "This is God's promised child, and when he is old enough he is to serve in the temple."

That year Elkanah went to the temple with Penninah and her children as usual, but Hannah said, "Let me wean Samuel first, and when he is weaned then I will go up with you and we can give him to God." Elkanah agreed readily, and they did just that. This time when they went, Hannah led her sturdy son by the hand and took thank offerings to Jahweh. Seeing Eli she said, "Remember me—how I prayed God for help? He has answered my prayers, so I am bringing him this child to be his and serve him." So Eli took charge of Samuel. Each year Hannah would come with Elkanah, and each year she wove a new tunic for Samuel and brought it to him. She delighted in seeing how tall and wise he grew. God blessed Hannah beyond her wildest dreams, because once she had begun a family she had three sons and two daughters after Samuel, and when they went up to Shiloh to the sacrifice, her portion was as great as Penninah's.

Samuel served Eli faithfully, and that's how it happened that he lay one night near the Ark of the Covenant outside Eli's door. Eli was nearly blind and used to call Samuel when he needed anything. Samuel had just fallen asleep when he heard a call. He was wide awake in a minute. "Yes, master, did you need me?" But Eli said, "I didn't call you, child." So Samuel went back to bed. He seemed hardly to have lain down when he heard it again, "Samuel! Samuel!" and he got up and ran to Eli. "Here I am! What is it?" But Eli said, "Perhaps you dreamed it. Go lie down."

The third time Samuel heard the call and went to Eli, the old priest had given the matter some thought. It had been a long time since Jahweh had spoken directly to anyone, he mused, and yet Samuel was a very special boy from his very conception. Eli began to realize that this was no ordinary mistake. When Samuel said, "You called?" Eli said, "No, son, I didn't call you, but I don't think you're just hearing things. Go back to your bed, and if you hear that voice again, it's surely God calling."

Samuel was excited and not a little scared. "What should I do?" he asked. "When it comes again, you should reply, 'Say what you want to me, Jahweh, because I'm listening to you,'" said Eli.

Samuel went back to his bed, and Eli lay musing as an old man will when he cannot sleep. The boy was good, and a joy to him. His deepest grief was his own sons' behavior. They should, by now, have been doing the whole service of the priesthood and standing before God for the people. Instead of serving as they should, they had become greedy and cynical. They took meat that was supposed to be sacrificed for their own food. They accepted bribes to give false judgments, and people had more than once complained to their father of their evil ways. What a contrast this dutiful child was to them.

Listening as he had been told to, Samuel heard the voice again, but this time he lay still and replied as he'd been told. God told Samuel a terrible thing. "I'm disgusted with the way Eli's sons are behaving," said God. "They can't be my priests any more. They simply aren't fit. Eli has known it too, and hasn't rebuked them, so I will wipe his name out. No sacrifice will remove that guilt." Then Jahweh left and Samuel lay quietly until it was morning and time to open the doors.

Samuel would have liked to forget the whole vision. He loved Eli, and the idea of causing the old man grief troubled him. "Maybe," he thought, "if I don't mention it, he'll forget." But Eli called him almost at once.

"What did God say to you, Samuel? Don't be afraid to tell me. If you leave out any at all, it will be a curse on you, so tell me honestly." When Eli put it that way, Samuel realized he had to tell him, and as gently as he could, he told Eli the whole thing. I don't think Eli was much surprised. He just bowed his head and said, "God is God. He must do what he sees is best." From then on Eli poured all his efforts into raising Samuel to be a holy man. He did well, too, for Samuel grew up wise and good, and Jahweh spoke to him often. All the people of Israel consulted him and heard what he said with respect. Hannah, watching her firstborn grow in strength and wisdom, praised Jahweh for it and was well content.

# Samuel as Leader

WHEN SAMUEL HAD GROWN to manhood, all Israel respected his wisdom. He was known as a prophet of Jahweh, but still he served under Eli. Israel, at this point, was at war with the Philistines, and doing very badly indeed, so the leaders said, "Why doesn't God go out with us as he used to with our fathers?" So they sent to Shiloh for the Ark of the Covenant.

When the summons came to Shiloh, Eli's two sons took up the ark and carried it out to battle. Israel, seeing it among them, gave such a shout of joy that the Philistines in their camp were frightened and sent out spies to see what had happened. "It's their God," the spies reported. "Now we're really in trouble! Their God lives in that box—the same that brought them out of Egypt and established them here!"

Israel's confidence surged, but wiser heads among the Philistines counseled, "If we stand up and fight like men we may yet win, but if we let that scare us, we will be their slaves as they have been ours." When battle was joined, Israel was routed and—as God had warned Samuel—Phinehas and Hophni, Eli's sons, were killed. The worst of the mess was, the sacred ark was captured and taken back to the Philistine city of Ashdod. There they placed it beside the temple of their god, Dagon.

When the news of the battle was brought back to Shiloh, Eli, who was very old now, fell from his seat by the gates and broke his neck. So all the grown men of the family of Eli perished that day as God had said, and Samuel became priest to Israel. The ark stayed in Philistine hands for seven months, and everywhere they took it, disaster struck. In five cities, one after the other, there were plagues of rats and tumors. The wise men of the land said, "Their God is doing to us just as he did to Egypt! Let's not be any stupider than we need to be!" So they put the ark on an ox cart and headed it back toward Israeli territory with a guilt offering of gold tumors and rats on it at their seers' advice.

When the harvesters at Beth-Shemesh saw the ark coming, they shouted for joy. They made an offering then and there of the beasts who drew the cart. For some reason, Jeconiah's sons did *not* rejoice ("So it's back. Big deal!"), and God struck them dead—seventy of them.

Samuel ruled as a judge over Israel for twenty years before they gathered under Jahweh and defeated the Philistines. As he became older, the work of the judgeship became too much for him, and he appointed his sons to help. Ironically, they went the same way as Eli's sons before them—bribery, corruption, greed, and oppression of the people. So the people came to Samuel and said, "Give us a king like the peoples around us. You were fine, but your sons are a mess! Give us a king."

Samuel was disgusted! A king indeed! When he asked God about it, though, God said, "It's not you they are rejecting, but me. It's I who have ruled over them since Egypt. Just warn them, though, that kings have grand ideas. They cost money and take the finest young people for their servants. Remind them that when they find their king a burden and yell for help, I'm going to turn a deaf ear to them." Samuel did tell them, but they had their hearts set on "being like other folks," so Jahweh said, "Do as they say, Samuel."

How do you choose a King? Well, if you're Jahweh's prophet, you wait and listen and trust. Presently God spoke to Samuel, "I'm sending you the man I've chosen."

Saul came down from the tribe of Benjamin on a purely mundane errand. His father's donkeys had strayed, and Saul and one of the servants set out to find them. The stupid beasts seemed to be over all hills, and finally they'd gone until they were out of food and Saul said, "We'll turn back, or Dad will stop worrying about the beasts and figure he'd better send out a search party for us." But the servant proposed, "There's a seer in the next town. We might as well see whether he can help us. I have a bit of silver we can offer him."

They met Samuel at the city gate headed for a sacrifice. They asked for the seer's house and he said, "I'm your man, but come along to the sacrifice and eat with me." When they did, Samuel gave Saul the choice portions of meat and the place of honor. Saul stayed the night with Samuel too, and next morning Samuel walked with him beyond the gates. When the servant had been sent on ahead, Samuel said, "God has chosen you to be prince over Israel." And he kissed Saul and poured the holy oil over his head. Saul didn't know what to think, but Samuel gave him three signs to prove God's favor. First he would meet two men who would tell him the donkeys were home. Then he would meet three who would give him food. Finally, he would meet prophets in an ecstasy and God would seize him with the same spirit.

It all happened just as Samuel said. Saul returned home and told no one of Samuel's anointing. Presently Samuel called all the tribes up to Mizpah and cast lots over them—tribe by tribe down to Benjamin, family by family to Kish, and man by man until the lot fell on Saul. Saul wasn't to be found. Finally someone spotted him hiding among the baggage. There wasn't much he could do, then, but stand up near Samuel. Saul was a big, handsome man, and all the people cheered, "Long live King Saul!" Samuel explained the royal constitution and made it all legal. When Saul went home to Gibeah, a huge force of fighting men gathered to him. Within the month they had roundly trounced the Ammonites. Israel was wild with delight.

Samuel called them together once more and said, "Now you have your king and I'm getting too old to lead you. It's a wicked thing you've done, rejecting God's kingship, but if you and your king follow Jahweh's ways, it will still work out and he won't desert you."

Saul won some impressive victories for Israel, but he had one particular fault. He was far too easily swayed. God would say one thing, the people another, and Saul would give in to popular opinion. God called Samuel and said, "I'm sorry I ever made that man king! We will choose another one who will rule as I want him to."

Samuel went down and told Saul about it, and then he never saw him again, since Jahweh had deserted him. After a long life, Samuel died peacefully at his home and all Israel gathered in tribute. They mourned the grand old man who had been the last of the judges of Israel, and buried him there in Ramah.

# Ruth

ONCE AGAIN THE GRAIN crops had failed in Bethlehem, and Naomi saw the worry on Elimelech's face finally give way to decision.

"Wife," said he, "there's no way we can live on what's here. In Moab, they say, there is plenty, and work to be had. We will just go for a few years, and when the Lord's favor returns to Judah's fields, we can come back." So Naomi packed their few belongings and with their two small sons, they set out for Moab.

They missed family and friends, but time brought new friends, and there was plenty, so Elimelech decided to build up a little nest egg before they returned to Bethlehem. The years slipped by, and Chilion and Mahlon grew to tall young men, and each year they'd think of getting back, but now there were roots in Moab. Then, quite suddenly, Elimelech wasn't going anywhere, and the newly widowed Naomi, moving through a haze of shocked grief, simply lived from day to day. The boys hardly remembered the home of their childhood. They had good jobs here and were, besides, courting a couple of local beauties, and when Ruth and Orpah came home as their wives, Naomi settled quietly to live her life out in Moab.

Ten years went by in just ordinary living, and Naomi was content, except she fretted a little that there were still no grandchildren. But then, the kids were young. There was still plenty of time. Then one of those fearful plagues came along and within the week Mahlon was dead. Chilion was stricken soon after, and now there were three widows in the house with not a man to support them, and once more Naomi's thoughts turned toward home.

Naomi was getting old. She could tell by the stiffness in the morning and by the way she got only half a day's work out of a day, but most of all, by the way the older days looked so much brighter than now, and the home of her childhood beckoned. She hated to leave the graves of her husband and sons there in Moab, but back in Bethlehem, dear Bethlehem of her childhood years, there she had been a bride and had her babies and such happy times before the famine that drove them into Moab. There in Bethlehem there were live brothers and sisters and children of their children—her own flesh and blood— since she herself could never have grandchildren now. And finally the desire was overwhelming. Naomi packed up her few personal things and got ready to go. Quietly, resolutely, her sons' widows packed theirs too. They had been her household for over ten years now, and the three women had clung together in the fresh grief of Mahlon and Chilion's deaths until time had healed the sharpness to a dull ache.

For a while they walked in quiet and then Naomi—loving them, and wanting their joy—said, "Go home, now, to your own families. May you find good husbands and happy homes! You're dear girls and deserve it!" They both cried and said, "No indeed!" and Naomi chuckled a bit and said, "Do I look like having more sons to be your husbands? Even if I married this night and started on the project it would be a right long wait!"

Well, Orpah was a sensible girl, and she wept bitterly, but home she went. I hope she got a good man and had a brace of kids! But we never really know because the story goes on with Naomi and Ruth. Naomi wiped away a tear and said, "There, love, she's gone like a sensible girl; you need to run on too." But Ruth threw her head up and her eyes got very bright and she said, "Don't ask me to go back! It's not right any more. I'll live where you live, and your family will be my family. I am a worshipper of Jehovah and may *he* punish me if I ever go back on my determination." Naomi smiled a little at her vehemence, and a frozen corner of her heart thawed a little. She was secretly glad she needn't go all alone. It was like having just a little of Mahlon with her, and whatever problems existed for one lone woman could scarcely be worse for two.

At first folks were terribly excited about seeing Naomi, and they thought Ruth a real dear to come and care for her. But when they would hug Naomi and say, "Is it really *you*, Naomi? God is good to send you back," the swift tears would brim over and she would reply,

"Don't call me Naomi any more (which means pleasant), but call me Mara (that is, bitter), for I left in plenty and the Lord has sent me back destitute!" And they would leave welcoming gifts and go away, shaking their heads.

A lot of gossip went around that Ruth was kind of foreign looking, but rather a lovely young woman, and she proved to be practical as well as lovely. One bright morning she said to Naomi, "I'll just go out and follow the harvest and get us a small store of our own for winter." And Naomi, who hadn't been quite sure what they were going to do, said, "You do that, Ruth! You're a good daughter to me."

So Ruth joined the women gleaning Boaz's field, and by mid-morning when Boaz came out to see how things went, she had already earned respect as a darned good worker. His heart smote him a little. He had meant to get on over and pay a duty call on Naomi. He was close kin to her husband, but for a shy middle-aged bachelor, those things don't come easily.

But he was innately a kind man, and he walked over to where Ruth stood resting a minute and told her she was welcome in his fields, and she looked up at him so gratefully he reproached himself for not having done something sooner. (And I'm not saying, mind, the beauty of the face didn't smite his heart a bit, too.) He was a humble man, and tongue-tied with the village beauties, so he just said why didn't she stay with his servant girls, and he'd see she was kept safe from being bothered and she could drink from their water skins; then, noticing the thinness of her face, he added, "And please come and eat lunch with us, too." And when she did, he saw her slipping some of her portion into the folds of her dress to keep and figured, rightly, that she meant to share with Naomi, and he saw to it she got more than two girls her size could eat.

By sundown Ruth was terribly tired, stiff and sunburned into the bargain, but talk about *triumph*. She couldn't remember when she'd been so glad as she was to lay twenty-five measures of barley before Naomi and pull out the food she had saved from lunch. Naomi hugged and praised her, and got water to wash her tired feet (over her protests). As she washed them she looked very thoughtful. Twenty-five measures was beyond what anyone could hope to glean unless somebody left some on purpose (which was, of course, exactly what Boaz had done), and Naomi said, "Honey, whose field was it?" Ruth tumbled out the whole story, and Naomi actually smiled. She was a wise woman and kept her own counsel, but she did tell Ruth that Boaz was a kinsman, and to do as he said and stay with his folks through the harvest.

As the harvest season went on, Ruth went every day, and she tanned a little darker with sun, but her face filled out with the extra food Boaz urged on her, and by the time the barley harvest drew to a close, there wasn't any worry about food for the year. Then Naomi told Ruth her plan.

"It's time you married again and we had a few kids around the place. Boaz is a good man, but if you wait for him to ask you to marry him, you'll be as old and gray as I am! Tonight you pretty yourself up and use some perfume in your hair and wear that yellow scarf that sets off your dark eyes, and when Boaz has finished the threshing and goes to sleep out on the straw by the threshing floor, you go curl up under the blanket at his feet and when he wakes up, *you* do the asking. Remind him he's next of kin to us and should do a kinsman's duty."

Well, Ruth didn't mind a bit! Boaz might not be the finest figure of a man around, and he was almost laughably shy with women, but she had seen his eyes follow her around and say what words couldn't, and she thought again of his kindness those first scary days in the fields, and she looked quite flushed and happy as she replied, "Yes, Mother, I'll do just as you say!" So off she went, and after Boaz sacked out, pretty pleased with himself over a good harvest, and sleepy from feasting after the hard work, Ruth slipped in. When he turned over about midnight he was really surprised. Ruth, suddenly shy herself, blurted out her request.

Forgetting his own shyness to comfort her, he wrapped his cloak around her shoulders against the night chill and told her she was wonderful and he never thought an old bachelor like him had a chance and that she was as good as she was lovely but there was a man ahead of him as next of kin, but not to worry, he'd get right at the deal in the morning. Just before dawn he sent her home again with a gift of fifty measures of wheat for Naomi (who had, after all, *sent* Ruth to him), and he got up a little business meeting and coyly explained to the other man that Naomi wanted to sell a field and he had first option unless he wanted to let Boaz buy. It was a decent piece of land and things looked bad for a minute, and then Boaz said, "But Ruth the Moabitess goes with it to marry its owner and keep the land in the family and raise up an heir to the family name and property." Well, the cousin had a wife and a houseful of kids already (which was why he *needed* more land), and so he said, "No thanks." And Boaz should go right ahead, and they sealed the bargain.

For a shy man, Boaz didn't waste any time. He was on Naomi's doorstep that very day. And before the year was out, there was the babble of a child in the house, and Naomi, rocking him in her arms, thought of her own little ones long ago and she looked at Ruth blooming with the serene joy of a very happy woman and said, "Daughter, you've been better than seven sons to me!" and meant it. She no longer spoke of God dealing bitterly with her, but said to her friends, "God gave me a new son, and my dear Ruth as well. Surely he is a God who remembers those who trust in him to bless them."

# Esther

IT ALL STARTED WITH A HOUSEHOLD SPAT—on a rather large scale, but still a real husband-and-wife squabble. King Xerxes had been making a feast for almost half a year, and the food was the best and the wine flowed like water and all the men in the city came. Queen Vashti put on a spread for their wives and daughters at the same time, and the palace sounds like a description of the bash of the season from the social pages. One day, late on in the afternoon, when King Xerxes got to feeling very happy (mind you, he wasn't drunk—just happy), he decided he'd like to get Vashti all tricked out in her crown and jewels and silks and let the boys see what a beauty she was. Well, when his servants came in to get her, Vashti balked. She was having her own party and she had maybe had one more than was wise herself. She stamped her dainty foot and ordered the king's eunuchs out of her rooms and said she wasn't coming.

The king was furious! Here he'd promised all his guests a look at the queen and he couldn't even rule his own household. How did that look for the empire? So the men who advised him said, "You'd better do something! Pretty soon all the women will think they can act that way and we'll have women's lib on our hands … All the husbands will be angry and we'll have no domestic peace at all. Tell her she can't be queen anymore." So he did just that, and sent out a proclamation that a man was boss in his own house, and Vashti wasn't queen anymore.

After a while Xerxes began to get lonely and to have second thoughts about the lovely Vashti. His advisers took hasty council and they said to him, "What you need is a brand-new queen!" So he agreed, and they collected all the loveliest girls in the kingdom, and after a year of the ancient equivalent of the Helena Rubinstein treatment, each of the girls was brought to the king. She had from dusk until morning to charm him and then she was sent away. Only if he asked for her by name could she come again.

Among these beauties was Esther, a Jewess. She was an orphan, but a cousin had adopted her and been a father to her, and she still lived under his roof. Mordecai was a canny man, and he told his lovely ward, "I wouldn't mention being Jewish if I were you. Just concentrate on being beautiful." There were many lovely girls, but Esther was as lovely in mind and soul as in body, and so she became Queen Esther. Xerxes was mightily pleased and Mordecai was content, and he slipped into the outer courts to see how things went for her and to keep her up with the news. That's how he heard the plot on the king's life between two eunuchs. He told Esther, and when the plot was foiled she gave him credit and the king duly recorded it in his books, and he valued the exquisite Esther even more.

Months passed, and the novelty waned, and then an awful thing happened. Namaan, an official close to the king, got his ear and said, "There's this strange bunch of people in the kingdom. Their ways aren't like ours and they worship peculiar gods and, well, they're *different*, and if we were to do away with them, I could really make your treasury look healthy." Well, the king agreed and handed Namaan his signet ring to seal it.

The Jews were horrified, and Mordecai looked grim when he saw his lovely cousin that day, and he said, "Can't you stop him?" But Esther said, "Nobody goes in there unless he calls for them or they're dead!" And they both remembered Vashti. But Mordecai said, "Esther, it may be for this that God brought you to be queen, and if you let us be killed it's only a matter of time before they remember you're one of us and your life won't be worth a row of pins!" So she said, "I'll go! Tell them we will all fast and pray for three days, and maybe he will pardon my coming and hear me." So on the third day she dressed in her loveliest clothes and came to the door of the king's hall. The king—struck again by her beauty— pardoned her on the spot and asked what she wanted. Well, she fooled around and took her time and let him wonder and eye her soft curves and smell her perfume and then she said, "Come to my dinner party tonight, and oh, bring Namaan!"

The king knew as well as you do that wasn't all, but she was very alluring, and he knew she planned something pretty special, so he agreed. Namaan? He went out and bragged about the favor. The only one that didn't scrape and bow about it was Mordecai. He just sat at the palace gate and looked through Namaan like he wasn't there, and Namaan was furious.

That night at the banquet, when Esther herself leaned over the king to pour another glass of wine for him, he said, "Esther, I know you want something. What is it? And it's yours up to half my empire." Esther smiled demurely and said, "Well, you're right, and if you'll come to another banquet tomorrow night—both of you—I'll tell you." But Namaan went home in a rage because of Mordecai, and his wife and friends said, "You've got the influence, hang the scoundrel!" Namaan listened and built a tall gallows, and Esther heard and went on quietly with her plans—now with her heart more in them than ever.

When Namaan came to the king in the morning, both had spent a sleepless night. The king had fretted over what Esther might be brooding about and so—nothing new—he had his records brought and tried to read himself to sleep. There was the account of Mordecai's uncovering the plot on his life, and he thought to himself that the man had never been rewarded, so he burst out to Namaan, "If I want to give someone great honor, what would you suggest?" Namaan was a vain sort, and couldn't imagine the king honoring anyone but him, so he really laid it on. "Why, give him a suit of your clothes and mount him on your horse—with the crown on the bridle. Have one of your noblemen lead him and proclaim, 'See how the king honors those he delights in...!'" And the king said, "Super! Namaan, you're a smart fellow! Do just that for the Jew Mordecai—oh, you'll find him sitting at the palace gate. You lead the horse." And Namaan, smiling blandly, inwardly cursed his stupidity and went to do the king's bidding—unable, obviously, to hang Mordecai for this day! He went home in a real tizzy after he had done with that chore, and all his friends said, "That man Mordecai will get you yet!" But just then the eunuchs came to hurry him off to Esther's feast.

Esther leaned over to pour the wine for the king again and he coaxed, "Baby, tell me what you want. It's yours up to half my kingdom!" And the lovely Esther straightened up and looked him in the face for a minute and the room was so silent it hurt. Then she said, "If it please you to grant my humble request, I'd like to stay alive—I and my people, who are about to be slaughtered by one of your officials." The king was aghast. Who in this court would dare threaten his beloved queen? And Esther turned to Namaan, who cowered like a rat in a trap, and said, "There he is!" The king strode into the garden in fury; Namaan, in a last-ditch effort, cast himself on the foot of Esther's couch to beg mercy. Can you blame the king if, entering at that moment, he saw only the threat of the gesture, and accusing Namaan of attempted rape, condemned him to death on the spot? And the eunuchs, having no fondness for Namaan's arrogance, told of his gallows and his plan to hang Mordecai, so the king said, "Hang Namaan on them!"

Esther was given Namaan's property, and Mordecai his position at court, and when Namaan was dead the king's anger cooled. Then once again Esther begged, "What about my people?" And the king said, "You can't unsay a royal decree, but whatever you two see fit to do, proclaim it, and Mordecai has my ring to seal it." (For by now Esther had told him Mordecai was her kinsman.) So the Jews of the empire were told to arm and fight back with the king's favor supporting them. Fight they did, and they won. And they held a mighty feast of joy and thanksgiving to the Lord. That is why to this day the feast of Purim is celebrated by the devout Jew in honor of the fact that God is a God who frees his people from their dangers and troubles.

# Job

CAN YOU IMAGINE A MAN so good that even God brags about him? That's Job. He was simply *good* in every sense of the word, and what's more, he worked at pleasing God. Then Satan (who can't bear to see a good thing let be) said, "Huh! He's good because he is your pet! Why should he be bad when he has it all his way?"

So God let Job be tempted. His crops were taken, his animals stolen, his property destroyed, and even his ten children were killed. From disaster after disaster *one* servant, only, escaped to tell him. And Job bowed his head and said, "God gave it! God has taken it away. Blessed be God's name!" And Satan was angrier than ever and so he said, "Huh! That's nothing! He is still comfortable and respected—touch his precious hide and watch him curse you!"

So God let Job be afflicted with terrible sores on his skin that itched and festered and stank, and Job went out and sat by the trash dump in the dust, and he was so maddened with the itch that he picked up a bit of broken pottery and scraped at it. And Job lamented, "God, why...? I have done my best. I've kept your law as I saw it. I've never knowingly offended you. Why are you letting this happen?" But he got no answer and he pondered, "If God is God then he isn't good! If God is good he isn't God!" And he asked and listened and there was silence except for his wife, who stood a ways off because of the stench, and said, "Curse God and die!" And Job, shifting his painful body uneasily, said, "No, I can't do that. I've always trusted God, and I'll go on trusting him—even if I die before I see it come to light."

She shrugged and went off, and presently three of Job's friends came to commiserate with him. Now mind you, there weren't many left who would. He had no money; he looked repulsive; all his conversation consisted of trying to figure why God would do this to him. I believe these three deserve much better than the lousy press they usually get. They commiserated and they moaned for seven days and then it began to get a little thick—Job's carrying on—and one after another, they offered what seemed to them good common sense. If God was mad, God had reasons. Job had better just admit he had sinned and beg pardon. Job went on lamenting. No, indeed, he won't admit to *sin* in general. If he has done wrong he doesn't know it, and as God is an honest God, he surely doesn't want a fake confession. They go on urging and exhorting that Job must be a sinner, and Job said, "If God will just talk to me, let me know how things are, I'll accept his judgment, and surely he'll judge me innocent, because God is fair." (Which, he added mentally, men certainly are not!)

So Job went on bemoaning and hollering at God to hear and answer until even a teenaged neighbor (we know the kid that has all the answers) came over and said, "Look, Dad, God isn't like that. He's surely speaking to you somehow and you're caterwauling so loud you can't hear. Now surely if you confess your sin he will restore you to prosperity!" And he began to rehearse the greatness of God as a thunderstorm blew up. Everybody ran for cover, and there sat poor old Job by himself.

But now, at last, God came and he said, "Job, are you really arguing with *me*, your creator?" And God rehearsed the strange and wonderful things of his world, and when he was done, Job said, "Yes, Lord, I understand. I understand that I am too unwise to understand." And God turned on the others and said, "You're a pack of mealy mouths! Job at least was honest about me, and if you'll have him pray for you I'll forgive you!" So, of course, they very meekly did. Marvelous! When had anyone asked Job's prayers since his disaster? And he felt warm and respected. And his sores healed, and his wife got pregnant, and folks came to rejoice and brought him gifts, and with one thing and another, Job became a rich and respected man. He owned twice what he had before, and his seven sons were strong and handsome and his three daughters so lovely he left them money as if they were men. And he lived to see their children's children and died happy in his bed at a ripe old age. But Satan retired routed.

# Jonah

A PROPHET—OH, YES INDEED! A man of God who speaks the word of
the Lord against all odds and with bravery even to torture and death,
and here, tucked in among them, is Jonah. Oh, he *is* a prophet all
right. God considered him so, and likewise the Hebrew and then the
Christian Canon of Scripture. I like Jonah. He is the sort of prophet
I would be, I'm afraid. "Go preach to Nineveh!" said God.

"Oh no! It's a lost cause!"

"Go!"

"But you'll just forgive them and make a fool of me!" So Jonah
sailed off for Spain, without a qualm yet. Peacefully asleep, he was
unaware of the storm God was pursuing him with until the captain
hauled him awake. The boat lurched and slued sickeningly. The wind
howled, the lightning glared, everybody prayed, the sailors (simple
sensible guys) knew God must be mad at somebody, and, casting lots,
found out, sure enough, it was Jonah. Still, he paid good money for the
ride and he was an affable cuss, and so they tried again to row on to
land. No way. It just seemed to make God madder, and the fury of the
storm redoubled, and when queried, Jonah said, "Well, yes, I guess I'm
to blame, I'm a Hebrew and I worship the God of all creation and he
said to go preach to Nineveh and I didn't want to and so I figured I'd
go hide out in Spain in hopes he'd lose track of me and it would slip his
mind." The sailors, wide-eyed with terror, turned on him and said,
"Oh, my! That was an awful thing to do! How shall we fix it up?" Well,
Jonah was a decent sort, and if God was going to hound him anyhow…
So he had them pitch him overboard. They did it reluctantly enough.
After all, they hadn't done anything, and they just wanted to live, and
all the time they were doing it they said, "Now please, don't hold us
guilty of murder! He said to!" It occurs to me Jehovah made a little
conversion mission even out of this side trip!

Anyhow, poor Jonah sank down and down into a sea now calm as glass—but that's not much use to you if you're "at the roots of the mountains and entangled with seaweed." That's how it looked to the terrified Jonah, anyhow, who was suddenly not so sure he wanted to be dead, and suddenly God's Holy Temple—source of all life—looked very dear, and God's wishes no longer unreasonable as they had been, and Jonah (mentally at least) cried, "Lord, I'm sorry, I didn't mean it, I'll go if you want me to. I love you and worship you and you are my life! Don't let me die!" And God forgave Jonah then and there, and sent a huge fish to swallow him. But he knew his man, and Jonah was three days in that dark place thinking it over before he was let out on dry land in sun and fresh air! And as he took a few deep breaths and began to feel himself again after his terror and uncertainty, God said, "Now, Jonah! About Nineveh...!" So Jonah obeyed God and went to Nineveh.

He went, all right, but not too enthusiastically. Three days it took to walk the length of that city... hmmm... three days again! And it took a whole day of walking before Jonah opened his mouth. But the second day he did begin grudgingly to say, "You people really are awful. You'd better say you're sorry and shape up, because Jehovah is going to destroy this place in forty days for your sins!" Grudging or not, they believed him, and the people did repent. They fasted in sackcloth and ashes—the king proclaimed it; even animals mustn't be fed, and, he added, everyone should pray to Jehovah. What a fantastic sight—what a revival—a whole city lifting its prayers to God in repentance.

Jonah didn't see it. He went on out and sat on the hillside and said "Okay, God! I'm waiting! Where is that destruction you promised?" And God, of course, forgave his people in Nineveh—just as he had forgiven Jonah, just as he forgives us, and Jonah sulked. "See, I told you you'd go soft and not do it after I said it." But God wasn't done with Jonah either. Jonah built a little lean-to for protection, and God covered it with an opulent green vine, and Jonah was delighted with its coolness without much thinking where it came from. Then a tiny worm chewed off the stem and a hot desert wind came up from the east, and Jonah was faint with heat, and he was furious, and God said, "Jonah! Don't tell me you're angry?" And Jonah said, "Angry enough to die!" (Haven't we heard that before Jonah?) And God said, "Angry enough to die, are you? And over a vine you did nothing to get for yourself and enjoyed for a day? This great city of people I made and gave life to—both adults and innocent children, and animals. How much more should I hear their prayers to me and keep them in life?" And there the story abruptly ends. I like to think Jonah saw not only the "reasonableness" of it, but also the parallel. He too had cried to God to be kept in life and God had heard him. Jonah? Are you listening?

# THE REIGN OF SAUL

# David and Goliath

YOU KNOW HOW IT CAN BE in a family when there are kids older than you are? Everybody expects the honors to go to the big kids first, and they keep saying things like, "You're too young to do that," or "That's a kid's job, let him do it." That's how it was with David. *He* was the last of eight sons and nobody knows how many daughters. Since girls can't be kings, nobody put *that* down. Well, anyway, when Samuel the priest came to hold a special sacrifice to God with Jesse and his sons, poor ol' David was—wouldn't you know—shooed off to the fields early to keep track of the sheep, while everybody else got all dressed up for the feast. Now Jesse was mighty proud of his strong sons, and he didn't mind a bit parading them for Samuel one after the other. Samuel had slipped the word to him that one of the lot was God's chosen king after Saul.

One after the other they came in, and each one was tall and strong and handsome. Jesse's heart swelled with pride and Samuel said, "God, is it this one?" (In fact, he only said that after the first.) He looked on Eliab, the eldest, and said, "Well, yes, I see, God, why you've chosen this man!" and God said, "Hold on there, Samuel! Don't get carried away! He's a right nice-looking specimen, but that's no guarantee he'd be any use as a king. I look a lot deeper than you, and this man just isn't what's needed!" Well, one after another they came and left, and God kept saying, "No," and things got a little strained between Jesse and Samuel. Number seven left after God had said "No," and again Samuel turned helplessly to Jesse and said, "God hasn't picked any of those—are you sure that's all?" And Jesse said, "Well, of course there's David, but he's not much more than dry behind the ears yet; besides, he's out with the sheep on the far hill." Well, like it or not, Samuel said they'd simply have to wait dinner until he got there. So some of the hired help was sent out to take his place and David came on in. His clothes were rough everyday stuff, and he smelled like, well, sheep aren't roses, and his feet were dusty with the long walk home, but he stood straight as a young sapling, bright with color under the dust, and there was a twinkle in his eye, and his voice when he spoke was clear and sweet and strong. What with one thing and another Samuel wasn't at all displeased when God said, "*Now*, Samuel—this one." And Samuel poured the oil of God's anointing over David's head, then and there while his brothers and father looked on, and even in his dusty shepherd's clothes it was clear that God's spirit rested especially on this young man. Jesse pondered God's strange choice, but he loved all his sons well, and David no less than the others, and suddenly he saw David *wasn't* a child anymore, and when Saul sent for him a few weeks later to come play his evil moods away (half the countryside knew David's harp songs), Jesse sighed and sent him off with the sad tug at his heart of the youngest going off on his own. Soon they all went.

Saul was having a war with the Philistines and all the able-bodied men in the countryside were drawn in. David came quietly home then, and went on keeping sheep, but now and again Jesse sent him down to camp with food for the older boys and a little present for their commanding officer (just to keep on the good side).

That's how the Goliath affair came about. The man really was *huge*, and every time they told it he got a little bigger, and every day he'd come out and do his little act. He'd stomp around and shout insults at the Israelite camp and tell them to send a man out to shut him up if they dared, and of course they didn't, till little old David (maybe remembering the spirit of God at his anointing) shouted back that *he* would come, in God's name, because if a man had God he didn't need to worry what else he'd got. Well, Saul tried to tell him not to, and his brothers sneered a few brotherly put-downs and told him to get back to his sheep—this was a job for real men. Well, David mentioned how he hadn't seen any of *them* doing it, and he had killed lions and bears, and God would defend him against this giant too. Saul tried to put his armor on David, but it felt heavy and strange and David said no, he was no seasoned warrior—just a shepherd who believed Jehovah would win the battle for him.

So out he went, and if his legs trembled you couldn't see it, and if his jaw was clenched a little tight, his eyes were clear and his hands were steady. Like a child playing skip-stones he scooped up a handful of pebbles and tested them in his fingers, choosing one in particular to keep near at hand, and then he walked steadily on up toward Goliath. That gentleman was amazed and a little nonplussed. He wasn't terribly bright to start with, just *big*, and he was used to people in armor running away from him, and here was this pipsqueak in shepherd's clothes just walking right at him. He did his usual thing and shouted a few insults, adding the names of his favorite gods and his intent to leave David's worthless carcass for the buzzards, but David talked right back. He said that Jehovah was his defense and if any carcasses were to be left, he was going to leave them in the name of Jehovah so the whole earth would know who was *really* God.

Well, Goliath was *furious*, and he strode forward ready to squash that pipsqueak with his bare hands when he got him. The thing is, he never *did*, because David took a few running steps toward him and swung with deadly aim and the huge giant staggered and crumpled to the earth. Fleet-footed from his years of scrambling after sheep, David was on him before he could even hope to know what hit him and, pulling Goliath's own sword, dealt him his death blow.

Well, Saul was mighty impressed, and David never went back to the hills and fields of his father, but stayed in the military entourage of King Saul, and God was with him.

# David at Saul's Court

DAVID WAS IN A VERY STRANGE POSITION. Samuel had anointed him king—quietly, as had been the case with Saul at first. Now he was a resident of the house of the reigning monarch. If that wasn't sticky enough, David and the crown prince were dearest friends.

After Goliath's death at David's hand, Jonathan gave him his own cloak. He gave him armor and a sword, too, and all the trappings of a fighting man. They made a solemn pact, these two young men, to be like blood brothers to each other. Saul wasn't pleased. He had this uneasy feeling about David. Oh, he found him winsome enough around court, and clever. That was part of the rub. He was too clever and too winsome.

The whole uneasy situation came to a head one day when Saul's troops returned from battle. David had been leading out raiding parties, and his exploits had gotten back to the home folks. They were delighted with his prowess, and the girls giggled and whispered behind their hands, "And, my dear, they *do* say he's handsomer than Saul used to be before he got that potbelly and started losing his hair and—" and they would go off into another gale of giggles. Anyhow, when the fighting men came back in a sort of triumphant procession through the towns of Israel, these same girls came out to meet the heroes. They'd made up a song; their sweet voices caroled it against the sound of their tambourines.

*Saul has killed his thousands*
*David his tens of thousands!*

It wasn't very tactful, to say the least, but they were silly young things, and each cherished dreams of someday being David's wife.

Saul went home and brooded over that song. The sweet voices echoed tauntingly through his dreams. It wasn't fair! Jahweh had deserted him, and David had it *all*. He was young and handsome

171

and a hero and—he had everything *but* the kingship! Next day David was playing his harp and trying to lighten Saul's black mood when Saul was seized with a jealous rage. Looking up suddenly, Saul brandished the spear in his hand and said, "I'm going to skewer you to the wall like a piece of meat!" Twice David sidestepped the angry Saul's thrusts, and then he slipped away. Saul sent David out of his sight after that, giving him battle commissions. All that accomplished was to give David more glory so that people idolized him even more than before.

When David returned, Saul said, "Look, here's my oldest daughter, Merab. You can have her as your wife." David made polite noises about his unworthiness, and just before time for the betrothal Saul changed his mind and let someone else have her.

While the talk of David marrying Merab was going on, all the girls in the palace had fluttered and moaned over that romantic idea; but one, Michal, fell fiercely in love with David, and she didn't care who knew it. Saul, hearing of it, decided to use it to his own purpose. "Tell David," his servants were instructed, "he's a fine young man and I'm really impressed with him and want him to marry Michal." Saul knew very well that David would go all touchy and protest that he had no bride price. "Tell him," said Saul, "all I want for Michal is the foreskins of a hundred Philistines." Saul heard that David and his men had headed off to get the bride price, and sat back to await news of David's death—and it wouldn't even be Saul's fault!

For Saul, things couldn't have gone worse. Not only was David not killed, but he returned with the foreskins of *two* hundred Philistines. The country rocked with delight over it. Even more than before, David was their darling. What could Saul do but marry the beauteous Michal to the young hero with such show of grace as he could manage? Jonathan was openly delighted. Now they were "brothers" indeed.

Every time there was a dangerous mission to lead, Saul sent David, but David seemed to lead a charmed existence. Clearly, Saul admitted to himself, David enjoyed Jahweh's special favor as well as the adulation of all Israel. Saul openly became David's enemy. He spoke to his servants and to Jonathan about killing David.

Jonathan, of course, went straight to David and said, "Make yourself scarce until I can find out what my father really intends. If it's all right, I'll call you back. If it's not, you'll be where you can slip away." David hid in the fields, and Jonathan went to Saul.

"Father, why do you hate David? Don't you recall how bravely he has fought? Remember how he felled Goliath? What about that business of the two hundred Philistines? Israel has seen great victories since he took the field in your service. Surely you don't want to spill innocent blood!"

"Son, you're right" said Saul. "These fits come on me and I'm not myself. As God lives, I will not harm David!" So Jonathan hurried out to get David, and once again David lived in the royal household and served Saul.

All went quietly for a time, then there was another Philistine raid, and David was sent to quell it. He did, too, and when he returned home, all Saul's old jealousies came back. Once again, as David stood playing his harp, Saul tried to kill him. David ducked, the spear stuck quivering in the wall, and David ran from the palace to his own house.

Michal was nobody's fool, and she had a reason to know her father's moods perhaps even better than David. She put up some food for him and an extra cloak, and as soon as darkness came, slipped him out a back window. "If you're here in the morning," she said, "you're as good as dead!" Then she set about seeing how much extra time she could gain him.

First thing in the morning Saul's agents were banging on the door to arrest David. "You can't take him, he's sick in bed," said Michal. It sounded fishy to them. He had looked fine yesterday. So she led them to his room, and sure enough, there he lay in dimness, rolled up in a blanket, his rough reddish hair just visible in the half-light from the shaded windows. They trooped back to Saul. They didn't hurry, either. Truth to tell, they weren't any too anxious to see David killed, and while they couldn't refuse the king, they didn't have to be too eager.

Saul turned purple with rage at their news. "Sick, is he? He's going to be a good bit more than that! Idiots! Pick up his bed and bring it here so I can see him killed with my own eyes!" They trudged dutifully back to David's house. Michal met them at the door and showed them to David's room. That's when they found out the form in the bed wasn't David at all, but the household teraphim with a wig of goat's hair. Now they were really scared. "He'll murder us!" they said to Michal. "You'd better come along and explain this!" So Michal stood before her father, Saul. "Why," said he, "did you, my own daughter, let my enemy escape and even *help* him?" Michal, as we've said before, was no fool. She raised her melting dark eyes to her father's face and let them fill with tears. Her pretty warm mouth trembled a little, and she murmured, "Father, I couldn't help it! He threatened to *kill* me, the beast, if I didn't aid him!" So David made good his escape to Samuel at Ramah, and Michal returned to her own house.

# David as Fugitive

DAVID WAS ON THE RUN AGAIN. There had been a brief respite after the Ramah affair. Jonathan had coaxed Saul and reminded him of David's service to him, and Saul had repented his anger and let David sit again at the king's table. Saul's favor was short-lived, and once again David ran for his life.

When he heard Saul begin to shout his usual imprecations, David had called Jonathan aside and said, "I've got to know how the land lies. I'll stay away, and if he notices, tell him I asked your leave to go home for the ritual sacrifices. Then come tell me how he responds." The first night Saul didn't say anything. "He has probably incurred ritual uncleanness," he thought. "He will be here tomorrow." The second night Saul asked Jonathan about him, and Jonathan made the agreed-upon excuse.

"You bastard! Worthless son of a faithless mother!" screamed Saul. "You are in league with my enemies. You silly fool! Don't you know that neither your life nor your succession to the throne is worth a damn while that man lives?" Once again Jonathan sought to reason with his father, but the enraged Saul roared threats against Jonathan's life as well, and seemed likely to spear him in David's stead. Jonathan hurried out to David's hiding place and sent him away in haste.

David was even less prepared for a journey than when Michal helped him to escape, but he had his wits. Saul hadn't actually declared him officially a fugitive, and even if he had, news didn't travel fast. When David reached Nob he went to the priest there as if he had the right. Ahimelech assumed he was on Saul's business, as always. "Why are you alone?" he asked. "Secret business for the king—I'm meeting my men over yonder," replied the clever David.

David went on to ask for food and a weapon "because the king's business was so urgent I didn't stop for either one." There was only the consecrated bread, but David assured the priest they were ritually clean. Finally—irony indeed—he took Goliath's sword, which was the only weapon there, and slipped away to seek asylum in Gath. That didn't work out. The king's servants promptly reminded him of that nasty ditty about David killing "his tens of thousands." Hearing them, David was scared. When they brought him to the king, he did a grand imitation of madness, banging on the doors and drooling. Achish, the king, was entirely taken in. "Do I need extra lunatics in my court? Is that why you've brought me this fool?" he roared. "Throw him out!" And to David's relief, they did.

David began to realize he needed to hole up somewhere and make a few plans. He hid in the cave of Adullam, and gradually all his brothers joined him. The company was also joined by many who were dispossessed or out of favor or in debt, until there were about 400 men. It was then that David quietly moved his parents out of harm's way, finding them asylum in Mizpah with the king of Moab; then he moved his men back into the wilds of Herath in Judah.

About this time, Saul found out that David had a force of men and was moving back into his territory. That's how it looked to him, anyhow. He never doubted that David was as eager to kill him as he was to kill David. Bitterly, he berated his courtiers: "None of you told me when my own son made a pact with that fox! Not one of you warned me when he incited my servant to become my enemy."

Saul's men stood silent, exchanging sly glances. The king was at it again—really paranoid! All except Doeg, that is. One suspects that Doeg the Edomite was the sort of greasy little talebearer we all hated in grade school. "I saw David, master. I saw him when he came to Ahimelech in Nob. I actually saw the priest give him food and the sword of Goliath. He consulted Jahweh for him too, master!"

Here was a target for Saul's rage that he could get his hands on. The whole family of Ahimelech was summoned before Saul. "What do you mean, you traitor, consulting God for my enemy David? What sort of man are you to give food and weapons to a man who is rebel against the king?"

"My lord," replied the startled priest, "who is more faithful to the king than your son-in-law? Why, he's not only that, but he's captain of your personal bodyguard. He eats at your table! I've always consulted God for him when he set out on campaigns for you. Why wouldn't I this time? Surely you aren't bringing charges against me. I acted in good faith, having no idea there was anything wrong."

"You helped him, and you'll all die for it," raged Saul. Turning to his guards, he ordered, "Strike them all down! Kill them, because they helped David escape. They knew! They all knew, and not one of them told me he was there."

Even Saul could go too far. He was God's anointed, and they could not openly rebel against him, but the Israelite guards refused— to the man—to strike down the unarmed priests of Jahweh. Saul was nearly apoplectic with rage. Turning to the tattling Doeg, he screamed, "Kill those traitors for me!" Doeg was an Edomite. He had no qualms at all in striking down eighty-five men who wore the linen ephod. Somewhere Saul found enough soldiery without qualms to utterly destroy the town of Nob. Every living thing in it was put to the sword, and the place was burned to the ground.

There was one son of Ahimelech who escaped the carnage. Abiathar fled for his life, and like other outcasts and fugitives before him, he found his way, little by little, to David's hideout. "My father and all my brothers died at Saul's hand," he said. "If he knew I lived, my life would be worthless. May I stay with you?"

"I knew it!" groaned David. "Doeg the Edomite is a wretched, sniveling talebearer. I saw him there that day and knew he was Saul's spy. I have been the cause of the deaths of your father's whole household! Indeed you *shall* stay with me. They will take your life over my dead body!"

Once David slipped out of hiding and harried the Philistines at Kielah. Saul got wind of it and started down to seize him, but David and his men slipped back into the wilderness. That's where Jonathan found him. Jonathan had none of Saul's illusions. By now he knew he wasn't meant to be king, and he really didn't want to be.

"Take courage and rely on Jahweh," he told David. "My father, Saul, won't be permitted to harm you. It's your destiny to rule Israel. We both know that. Look, I'll be glad to be your second. Saul knows this, and even though it angers him, that's how it will be." They made a pact before God there in Horesh, renewing their bond of loving friendship. Then Jonathan went quietly back to Saul, and David settled in to wait for God's will in the matter.

# David Spares Saul

SAUL'S OBSESSION WITH DAVID'S CAPTURE made his life a constant uneasy game of dodging. Saul was God's anointed, and even to free himself of the nightmare of his constant jeopardy, David would not raise a hand against Saul. Once the residents near the wilderness where he hid offered to deliver David to Saul. "We know his haunts, you just come and get him," they said. Saul brought a force out and they started after David. Saul marched up the mountain with his force, while David slipped from cover to cover on the other side of the same mountain. Just then a runner brought news of a Philistine invasion, so Saul had to turn home.

David moved, then, to the wild places of Engedi. As soon as Saul had finished battling the Philistines, he was after David. It was simply hopeless! He had 3,000 men handpicked for the job and God only knows how many willing informers in the surrounding countryside. They could have found a pygmy flea! And of course, Saul found David, but not quite as he expected.

They were stopped by the sheepfolds, sort of taking a break and planning how to comb the area, when Saul felt the need to relieve himself. He slipped away for privacy into a cave that was right there. David and his men were crouched hiding in the far corners of that very cave, and when they saw Saul walking in their direction, the men were jubilant. "God *said* he would deliver your enemy into your hand! Today's your day!" they exulted. "God forbid that I should harm his anointed king!" replied David.

When Saul squatted down, half blinded by the darkness of the cave after the sun outside, David moved stealthily toward him. His men wondered what on earth he meant to do. Had the man lost his wits? If he refused to harm Saul, what was he moving toward him with drawn sword for? Swiftly David bent near the squatting king and, catching a corner of his cloak, sliced a piece off with his razor-sharp sword. Then David melted silently back into darkness. Saul rose presently and moved back out into the light, and when he did, David's men really had cause to wonder, for David leaped to the cave's entrance after Saul and cried in ringing tones, "My lord king!"

The startled Saul whirled to look behind him. Surely that was David's voice? What he saw was indeed David, bowing to the ground in homage. David had repented even such a small thing as tearing the cloak, and forbidding his men to touch Saul, had gone out to speak to him.

"David? David, my son, is that you?" asked Saul. Forgetting for the moment his fears and suspicions, Saul remembered the winsome young man he had married to his daughter.

"My lord Saul," said David, "it certainly *is* me. What's more, you are mighty lucky it is! See what I have in my hand?" (Here he waved the piece of Saul's cloak border he had taken.) "All I've taken is a scrap of your cloak. It could just as well have been an arm or a leg—or your life! But I said, 'I won't harm the Lord's anointed, no matter how much he has hounded me!' Now let Jahweh judge between us!"

Saul shed bitter tears. "David, my son, you have paid back my suspicions and my persecution of you with loving kindness. You have honored and protected me in spite of my ill will toward you." Then Saul made one of the hardest admissions of his life. "David, you are the better man of us, and now I understand that God will make you king, and that Israel will be secure in your hands. One thing, David, if you will do me one more favor," said Saul. "Please promise that you won't do as so many kings do and wipe out the members of the former ruling family. You can have the kingdom, David. That's as God wants it, but don't wipe my name from the face of the earth."

"My lord Saul," said David, "I give you my word I'll honor and protect your descendants as I have yourself." So Saul left, and I don't know what he told his troops, but he called off the manhunt and David and his men went back to their stronghold.

# Abigail and David

DAVID MOVED, AFTER A WHILE, down to Maon, to another wilderness where the flocks of Nabal pastured. Nabal was a rich man, and David saw a chance of maintenance for his troops. At shearing time, when there was usually a real wingding—lots of food and wine, and handouts for those in need—David sent ten men down to Nabal's place with a message. "Tell him I, David, send him wishes for peace and joy and prosperity. May his days be long and prosperous, and in Jahweh's name, can he spare us a little food?"

It was a common custom for those who were wanderers without land to ask for food from the local people. It was considered a sacred responsibility to give them what they needed. Nabal, however, was tight fisted and a bit of a klutz. He flatly refused the request, even though they reminded him they could easily have robbed his shepherds blind in the pastures.

"Who in the hell is David?" Nabal exploded. "Am I to take the food I've fixed for my feast and share it with every ragtag and bobtail runaway slave that comes begging?"

The ten went back to David with the answer. David had a temper of his own, and he said, "I'll *stomp* that klutz! Not a man of his household will live to tell about it either!" And his men armed and mounted to start for Nabal's place.

Now Nabal had a wife, Abigail, who was wise as she was beautiful. When he was so insulting to David's men, some of the wiser servants went to her and said, "Look, Nabal's just *asking* for it! All the time the flocks were in his area, David not only kept his hands off, but he also protected us from other marauders. His request for provisions is reasonable. Besides that, the man has a temper, and when Nabal's insults reach him, he's likely to descend on us like the wrath of God!"

181

Abigail moved fast. Two hundred loaves of bread, two skins of wine, five sheep prepared for cooking, roasted grain and raisins and figs were all gathered and loaded on donkeys before the hour was out. "Now," said she, standing back to survey her gift, "you just start out toward David with those, and as soon as I tidy up a bit I'll follow along to do the talking."

The servants headed off and Abigail smoothed her hair and slipped into something pretty. She rubbed a few aromatic herbs on her warm skin, too, then she mounted her donkey without telling Nabal and hurried off after the servants. She caught up to them just about the time they met David. David looked at the plentiful food and then he looked at the lovely Abigail. "My lord," said she, "my husband has no manners and less sense! Please take these few little gifts I've brought you, and distribute them among your men. Don't soil your hands with Nabal's blood in vengeance. Jahweh will protect and keep you safe always because you are a man without fault and fight his battles!"

David said, "You're right! Bless you for your wisdom and for stopping me from doing this evil thing. Your gift is generous and has stayed my anger. Go home in peace, my dear. I would not harm you or yours for anything!" And he watched wistfully as she rode away.

Next morning, Abigail told Nabal what she had done. He was seized with such vexation that he had a stroke, and ten days later he died. It seemed, clearly, to be God's vengeance.

Abigail had evidently borne little love for her husband, Nabal. In fact, she had said scornfully to David that the very name Nabal meant "brute," and that the man really lived up to it. Still, she was a just woman and she saw to it that he was properly mourned. She buried him according to customs of the day, and David, hearing of the affair, bided his time.

David, you recall, had been married to Saul's daughter Michal, but when he became *persona non grata* at court, Saul could see no point in wasting a perfectly good daughter. (Women were used as chattels to make favorable alliances at this time.) Saul took back his bargain with David, and gave Michal to a man by the name of Palti.

David had married a girl from Jezreel named Ahinoam, but the custom was that a man kept multiple wives to increase and insure his tribe against extinction. When the proper period of mourning was over, David sent his servants to Abigail with a proposal of marriage. She was still young and lovely, and she knew she was likely to end up married to someone chosen for her as Nabal had been if she sat around long. Besides, she had been impressed with David, and she knew a good thing when she saw it, so when David's servants came, she wasn't a bit coy.

"I'm entirely at your disposal," said the decisive Abigail. "Just let me get a few things together, and we can start off." She wasn't waiting around for any of the menfolks to find out and interfere. Next day she mounted her mule with a glad heart. Once again she was riding out to meet David, but this time free of the sulky and difficult Nabal. So Abigail became David's wife, and if I can't say they lived happily ever after, I *can* say that she must have had a lifelong satisfaction in one thing. For a woman of Abigail's day, it was a rare privilege to choose her own husband. And frankly, if the men who could have intervened had any thoughts of doing so, I should suppose that one look at the idea of snatching her from David's stronghold quelled them.

# Wilderness Exploits

ONE OTHER EVENT OCCURRED at the cave of Adullam that helps explain how David inspired such fierce loyalty in his followers. It appears as a small "hero tale" in the long listing of his "thirty and three" special warriors whose bravery the people of Israel especially remembered. This particular escapade involved the three, and it's almost like a prank. It sounds like the stuff that men of all times have done to relieve the pressure and boredom of waits between battles.

David was bitterly homesick sometimes. He was cut off from all settled existence of home and family. He could not return to his wife Michal, and he couldn't visit the people of his hometown, Bethlehem. There was no end in sight, either, but to wait for Saul's death, since he wouldn't cause it himself. One day, in this mood, he mused nostalgically, "What wouldn't I give for a drink of the sweet water from my childhood! Oh, if I could only go down and draw up a drink from the well of Bethlehem!"

The three caught each other's eyes and slipped away from the company. If David wanted water from Bethlehem, he should *have* water from Bethlehem. Never mind that the whole area was occupied by Philistine troops. Wouldn't it be a lark—a real feather in their caps—to slip into the town and get a skin of water without getting caught. They could just see themselves strolling up casually to David and saying, "Oh, by the way, here's that water from Bethlehem you fancied."

It was the beginning of the harvest, and the valley was lousy with Philistine troops. In fact, Bethlehem was one of their garrisons. The three men managed, somehow, either to blend with the landscape or to slip in under the cover of darkness. It isn't recorded how they did it. What is recorded is simply that they came back to camp triumphant and handed David water from the well at Bethlehem's gate.

David sat holding that water skin in his hands, with thoughts and impressions chasing each other through his head—the cool drinks from that well in his early childhood days; the choking grip of Philistia on that beloved ground; the dearness of the men who had risked their lives to bring him fulfillment of the desires of a chance word.

A great stillness had fallen on the men who had gathered to "see the fun." David looked up into the expectant faces of the three. "What can I say? It isn't water I hold in my hands. It's your lifeblood risked to satisfy my whim." Then he rose to his feet. "This is far too costly a gift. It would be like drinking blood! It is appropriate, surely, as an offering to Jahweh!" And slowly, reverently, he poured the precious stuff out on the earth before God.

When it came to risky pranks, David was no slouch himself. Once more, Saul had decided to hunt David down; once more he had encamped in the valley with a chosen 3,000 men. David's spies had confirmed that they were bivouacked in the valley with all the troops grouped around Saul's tent. They felt quite secure, and hadn't even bothered to post sentries.

This time, David didn't wait for Saul to come up to him. He asked for a volunteer—someone to be a witness, one suspects. Abishai, son of the massacred priest of Nob, offered, and as night deepened, he and David slipped into the sleeping camp. Right up to Saul's tent they went, moving quietly among the troops. God had made a deep sleep fall on them, and David and Abishai stood at their center looking down at the totally vulnerable king.

"Surely this is your moment," whispered Abishai. "He's in your power, and now certainly you can deliver and avenge us both!" But David shook his head. "He's still Jahweh's anointed. Far be it from me to lay a hand on him!" But with a schoolboy grin he reached down and took Saul's spear, which stuck in the ground by his head. He picked up the water pitcher, too, that stood ready in case he should be thirsty in the night, and handed it to Abishai. "When his time comes," he said, "Jahweh will bring his end. Surely we don't want to bring Jahweh's curse on us by causing it."

When they had put a good safe distance between themselves and the camp, David turned around there on the side of the mountain and let out a mighty shout. "Yo! Abner! Answer me, Abner!" Abner woke from sleep with a start and rushed out of his tent. "What? Who's that calling?"

David replied, "Are you men or sissies down there? Why don't you keep a decent guard on the king's life? A man of Israel came in to kill him, and there you all were sleeping like the dead—sleeping like the dead you deserve to be since you left his life unguarded. Where is the king's spear, and the jug of water that stood at his hand? That's pretty sloppy work, old boy. Not well done! Not well done at all!" taunted the irrepressible David. (He'd headed the king's bodyguard when he was in favor, if you remember.)

There was a general scramble toward the king's tent, but just then Saul himself called out, "Is that you, David? David, my son, is that your voice?"

"It is, my lord king," David replied. "Why do you harry me? What evil have I done? Have I harmed you that you hunt me like wild game? Your men want to cut me off from the heritage of Jahweh. Go serve other gods, they say. As God is my judge I am innocent of wrongdoing!"

"David, my son, you are right. I've pursued an evil course! I'm a confused and cruel old man, and your care of my life shames me. I promise I won't harm you. Come back, and I won't harry you anymore or try to kill you, and God will indeed bless you."

David had heard *that* line before, and he didn't believe Saul's repentance would last any more than you and I do. He had what he wanted though—respite for the present. "Well and good, my lord. God rewards men according to their deeds. *He* will prosper and defend me for my righteous dealing," called David. "Send a man over to get your spear, and all's well between us." So the chagrined Abner sent a man to run up to where David stood and bring back the king's spear. I don't know what happened to the water pitcher. If I were David I'd have kept it. Can't you imagine the gathering around the campfire that night, and Abishai chuckling, "And then David said to Abner—" and "But we kept the water jug that stood right at his fingertips as a little souvenir."

# David in Philistia

THE TIME OF DAVID'S being a fugitive in the wilderness lengthened. Abigail and Ahinoam were good wives, but they longed for a settled household existence—and said so. His men were loyal and steady, but many of them had families who needed security; they, too, spoke of it with longing. David himself was weary of being always on the move, always hunted. Soberly he assessed the fact that one of these days his luck would run out and Saul would kill him.

It was no small thing to desert Israel when Samuel had anointed him to be its future king, but Samuel was dead. Saul was very much alive, "And," David reasoned, "a dead king and a dead dog are equally useless!" So he made the decision once again to go to King Achish in Gath. David, with an available fighting force of 600 men, looked a lot better than had David the lone fugitive. Achish spoke fair words and received David as a resident alien in the capital city.

David played fair. He fought Achish's battles, and when they raided surrounding tribes, he brought Achish spoils from the raids. Ahinoam and Abigail settled in contentedly where there were other women, and it was good not to have to beg for food and keep a sharp eye out for traitors. Saul, when he heard David was in Gath, breathed a sigh of relief and forgot about running him to the ground. David still felt a little uneasy perched in Gath, though. There he was at the king's whim and far too visible. So he said to Achish, "Give me a place in one of your smaller cities—me and my men—where we can settle our families and live on our own ground."

David had one really nasty practice on his raids. Wherever he went to take spoils, he killed all the people and laid the land waste. Animals and possessions he kept as spoil, but he operated on the basis that dead men tell no tales, and he wanted no tales told. Achish reasoned that since some of David's raids had been into Israeli territory, they surely hated him enough by now that he couldn't help but stay loyal to Achish. In light of David's service, Achish gave him the town of Ziklag for himself and his people.

For a year and four months David stayed in Philistine territory, and then the Philistines mounted a force to attack Israel. David and his men went with Achish's troops and the other chiefs raised a stink. "Oh, no! Do you think we want a fifth column in our midst? In battle's heat they will turn their swords against us." Once again they reminded Achish of that fateful ditty the maidens sang:

*Saul has killed his thousands,*
*But David his tens of thousands.*

"Well, said Achish, "I find no fault with him, but if you're going to be *nasty* about it—." And he sent David and his men back to Ziklag. It was as well for David that he did. When they arrived home three days later, "home" was a heap of smoldering rubble. The Amalekites had raided the town and carried off possessions and livestock. They had taken quite a few slaves, including David's two wives. The people left were furious. They figured (and probably they were right) that it was precisely because Ziklag was the town of the marauding David that it had been sacked.

David mourned his loss, then he called Abiathar. "Ask God for me whether I should pursue these raiders." The answer came, "You should. You will certainly overtake them and rescue your people." Six hundred men set out and marched until they came to the river Besor. Did I say marched? They half ran. Their only hope was to catch the raiders by surprise before they reached home.

At Besor, 200 of the men were too exhausted to go on. David made a quick decision. "If we don't catch them today or tomorrow, we've lost our chance. Let these men stay with most of our supplies. Moving light, we will have a better chance of catching up." So, taking only food for the day, they set off at an even quicker pace.

As they moved out into open country they found a young Egyptian lying in the fields. They brought him to David. The exhausted man was given food and water. He ate as if he were famished! Someone added a piece of fig cake and two bunches of raisins. He gobbled those too, and when he had eaten he told his story.

"I'm a slave of one of the Amalekites. I fell sick three days ago and he left me here to die. We had raided Judah and Caleb and burned Ziklag. Yes, I know where they are camped, and if you'll not turn me over to my master and swear not to kill me, I'll lead you there."

"Kill you?" said David, "Man, if you find them for me, you shall live free among us or go where you like, taking your share of the spoils with you. I am David of Ziklag and they hold my wives!"

When they came to where the raiders camped, they were holding a real bash to celebrate all their spoil. They were entirely off guard, and most of them were probably not a little drunk. David and his men swept down on them like the wrath of God. They slaughtered the Amalekites right and left, and only 400, who managed to mount camels and flee, escaped. They, of course, had no time to gather any of the booty. It was all there to the last woman and child. Even the flocks were gathered up and driven along by the returning people.

The men went jubilantly shouting, "This is David's booty!" David let them holler to their hearts' content, but he did some long thinking. He had got back his wives, and there was plenty there. No need to be greedy. When they got back toward the river some of the men began to say, "No booty for those who did not fight! Oh, they can have their brats and their broads back, but the *rest* goes to those of us who did the work."

David nipped that in the bud. "Shame on you, after Jahweh has blessed us with such success!" he said. "The men who kept the baggage safe served too, and must have their share." He made it a law for Israel that day, and so it remained.

David also saw rather clearly that Philistia wasn't entirely good for his health, and he might want, someday, to return to his own people. So he sent a portion of the spoil to all the towns of Judah with the message, "Here is a present for you from the booty taken from the enemies of Jahweh." David was nobody's fool, and time was to prove this one of the smarter moves of his life.

# Saul's Death

WHEN THE PHILISTINES ENCAMPED at Shunem to make war on Israel, Saul collected his troops at Gilboa to give battle. Saul slipped down to a sentry point to have a look at the Philistine encampment, and when he did, an eerie thing happened. Saul was no youngster on his first campaign. Neither had he ever been known as a coward, but suddenly Saul's knees shook. This seasoned warrior was seized with a deadly premonition, and try as he would, he couldn't shake it.

"Jahweh," prayed Saul, "how is it with us? What shall I do? Do we attack or wait?" There was no answer. Do you know that feeling you get when you pray and the words seem to fall dead from your lips into a dull, gray void? That's how it was for Saul. He called the priests with the Urim and Thummin, and they looked and found no answer. "Surely," thought Saul, "the Lord God will speak in a dream," but such sleep as he got was dreamless.

Saul was really desperate. The heavy sense of foreboding grew heavier still, and no answer came—none at all.

Finally Saul called his servant and said, "I want a medium! If I could just talk to Samuel he would know. Get someone who can call him up for me."

"But my lord King," the man protested, "the mediums were all killed or banished at your express order!"

"Never mind that!" Saul roared. "I want one *now*, and you know damned well that there's one skulking about the place somewhere!"

"Well, there *is* a woman down at Endor who has some skill at necromancy," the servant admitted. So Saul put by all signs of rank and, dressing himself like one of his foot soldiers, took two other men with him and went down to Endor that night, secretly.

"Foretell me the future by means of a ghost!" he demanded. "There's someone I absolutely have to talk to, and I want you to call him up for me. I'll make it worth your while!" And he jingled a palmful of silver. "Look," protested the medium, "do you want to get me in trouble? You know as well as I do that Saul would have my head if he heard I'd done that!" But she eyed the silver greedily.

"In God's name, I swear it, you won't come to any harm. You won't be counted responsible for a thing. The blame is all mine if it ever surfaces," promised Saul, and he pressed some of the silver into her hand with the urgent command, "Samuel! Call up Samuel for me!"

The medium began her ritual, and Samuel materialized, and somehow she *knew*. "My God! You've trapped me! You're Saul, and you've deceived me!"

"Hush, I'll not harm you! Tell me what you see!" said Saul. "In God's name, what's there?" And she described Samuel. Saul bowed in homage.

"Why have you conjured me up to disturb my rest?" said Samuel (or rather, his ghost, for so we must presume it to be).

"I couldn't help it! I've got to know what's to come, and I'm so frightened. God won't say a *thing*, and the priests read no signs. Samuel, you were always kind to me. Tell me what's coming!" cried the wretched Saul.

It was little comfort Saul got from his apparition. "Why call me," it snapped, "when God has deserted you just as I prophesied in life? What did you suppose *I* could do? There's *nothing* you can do to stop what God has purposed. The battle will go to Philistia, the kingdom to David, and as for you and your sons and many of your best men, by tomorrow night you will be with me."

Saul fell on his face, terrified by what Samuel's ghost had said and weak with hunger and fatigue. He had not eaten for two days. The medium was more than a little frightened herself. Here lay the royal monarch, the pride and strength of Israel and leader of its defenses, stretched out on her floor like one drugged or dead.

"My lord Saul," she pleaded. "My lord king!" And then she thought of a very practical feminine remedy. "You're hungry." She coaxed almost like a mother with a fretful child. "Let my lord rise, and take food for strength for your return journey. It will look better when you've something in your stomach!"

At first Saul refused. If he was a dead man by sunset tomorrow, why bother? Why bother with anything? But his servants pressed him as well. "Lord king, your forces look to you. Surely you need strength to return to them." And as Saul began to stir, the woman urged the servants: "Help him to the divan there, where he can be comfortable. I'll hurry and fix a meal for you!" She prepared meat and bread with her own hands and fed them, and when they had eaten, Saul and his men went out into the night.

The next day's battle was disastrous. Saul's worst fears were realized, and his troops scattered like dry leaves before the wind. Saul himself fell wounded by an arrow, and thinking of the atrocities routinely committed on captive kings, he begged his armor bearer, "Please kill me and let me go to my grave in peace! Don't let these uncircumcised men gloat over me!" But his armor bearer could not bring himself to do it. Wasn't Saul, after all, Jahweh's anointed? Desperately, Saul lunged to his feet and fell on his own sword. The young man who bore his armor, seeing his king dead and the enemy nearly upon them, took his own life.

Saul, his armor bearer, and three of his sons died that day, and after the fashion of the time, the Philistines cut off the heads and took the armor to show with them in triumph. The bodies of Saul and his sons were fastened to a wall in Beth-Shan.

Once, in his younger days, Saul had delivered the people of Jabesh-Gilead from the Ammonites, and now they remembered their debt. Under cover of darkness they stole the bodies, burned them at Jabesh, and buried the bones with honor, and so ended Saul's life.

# REIGNS OF DAVID AND SOLOMON

# David's Return to Hebron

WHEN DAVID RETURNED FROM RESCUING his wives and the rest of those taken by the Amalekites, they had exactly two days of peace and quiet before a messenger ran in. His clothes were travel-stained and ritually torn, and there was earth on his head in token of mourning. He was, in fact, the ancient equivalent of the "letter edged in black."

Straight up to David he ran, and fell to one knee in homage. "Where do you come from?" asked David with an odd feeling in the pit of his stomach. "And what news?"

"I'm escaped from Israel's camp, my lord, and the news is grim!" gasped the messenger.

"Say on."

"King Saul and his son Jonathan lie dead, and the army is defeated. Those left alive are scattered in all directions, and many lie fallen on the field."

"Are you sure?" asked David. "Who told you Saul and Jonathan were dead?" (What a mixture of grief and relief must have been in that thought for David, if it should be true.)

"I saw it myself, my lord. I stood a little way from Saul on Mount Gilboa, and he leaned on his spear and cried out to me, asking who I was. I told him I was a resident alien. When he heard I was Amalekite he said he was mortally wounded and asked to be killed rather than taken alive. The enemy were almost on us, so I did what he asked. I've brought you his crown and arm ring, my lord David."

David and his men mourned for Saul and Jonathan and all Israel. The messenger was ill-rewarded, to say the least. David had him killed on the spot, "For," said he, "you are convicted out of your own mouth of killing God's anointed king!" Then David composed a dirge for Saul and Jonathan, and all the Israelites with him mourned.

When David had mourned Saul and Jonathan according to custom, he set his face to the future. Now that Saul was dead, that future need no longer be in Philistia. "Jahweh," prayed David, "shall I go up to my own land?"

"Go!" came the answer. "Your moment is come."

"Where am I supposed to go?" asked David. "Which city will receive me? Where shall I rule? Because you know as well as I do, Lord God, I go back as ruler or not at all, and so do they." And the Lord said, "Return to Hebron."

David and his household, his men and all their households returned to Hebron. Remembering the gifts David had sent them, the men of Hebron welcomed him, and the news went around Judah: "David is back. Now's the time!" All the men of Judah gathered at Hebron and crowned David king.

Saul was dead, and three of his sons with him, but he left sons at home, and his commander, Abner, still lived. Abner was loyal to Saul's house, and did what any reasonable man might expect. He set up the crown prince Ishbaal, eldest of Saul's remaining sons, as king over Israel. Now the kingdom was at war both within itself and outside.

David sent kind words to Jabesh-Gilead, praising them for Saul's burial and swearing his friendship. Gilead was in Ishbaal's territory, and Abner said, "If you let David be, he'll win your people from you, bit by bit. You *know* what a folk hero his escapades have made him, and if you aren't to look like an also-ran of a younger son, we'd better get down there and chase him out of Hebron. Judah had no right to crown him anyhow!"

Ishbaal assented to Abner's plan, and Abner gathered his troops and went on down to Gibeon, sort of pawing and snorting on the way to be sure the people saw that Saul's house was far from extinct.

Joab, who was David's commander (and also, incidentally, his nephew), gathered the men of Judah and did a little pawing and snorting of his own. There they sat, one party on each side of the pool, not facing Philistines this time, but their own countrymen. Those who had fought shoulder to shoulder were suddenly enemies.

Presently Joab and Abner met, and they resorted to the same ploy Goliath had used—a few in combat representing the many.

Twelve young men were numbered off from the tribe of Benjamin for Ishbaal. Twelve of David's followers came in his name. It was deadly sport. Still, for fighting men it *was* sport, and the kids were all do-or-die. All they saw was the glory. The wagers were laid, the rules were set, and when the signal was given, twenty-four of the finest young men in the land rushed together in deadly combat.

Have you ever seen two wrestlers so evenly matched or two sport teams so equally skilled that the contest literally isn't one unless someone makes a mistake? If you have, you've seen what happened here, and there were no mistakes. Each of those men fought to kill, and their training was superb. In one motion each caught an adversary's head with the free arm. In the second motion, only seconds past the first, each ran his sword home in the other's side. It was over before it had begun, and twenty-four young men lay dead between the stunned and silent troops.

The silence didn't last much longer than the deadly duel had, though. Someone, looking down at a dead brother, or son, or friend, let out a hoarse cry of rage and grief and lunged for the nearest man on the other side. It doesn't matter who started it, because every man on the field was in it as soon as he did. The battle was fierce and vindictive, and David's troops won the day.

Abner and his men fled—what was left of them—and that should have ended it, but there was a young hothead in David's troops called Asahel. He'd been known from his boyhood as a swift and tireless runner, and he took off after Abner. He didn't want anybody else, and he passed heavier and slower-footed men without bothering them. He wanted the big game. Wasn't he, after all, David's nephew and Joab's brother? When Asahel was almost up with Abner, he recognized the footsteps and he turned and called out, "Asahel, is that you?" "It is!" replied the young man.

Abner was strangely loath to strike this youth. He was a good kid—hardly dry behind the ears, and he was Joab's brother. "Turn aside," said Abner. "Kill someone else if you must, but turn aside. If you don't I'll have to kill you, and how could I face Joab?" But Asahel came on undaunted.

Abner was sick at heart, but he did what a seasoned warrior must with his life at stake. Coming to the spot later, Joab and Abishai found their young brother dead, with Abner's spear through his body. Furiously they took up the chase and kept on until sunset. By now, Abner had gathered his men, and he stopped and called out to Joab, "Is the sword to eat its fill forever? How long before you call these men off from killing their brothers?"

"If you hadn't said that," Joab replied, "I *never* would have!" They returned to their own cities then, and Asahel was buried in his father's tomb.

# The Kingdom Unites

IN SPITE OF ABNER'S WORDS of warning, war dragged on between the houses of David and Saul. It's hard to tell where it would have ended had it not been for a woman. Abner did pretty much as he pleased around the court. Ishbaal was no Saul. One begins to suppose, in fact, that he was pretty nearly Abner's puppet. One thing finally got to him, though. Abner decided he had an itch for one of Saul's concubines called Rizpah, so he took her. What, after all, was a woman more or less?

To Ishbaal this was the final straw in a heavy weight of arrogances. Even on a lowly concubine, some of the royalty had settled by the simple fact of her having belonged to Saul. It wasn't right that Abner should coolly usurp her, and Ishbaal complained. Abner knew darned well what he had done. He, too, knew it was inappropriate, but since when is a man reasonable over a woman he wants, like Abner wanted Rizpah; instead of apologizing and giving her back like he should have, Abner lost his temper. "Am I a dog's head?" swore the angry commander, "that you're so fine I can't get near your royalty? Do you quibble with me over a *broad*?"

Ishbaal was terrified. He knew he owed his kingdom to Abner, and he was about to swallow this insult along with all the others, but Abner couldn't let it be. He may have been pricked by his own guilt, or it may have been the full realization of the contempt he bore this weak son of Saul he had set up as a sort of paper king. "I've had it!" he spat out. "I'm going on down to tell David he can have the whole shebang! He'll make a *real* king! Didn't Jahweh promise him the kingdom? I might as well see that he gets it!" And he stomped out, leaving the speechless Ishbaal to wonder how he could be placated.

Abner wasn't simply being nasty. He had spoken in anger what had been brewing in his heart for a long time. Ishbaal *was* no king, and David had the experience and expertise and perhaps, above all, the charisma to unite the torn tribes into a solid kingdom. "Come to an agreement with me," read Abner's message to David, "and I'll bring you all Israel."

David knew his man, and when Abner gave his word, it was good. The return message was equally terse. "I'm with you, but only if you bring me Michal, my wife." All this time that had rankled—that someone else should have had *his* Michal! For Michal there *was* no choice. Women were chattels. For the two "husbands" involved, it was a "damned if you do—damned if you don't" situation. Abner simply went and took Michal from Paltiel, son of Laish, to whom Saul had wed her. Paltiel knew he couldn't fight the commander of the troops, but neither did he accept the situation calmly. He evidently loved the girl, and he followed her, weeping, to Bahurim. "This just won't *do*," said Abner. "She was *his* first, and he wants her back. *He* never said you could have her. Go on home and find yourself another wife and cheer up!" I don't know whether Paltiel did find another wife or not. I don't even know if he cheered up, but at least he went on home, and left Michal with Abner. Abner did his homework well. He called on all the elders of Israel and reminded them, "Jahweh promised that David's hand would deliver us from Philistia, and this Ishbaal is simply *worthless*. You've been wanting David as king for a long time. I'm going up to make our move."

Taking the lovely Michal (daughter of the dead king, remember) and twenty men as escort, Abner went up to Hebron. David was as good as his word. He made a feast for Abner and his company, and they agreed amicably that Abner should return to rally Israel to David's scepter. What was to be done with Ishbaal seems to have been largely ignored. Perhaps with the loss of Abner they figured he would revert to an ordinary citizen. More likely they figured Saul's house was not so popular that he'd be let to live long.

What David and Abner had not figured was that Abner wouldn't live to see sunset. David wished him Godspeed, and he left unhindered to return to Israel. When Joab and a party of soldiers returned later that day, they got the news. "Abner's been with David, and all Israel is coming over!" Joab went right in to David and howled. Was it perhaps a little jealousy? Was it the acrid taste of his little brother's unavenged death? "You fool! He's only speaking soft words to lull you and gain your secrets so he can attack!" said Joab.

David refused to hear Joab, so he took things into his own hands. Swift runners were sent to bring Abner back to Hebron. What David didn't know, Joab thought, wouldn't hurt him. There had been friendship between Joab and Abner. They had fought together against Philistia for years. Abner thought nothing about it when Joab drew him aside at the city gate to speak a private word in his ear. After that he ceased to think at all, because he was dead. Joab had avenged Asahel as he had longed to do.

It's hard to say whether or not David was angry. He was realistic enough to understand Joab's motives, and politic enough to know he mustn't let it look like his idea. He went into public mourning and ordered all the troops to do the same. He pronounced a public curse on Joab's house. He sang a dirge at Abner's tomb, and buried him with honor there in Hebron. Then the king fasted all day and he proclaimed, "I am so weak with sorrow and fasting I simply can't punish Joab as his deed deserves. Let Jahweh judge him and pay him back in proportion to the wrong he has done!" It sounds like a cop-out to me, but it pleased the people mightily (which is what David had, of course, intended).

Ishbaal did not long survive Abner. All Israel was shaken at the news of Abner's death, and some of the alien princes who lived in the land were sure they knew how matters stood. Their allegiance to the strong Saul had been tenuous at best, and for Ishbaal they shared Abner's contempt! What better way, they reasoned, to get David's favor than the gift of Ishbaal's head—detached from his body. They watched their chance, and one day as he napped after lunch, they slipped past the woman cleaning wheat on the doorstep (who had paused for forty winks herself). Ishbaal died without waking. Taking the slain man's head, they left for Hebron.

Admitted to David's presence, the men brought out their grisly gift. "My Lord David is avenged on Saul's house forever!" they said. "See, Jahweh has delivered Ishbaal into our hands. He tried to kill you, and now he is dead himself!" But David cried out in anger, "You have entered an honest man's house and killed him in his own bed! Your lives shall pay for your treachery, you bandits!" So the men were killed, and they buried Ishbaal's head in Abner's tomb (which, under the circumstances, strikes me as a bit ironic).

With Abner dead, there was no one to crown or defend another of Saul's descendants as king. No one really had much of a mind to have them anyhow, and if anything was needed to bring Israel to David's side, Ishbaal's death accomplished it. Israel came to David in Hebron. "We are your flesh and blood, and we remember Jahweh's promise that you should be king. Now rule over us, and let us have peace with each other," they said. So there, before Jahweh, they crowned David to rule over Israel as well as Judah. In the thirtieth year of his life, the shepherd from Bethlehem, youngest of the sons of Jesse, became king of all Jahweh's people.

# The Ark Brought to Jerusalem

WITH ISRAEL AND JUDAH REUNITED under David's kingship, the Philistines began to worry. They had reason to know David's abilities as a warrior, you may recall, and they figured the best way to catch him was to get him soon in the hope he would be off balance in his new power. So the Philistines mustered their troops in the valley of the Rephaim.

"Lord God," prayed David, "shall I go down against them?"

"Go, by all means, and expect the victory I will send you," God replied. David's first battle with his united men was such a rout for the Philistines that they fled, leaving even their gods behind! Delightedly, David and his men carried them off, remembering their own consternation when the ark had been taken some years back.

The Philistines were beaten, but not destroyed, and they took just long enough to get themselves organized, and once again they mustered in the Valley of the Rephaim. Surely they must get their gods back home. Maybe that first round was just luck on David's part. Or maybe, they thought, they'd been a little careless. This time they posted double guards, and there wasn't space where a healthy *flea* could get through between them and Israel without detection.

David said to God, "What about it, Jahweh? Shall I go up and fight?" and God said, "By all means, David, but not quite like it was before. Just you slip around behind, where they aren't looking for you. When you hear my feet going ahead of you in the tops of the balsam trees, then you will know I am there to fight for you."

Israel went out as God had told them, and the Philistines, with their attention entirely on the frontal attack they expected, were put to such confusion that they turned and ran. Israel pursued them all the way from Gibeon to the pass of Gezer before they turned back to their own cities.

Perhaps it was the capture of the Philistine gods that put David in mind of the ark of the covenant. Maybe he had meant all along to bring it up to the capital city just as soon as he got those pesky Philistines off his back. The capital city, by the way, was Jerusalem now. David and his troops had taken it from the Jebusites and, moving into the fortress, had built a strong wall around it. No doubt of it, David was enjoying the settled security of the kingship.

All the picked troops of Israel—30,000 of them—mustered behind David to escort the ark of the covenant up from Baalah of Judah. They had a brand-new ox cart for it, and Ahio and Uzzah were chosen as escorts to walk before and beside the cart. All the rest, led by David, walked along singing and shouting and dancing to Jahweh in celebration—and I do mean celebration. There were tambourines and lyres and harps. There were cymbals and castanets, and probably a half a dozen other noisemakers nobody thought to record. Israel had a real fortified city and a powerful king to defend it, and Jahweh's holy ark was coming home to it!

Just as the celebration was going strong, though, a really frightful thing happened. It had been a long time since Jahweh had put out his hand and destroyed someone as obviously as he had the idolaters in the wilderness. But as the ark lurched and swayed along near the threshing floor of Nacon, it looked a little unsteady. Uzzah, walking beside it, put out a hand to steady it. It was a forbidden thing to touch the ark itself, because it was holy, and Uzzah fell dead right there.

David was shaken, and not a little angry that God had struck Uzzah that way, so they turned aside and lodged the ark at Gath in the house of Obed-Edom. Three months it stayed there, and in that time the household prospered in an extraordinary fashion because Jahweh was rewarding them.

When David heard of this, he was reassured, and he set out again to bring the ark to Jerusalem. This time, in addition to the rejoicing, they offered sacrifices to Jahweh as they went. Remembering Uzzah's fate, all the men kept a respectful distance from the ark, handling it carefully by its carrying poles. They brought it into the city with the sound of ram's horns and dancing; David, in an ecstasy, leaped and danced before it, dressed only in a linen loincloth. Michal, Saul's daughter, looking out the window, was really turned off by it. "Well!" thought she. "If that isn't silly looking! Where is the king's dignity? Even at his worst my *father* wouldn't have run around nearly naked and cavorting like that!"

David saw the ark safely into the tent he had ready for it, and then he offered final sacrifices. When all this was done, he gave the people bread and dates and a raisin cake for every man and woman there! They all returned to their homes rejoicing, and David started back to bless his own household.

Before David got to the door, Michal went out to meet him. "Well!" she sputtered. "If you aren't a fine one! You've made an absolute *fool* of yourself cavorting around out there before all the maids in the kingdom—and you nearly naked! Does the court lack jesters that you feel you need to play the fool? What will people think?"

David was distinctly taken aback by her vehemence, and more than a trifle annoyed. "I wasn't dancing for the people!" he protested. "I was dancing for Jahweh alone! And," he added, "as Jahweh lives, who chose me to be king instead of your father, I'll dance that way again. If my honoring him like that lowers me in your eyes, that's *your* problem. But by those you speak of, I will surely be honored!" And he turned his back on her and stomped into the house.

It is a matter of history that Michal never bore any children. It could possibly be regarded as a curse of God on her for her rash words. It could also be that David, having several other wives, found them inclined to be more tactful. He could not, for reasons politic, openly put Saul's daughter out of his house. But he could (and I suspect he did) put her out of his chamber. She had let him know much too clearly that she despised him. And whether from natural or supernatural causes, she bore the reproach of a childless wife in Israel.

When David brought the ark up, he put it, with all honor, in a tent. That was fine except for one thing. Hiram of Tyre had sent up envoys with material and craftsmen and built David a house of stone and cedarwood, and his conscience was uneasy. "I live in more luxury than God's holy ark," he said to Nathan the prophet. "I should build Jahweh a house too, now that we've brought the ark home."

"Why not?" said Nathan. "Jahweh is, after all, with you!" That night the word of God came to Nathan. "Tell David he is truly in my favor and I will make him prosper and keep the kingdom safe in his hands. I will not only keep him safe, but his sons will rule after him, and be as if they were my own sons. But tell him this, too. Jahweh says, 'Did I ask you for a house?' For that matter, in all these years I've been establishing leaders, did I ask anybody for one? To which of the judges did I ever say 'Build me a house of cedar'? No indeed! I never asked for that. Besides," said God, "David is a man of violence, and it is a man of peace who will build my house. Tell him once more that I will establish the son of his flesh on the throne of Israel, and it is he who shall build my house in peace." So Nathan went and told David all God said.

"Lord Jahweh," prayed David, "I'm honored and blessed, and I understand. You are building my household and that of your whole people of Israel. It's like nothing in the world's history, the care you've given us. Only be pleased to continue your blessing!" And quietly David put aside his plans to build a temple.

# Mephibosheth and Bathsheeba

FIRMLY ESTABLISHED IN HIS FORTRESS at Jerusalem, David set about methodically extending his territory. He defeated the Philistines and Moabites. He reduced all the smaller kingdoms around him to taxpaying suburbs of Israel. With a firm hand he set internal affairs in order and made appointments of trusted men to all the public offices.

Finally, as the kingdom began to run smoothly and the pressures of battle to ease, David remembered Jonathan. True, he was dead and buried, the beloved friend of his youth, but David recalled the promise to care for his house, and he set out to find whether Jonathan had left sons.

When a new king comes to power in a warlike nation, if you are of the royal blood of the house no longer in power, the best place to be is somewhere else. So the one son of Jonathan who still lived wasn't exactly making himself noticeable. There was another reason, too, why he lived in retirement: Mephibosheth was lamed in both feet. He had been a child of about five years on that terrible day when Jonathan and Saul were killed in battle. It was only a vague memory now, how the people in the palace had panicked and run for hiding in fear of being wiped out in a general slaughter. Big as Mephibosheth was, his nurse had scooped him up in her arms and run with him. In her haste, she had stumbled and fallen heavily. His screams of pain were lost in the general lament over the fallen. Only much later did they realize how badly he had been injured.

When David began his search for Saul's household, he found among his retainers a man called Ziba who had served Saul. Ziba was a discreet man, and when he had made sure David meant Mephibosheth well, he readily revealed his whereabouts. "Get him for me!" said David. "Bring him here to court where I can see him!"

When Ziba returned, he led a young man who leaned heavily on him and hobbled painfully, but David wasn't looking at the twisted feet, but at the face so much like Jonathan's, and his heart turned over with love for the young man. "Stay here with me," he said. "Eat at my table and be as a son to me. Your father was my dearest friend, and you are much like him. Have you family? Are you provided for?"

"A wife and son," replied Mephibosheth. "We don't go hungry, my lord. We've had good friends."

But David called in Ziba and said, "All the lands of Saul are to belong to Mephibosheth now, and you and your sons and slaves are to work them. See that he and his family are well cared for! Mephibosheth himself shall eat at my table, for is he not Jonathan's son?" Ziba was well satisfied, and he and all his household managed the estates, but Mephibosheth lived there in Jerusalem, and was treated like one of the king's sons.

So David kept his promise to Jonathan with honor, but unfortunately, his honor didn't extend to some of his other relationships, and his actions were not all what Jahweh would have asked of his anointed. This was particularly true in the matter of Bathsheeba.

David was getting solidly middle-aged—no doubt about it. Kingship agreed with him, now that Saul was dead by another's hand and he was free to take his place as God's anointed. And after the lean, harried years of living as a fugitive from Saul's capricious temper, it was good to settle in the palace in Jerusalem and let Joab take over leading the troops to battle this spring. There was even time for afternoon naps, and this particular day he had slept luxuriously and risen in the long shadows of late afternoon to walk on the palace roof and survey his city. That's when he saw her! The most beautiful girl that ever made a man's blood pressure rise, stretching with indolent luxury in her bath. Well, David lost his head, the old fool, and he called a servant and said, "Who is she?" And the servant—it wasn't his business—replied that she was the wife of Uriah the Hittite. "Wife! Confound it!" thought David, but he said, "Well, bring her here anyhow. I could see her a little closer by and she could have dinner with me and a little wine. She must get bored while he's out fighting and all—we'll cheer the poor girl up!"

So they went to fetch Bathsheeba. She was definitely excited—dine with the king?! And she put on her loveliest silks and jewels and her most expensive perfume and her gold ankle bracelets and, well, with one thing and another, he cheered her up all right. He cheered her up so well that a couple of months later he got a frantic message saying, "I'm pregnant and I haven't seen Uriah for six months. I'll be disgraced!" David moved fast. Uriah was brought home from the front and asked for reports, and then he was flattered and told, "Take a couple of days off! Go home and get a good meal and see that (heh, heh) pretty little wife of yours." David had no doubt that once Uriah got there Bathsheeba could manage the rest. Trouble is—Uriah never went! The big boob went out and slept in the bachelor's quarters, "because," said he, "I can't loll around taking it easy while my buddies are out there getting hacked up!" So David said, "Bring him back!" And this time he had Uriah to supper, and if I do say so, the servants deserved Academy Awards for their straight faces. David made sure Uriah's wine glass stayed replenished, and he called his most voluptuous dancing girls to entertain and then he diplomatically pointed his slightly tipsy guest toward home and Bathsheeba.

No luck! Uriah stumbled down to the palace guardroom and said, "Move over boys." That did it! Uriah went back to the troops, and a messenger carried the terse order to Joab, "Get this man killed and make it look like an accident!" No problem! Uriah was hot on honors and do-or-die, and it was easy to just pull back a little and leave him exposed. Joab sent word back and that was the end of it.

Bathsheeba mourned the prescribed time and then what was more natural than that David should console his officer's bereaved widow—and she expecting and all? He consoled her so well, in fact, that by the time the baby was born she was his wife, and settled into the palace, and David congratulated himself on getting out of that one neatly.

Then one day Nathan the prophet came in and said, "I've got a story you should hear! There's stuff happening in this kingdom you'd hardly believe," and David said, "Say on!" And Nathan told the heartrending tale of the rich man with flocks and herds and lands who, to make a feast, took from his poor neighbor his only animal, a pet lamb he had raised from a few days old and used to feed from his own plate and give it milk from his cup as if it were a daughter.

David rose up in wrath and swore the scoundrel should die before the sun set; Nathan let him have his say and David said, "Where is he? Fetch him here at once!" And Nathan said, "You're wearing his skin, King David!" And then he reminded David of all God had done for him and given him and he said, "God will punish you for this because he is a righteous God and you have indeed been wicked!"

Now David was king, and he had killed one man and could have killed another, but David also cared very much about the fact that he was God's anointed, and that great man in all his splendor dropped his head and said, "God forgive me! I have sinned." And Nathan said, "God does forgive you; your own life is spared, but the child will die."

Nathan left the palace, and David heard with a heavy heart that his youngest son was ailing. Three days they watched the infant, and David shut himself in his chamber and fasted and wept in sackcloth. His court officials couldn't get him to eat or come out, so they were scared to death to tell him when the boy died. He guessed it from their faces, though, so he got up and dressed and went to the temple to pray, and he came home and ate a good meal. "Because," said he, "now I can't change God's mind, I leave him in God's care for I will one day join him."

And David went to comfort Bathsheeba—must have done a good job, too, because in the course of time she bore him another son, and David called him Solomon, but Nathan the prophet called him Jedidiah, "because," said he, "God loves this child especially, and that name means beloved of the Lord."

# The Rape of Tamar

IF EVER THERE WAS A MAN who showed real ability to weld a kingdom out of a gaggle of quarrelsome tribes, it was David. He ruled his subjects and deployed his armies with a positive genius. Unfortunately, the same was not true of his household. His sons seem to have been enough to disgrace any father.

Amnon, one of the princes, was at the age to fall hopelessly "in love." He had a real crush on Tamar, the sister of Absalom. Tamar was, of course, a virgin and a princess, and by the laws of Leviticus, Amnon couldn't marry his half sister (though ancient custom had allowed it). So Amnon pouted and moped and picked at his food and tossed on his bed nights until he worked himself into a real tizzy.

In a sense, Amnon isn't the villain of this piece. It was an older and should have been a wiser head that came up with a tricky plan. Jonadab was a cousin of Amnon's, and he was really rather fond of the youngster, so he coaxed, "Come on, Amnon, what's eating at you? Surely a prince of the royal blood can have what he wants!"

"Oh no, not me!" said Amnon. "I couldn't be so lucky! I have to end up wanting my half sister Tamar. Have you *seen* her, Jonadab? Gorgeous! Simply gorgeous! And she has to be my half sister and you *know* how sticky the law is about that. Without her, life simply isn't worth a damn! And I can't have her!" And the sulky Amnon kicked a jar so hard that it shattered against the wall.

Jonadab thought a minute and then he gave Amnon a shrewd look. "What if I tell you how you can have her without any trouble at all?" said Jonadab.

"No kidding? You can get me Tamar? Best of friends! I'll reward you richly indeed! When are you going to bring her to me?"

"I'm not," said the wily Jonadab, "The king is."

210

"The king? You're joking, Jonadab. He's all hung up on this law thing. He'd never hear of it if I were on my deathbed for desire of her!"

"I think he will," said Jonadab. So they made a devious plan. Jonadab went to the king and said "Uncle, I'm terribly worried about Amnon. He can't sleep, he's feeling awful, and now he's taken to his bed and won't eat a thing!" David wasn't too wise about his sons, but he loved them almost inordinately, so he got up right away and went, himself, to check on what ailed Amnon.

Amnon, meanwhile, had laid himself on his bed in his darkened room with his face to the wall. Every now and then he moaned a little for effect.

"My son," said David, "what ails you? Take a small sip of wine to strengthen you and tell me what hurts." Amnon shook his head and moaned again. "You're *thin*," said his worried father. "I know you're wasting away. Come, eat a little something. What can I get that will tempt your appetite?"

Amnon turned his head languidly and muttered hoarsely as if nearing exhaustion. "Tamar—my sister Tamar. If she makes cakes in my sight and ... feeds ... me ... with her ... own (gasp) hand." David loved his son, and besides, Amnon was his eldest and the pride of his life, so he said, "Why not? Jonadab, just run over to the palace and have the princess Tamar come right now."

Jonadab went, looking as innocent as if he'd never thought of it. Tamar came, and David said, "There's a good girl! Just fix some cakes for your brother here. He says he'll eat for you. I expect he's a little out of his mind, but if you can get him to eat, he'll get better, I'm sure." And David went back to the palace.

Tamar turned back the long sleeves of her gown, and they brought meal and oil and all the other makings and she kneaded the cakes right there at the bedside and baked them on the brazier. All the while Amnon watched covetously the curve of her bare arm and the way her clothes hung against her body and the curly tendrils of her hair damp from the brazier's heat. When the cakes were done, smelling as savory as only fresh-baked meal can, Tamar dished them up and offered them to Amnon.

"No," said he, "no, I can't eat with everybody standing there gawking at me. Out! All of you! Just leave Tamar to feed me, and the rest of you go!" The servants did as they were told, and then Amnon said, "They're still peeping! I *know* they are! Here, bring those into my inner room where I can be sure of privacy." And Tamar, humoring him because he was sick, followed Amnon to the inner room.

As Tamar moved close to the bed to give Amnon his food, he reached out and caught hold of her instead of the cakes. "Come on!" he said. "Let's make love! I'm crazy for you, Tamar, really I am!" Tamar tried to pull away, and at first he only held her and tried to fondle her.

"Don't!" she said. "Amnon, no! Men of Israel don't behave that way! Where could I go to hide my shame if we behaved like that? And have you thought of yourself? You'd be an outcast! Amnon, look, I like you a *lot*, and if you'll just ask the king, I think he will bend the rules for us. If I were your wife—"

But Amnon hankered after Tamar with a lust that wasn't going to listen to reason. He had her in his hands, and he didn't give a damn for anything but *now*, so he simply overpowered her and took what he wanted. Up to now, I suppose we might plead hot blood or youthful folly, but for the next thing Amnon did, there seems no excuse. He pulled away from the sobbing Tamar and suddenly he hated her as much as he had lusted after her before.

"You can get out now!" said Amnon. "I really don't want you any more. I don't care if I ever see you again!"

"No, my brother," pleaded the shaken Tamar. "To send me away now is an even worse wrong than the first!" But Amnon couldn't face either Tamar or himself, and he called the soldier who served him and said, "Put this woman out and bolt the door!" So Tamar put dust on her head and tore her robe in mourning and went wailing back to the palace.

Absalom did his best to comfort Tamar. "Just hush up and it will blow over," he said. "After all, he *is* your brother." Tamar remained disconsolate in his house, and Absalom, seeing the despair of his lovely sister, silently swore vengeance.

When David heard of the affair, he knew he'd been duped. He also knew Amnon had done a great wrong and should be punished.

But Amnon was his favorite, remember? Absalom had done a fierce job of shushing the affair, and Amnon certainly wasn't going to tell it. He knew by now how ugly it had been. So David swallowed his wrath and pretended he didn't know, and it looked as if the whole affair had blown over.

# Absalom's Revenge

TO ALL APPEARANCES, Amnon's rape of Tamar was forgotten, and if King David remembered it at all, it was only as an unpleasant little affair in the past. That's why, when Absalom came to invite the court to his shearing feast, he saw nothing more than a young man's wish to "swank it" by entertaining rather beyond his means. "Do come, Father, you and your officers!" "No, no," laughed David. "We would eat you out of house and home!"

Absalom had been fairly sure of that reply, so he pursued, "Well, then, if not you, send Amnon in your stead."

For a minute the king felt some vague sense of foreboding. "Amnon?" he said. "Why Amnon, of all people?"

"Just let him come in my honor since you won't. He *is* your eldest son," said Absalom.

"Well, all right," said David. "I'll tell you what—why don't you ask *all* your brothers? You young blades can celebrate and kick up your heels and that will be better than us old fogeys coming."

So Absalom bowed himself out of the king's presence, and all the princes were bidden to his feast. When they were all gathered at his place near Ephraim, Absalom set out a real feast. The food was plentiful, the entertainment lavish, and the servants had orders to fill Amnon's glass with wine as often as they possibly could. Somewhere midway through the feast the genial host rose from his place and, turning grim, shouted, "Now!" Before anyone could do more than wonder, two armed servants who had stood quietly in the shadows converged on Amnon. Their work was deadly sure and the other princes scrambled from their places and, mounting their mules, rode, as they supposed, for their lives.

Somebody else fled the feast too, and even faster than the galloping princes came the rumor. "Absalom has slaughtered his brothers. All the king's sons are dead at their brother's hand!" The stricken David fell on his face and tore his clothes. His sons were his *life*. All the men of the court tore their robes and wailed, and into this melee walked Jonadab. "Uncle, wait!" he said. "It's terrible, I know, but not nearly as bad as you think. Only Amnon will be dead. Absalom has had a grudge for him these two years past. It was written all over him. Believe me, your other sons are safe."

Just as Jonadab finished, a man from the watch ran in to report a group of riders approaching, and presently a second confirmed that they were, indeed, the princes returning. Jonadab, who had started the whole mess in the first place, seems to have slipped away scot-free. The court mourned Amnon, and Absalom went into voluntary exile in Geshur until his father's wrath should cool down.

Three years Absalom stayed away, and three years the king mourned his eldest. As time went on, though, it became more form than emotion, and David began to long after the son who lived. Amnon, after all, was dead. Must he lose Absalom as well? Joab, his commander, sensed this, and he sent a wise woman with a tale as good as that told by Nathan over Bathsheeba so as to lure the king to say one mustn't threaten *forever* a man who had killed in anger. David saw the ruse, once he'd fallen for it, but maybe he was looking for an excuse anyway, so he said, "All right, Joab. Bring him home, but not to court. I won't have a murderer in my *house*, but let him return in peace to his estates."

Absalom came back quietly enough, and for the moment he settled at his house in Jerusalem, glad to be home and unthreatened. He stayed away from the palace, all right, but there was no bar to his walking the streets and charming the people. He was a handsome man, was Absalom. His sister Tamar had come by her beauty honestly, and evidently Absalom favored the same lovely mother, but in a masculine version. We never hear what became of Tamar, by the way, but when Absalom had had three sons, he had also a beautiful little girl, and he named her Tamar.

When two years had passed and Absalom was still exiled from the king's presence, he summoned Joab. Now, Joab knew very well that Absalom meant to send him to coax the king. He figured he had already risked his neck for this prince once, and that was enough, so he simply ignored the summons. A second time Absalom sent for Joab and a second time he was ignored.

Absalom was furious! He was used to having his own way, and he meant to get it. Absalom just happened to have a field that shared a common boundary with one of Joab's. It was almost time for harvest, and Joab's barley stood dry in the field. "I'll get his attention!" said Absalom to his servants. "Just you go out and set fire to his field. I guess he won't ignore that!"

Joab did, indeed, come right over to Absalom's place. "What do you mean by burning my barley?" he roared. "What do *you* mean ignoring my summons? I had to do something to get your attention," retorted Absalom.

"Now go to the king and tell him for me, 'What was the point of my return from Geshur? It would have been better to have stayed there than be an exile in my own land. Let me come before the king's face, and if I am guilty, let him kill me, but if not, let me see his face again.'"

Joab went once more to King David and delivered Absalom's message. David knew that Absalom had killed, but hadn't he, after all, had provocation? And in his own heart David must have known that his laxity in not punishing Amnon had helped to bring about Amnon's death.

Absalom was sent for immediately; he came in and threw himself on his face before his father. Officially, at least, David had not seen this handsome son in five years. He rose from his throne and, raising Absalom to his feet, threw his arms around him and kissed him. So Absalom returned to favor.

# David and Absalom

IT WOULD BE NICE TO SUPPOSE that Absalom gained in maturity and kindness from his father's forgiveness. I'd like to be able to report that his presence was joy enough to justify David's bringing him back. Well, miracles do happen, but Absalom wasn't among them.

No sooner had David pardoned him and let his return to favor be known than Absalom began openly to do what he had all along. He had his eye on the main chance, and that meant the kingship of Israel. Kingship went to the oldest son, and with Amnon dead, Chileab still stood in Absalom's way. Besides, his father looked as if he would live *forever*, and Absalom wasn't a patient man. He hired a fine show of a chariot and horses and fifty men to run ahead of him, and the people, liking a good show, used to cheer the young prince.

The sneakiest thing Absalom did, though, was to wait on the road by the gates coming to the part of the city where the palace was. When anyone came in, he used to ask them their town and inquire into their needs. Then he would commiserate with them and assure them if *he* ran the zoo they'd certainly get their desires, but there wasn't much hope under the current regime. When people did him homage he would take their hand and embrace them and be generally folksy. Well, the common folks *loved* him, this handsome young prince. "And so kind!" they'd say. "*He* understands our problems, and he actually embraced me like a brother!"

For four years Absalom built his popularity this way. If David knew it, he chose to ignore it. He had a real genius for selective deafness, had David. So one day Absalom said to David, "Father, there's a little matter I need to see to. Remember when I was in exile in Geshur and dared not come home?" David nodded assent and wondered that Absalom should bring up that touchy subject.

"I made a vow to Jahweh there in Geshur," continued Absalom. "I longed so for my home that I vowed if he brought me back in peace I would offer special sacrifices at Hebron."

David was pleased. Was this troublesome son actually turning to Jahweh and showing both maturity and piety? So David blessed him and granted permission for Absalom to go to Hebron. But Absalom had something other than piety in mind. As he traveled he sent word through all the tribes of Israel, "When you hear the trumpets sound, you are to shout 'Absalom is king at Hebron!'" and he gathered strength as he went, so that he had a sizable force by the time he got to Hebron. He did, by the way, make the sacrifice he had said he was going for, but whether in thanksgiving for deliverance or as a request to Jahweh to further his plot's success it's hard to say.

Some of David's own counselors went over to Absalom, and the affair had gotten quite out of hand before someone who was loyal got hold of it and went to tell David, "You've been had! The hearts of the men of Israel are with Absalom now."

By the time David got wind of the uprising, it was big enough to make him believe that Jerusalem was indefensible, so he gathered his household about him and once again, as in Saul's time, took to the hills. He was no longer a young man, full of the sureness of the Lord's call, but old, tired, and unsure, and burdened by a great caravan of household. Perhaps one of the most heartwarming pictures of the old king is the one at the city gates when he offered to send back the 600 soldiers from Gath—with a blessing, yet. One wonders how many of these men were friends from the year spent in the king of Gath's service while Saul was still alive. What comfort it must have given him to hear Ittai swear allegiance by the living God! The priests, too, brought the covenant box. (Isn't the king, after all, Israel?) But David said no. They were to return the sign of the Lord's presence and favor to the city and let the Lord decide who was to be king. If David returned, then he would see the ark again. If not, perhaps God meant Absalom to replace him, even as *he* replaced Saul.

It sounds almost defeatist, but his actions were not those of a beaten man. He still set up his spy net, and almost by reflex, perhaps, joined in the battle plan. We see the faithful Joab leading the host.

One wonders whether he was cursing the day he wheedled Absalom back to favor. Along the weary march, we see both love and hatred for the king. There is perfidy and steadfast faithfulness and over all of it the studied greed and arrogance of Absalom. Yet David, driven from his home and forced to defend his very life, said still to his soldiers, "Whatever you do, don't hurt Absalom. He's still my son, so spare him for my sake." And then he settled for the hard hours of waiting out the battle, by the city gates at Mahanaim. It was the genius of Israel to see the hand of God in success and failure, and so when Absalom got his hair tangled in a tree, hanging there helpless when his mount bolted, that's what Joab saw. Perhaps he also saw the spoiled prince who had burned his barley even though he owed Joab his return to Jerusalem. Perhaps he saw the ungrateful son who had driven an aging father from house and home. Whatever he saw, Joab scoffed at the men who would have heeded the king's cry to spare him and had Absalom killed on the spot. But he wasn't a fool, and when an eager young noble asked to bear the "good news" back, Joab forbade it and sent an expendable slave instead. Finally, however, the young man was permitted to go too, and outrunning the slave, brought the news: "Battle's over! We won!" It was left for the slave to give an eyewitness account of Absalom's death, and David simply crumbled. He turned his back and retired into his private quarters, bewailing the death of his son.

So the soldiers, their victory snatched from their hands by the king's strange actions, sneaked back into town as if they had something to be ashamed of. Joab was furious! He blustered into the presence of the weeping king and dressed him down. "These men have followed you into exile, risked their lives to save yours, and now you set their gift at naught! Do you want the kingdom, or are you going to sit here blubbering over that traitor while your true friends are made ashamed of their very bravery?"

And David came to his senses. He dried his eyes and gathered the troops and praised them, and if his heart remained heavy for his son, yet it rejoiced that he was still the Lord's anointed king, and it was a king's progress back to Jerusalem. David pardoned and rewarded and generally spread peace and prevented bloodshed and hard feelings.

Joab, by the way, lost his command to another, but that's all that happened to him. And by the time David reached Jordan, Judah and Israel were fighting over who had most claim on him, like little kids playing "teacher's pet." So David entered, again, the holy city and saw, with joy, the Ark of the Presence. For many years yet the favor of Jahweh was to keep David's reign in power over his united kingdom, but beneath the splendor and the joy of that fact ached, always, the heart of a father who possessed his kingdom at the price of the life of his son.

# Solomon Crowned

KING DAVID WAS NEARING THE END of his days. Almost forty years he had ruled over Israel, and it had become a nation under his reign. But now he hardly left his bed, and he complained bitterly that he was cold to the marrow of his bones. "There are not enough coverlets in the world to warm me! They don't weave the wool as warm as they did in my youth," he fretted.

"He's old and feels death's chill," they whispered. "Let's find a maiden to warm his body with her young vitality and see to his care while he lives."

So they brought a very beautiful young Shunemite girl, Abishag by name, and she cared for the king and kept him warm with her own body, but she remained a virgin, for David was past sexual desires. He was past almost anything that took effort, and people began to worry a little over the fact that he had not named a son to replace him.

Some people worried about whom David would name as successor, but there was one who gave up worrying for action. Adonijah was the younger son of Haggith, and like his brother Absalom and his sister Tamar, he had great physical comeliness. Like Absalom also, he had an eye on the kingdom—a greedy eye.

"He's a senile old fool," thought Adonijah. "He put down Absalom, but that's because Absalom was premature in his try. I will have the kingdom in my pocket before he can totter up from his bed."

In one way you feel sorry for David. This was the third son to go wrong and the second to try to snatch the kingdom. In another way, it's the same old story. Adonijah knew he could do anything he pleased because he had done some mighty chancy things in the past and all David had ever done was chuckle, "Boys will be boys!" and turn his back.

Like his older brother, Adonijah hired a royal chariot and fifty runners to precede him. He didn't even bother to ask David's permission. He just invited the group of court officials and priests and general VIPs he was sure would follow him, and headed off to the Sliding Stone by Fuller's Spring to have a great sacrifice and proclaim himself King of Israel. He had some rather impressive support. He had his cousin Joab, who was David's army commander. He had Abiathar the priest, and he had all the royal princes but one, and that was only the youngest.

If Adonijah had important guests, however, he also had some important exclusions. Left home in the palace were Nathan the prophet and Zadok the priest. The young Solomon may have looked unimpressive to Adonijah, but his mother, the beautiful and beloved Bathsheeba, was a more formidable adversary than he had counted on, and she and Nathan both believed Solomon should inherit the throne.

"You get in there," said Nathan to Bathsheeba, "and tell King David what's happening. Remind him he promised the throne to your son. If you don't, I wouldn't give either of you much chance of living out the week. As soon as you are done, I'll go in and back you up."

Bathsheeba did her job well. "Didn't you promise Solomon the throne?" said she. "I certainly did, and he shall be king," said David.

"That's what I thought," said Bathsheeba. "I knew you were a man of your word, but Adonijah is out at the Sliding Stone making huge sacrifices and proclaiming himself king, and he's got some mighty important folks out there with him!" And she bowed herself out of David's presence and left him to think it over.

Nathan waited a slow count of ten, then he came in and repeated the performance. Now, Adonijah had made two mistakes. The first was leaving these two at court. The second mistake was the stupidest. He had taken David's physical decay for his dotage, and he was badly mistaken. David's mind was still sharp, and he moved with the decision of an old campaigner.

They called Bathsheeba in and David said, "Who did you say was around court?" When they had told him he said, "Good! Gather up everybody that *is* anybody. Put Solomon on my own white mule, and take my palace guards to attend him. Zadok the priest shall take the holy oils from the Tent of the Presence. All of you make a festal procession down to Gihon, and when Zadok has anointed Solomon king, blow the trumpets and shout 'Long live King Solomon!' Don't dally around, either. As soon as that's done, bring him right back and set him on my throne so there's no doubt in anyone's mind who Jahweh's anointed is to be."

They did as David had said, and all the people who hadn't been important enough for Adonijah to bother with gathered at the sound of the trumpets and shouted and stomped and cheered so it sounded like the earth would split. They escorted Solomon back and set him on the throne and all the court congratulated David and wished Solomon a reign even more glorious than his father's, and David praised God, "for," said he, "I have lived to see my own son ascend the throne in peace."

They had just finished the meal out at Adonijah's bash when they heard the roar of the people and the sound of the trumpets for Solomon. Joab jumped to his feet, feeling maybe a little guilty, and said, "What's that uproar in the city?" And just then, Jonathan, son of Abiathar, came in.

The young man evidently didn't know what Adonijah was about, because when Adonijah greeted him with the words, "You're an honest man. Surely you bring good news!" Jonathan replied, "Oh, yes sir! Our lord, King David, has made Solomon king. I came right out to tell you! *My*, it was grand! Zadok and Nathan poured the anointing oil over his head, and he rode the king's own mule, and now he's sitting on the throne, and everyone is congratulating King David!"

The poor young man must have wondered what ailed people when his "good news" had the effect of scattering them in all directions as if he'd brought a case of the plague in with him. Each man rushed off to his own home and tried very hard to look as if he'd been there all along. Each, that is, except Adonijah. He knew, suddenly, the abject helplessness his brother Absalom must have felt hanging in that fatal tree. Adonijah made a run for the Tent of Presence, and there he knelt, clinging to the horns of the altar, for there, in Jahweh's presence, a man might not be killed.

It didn't take long before someone brought Solomon word. "Adonijah is clinging to the horns of the altar. He says he won't stir a step until you swear by Jahweh you won't put him to the sword."

This was Solomon's first judgment, and surely the whole court waited to hear what sort of king they had. He must have wondered a bit himself. The man had, after all, been within a breath of seizing the throne. "Tell him," said Solomon after a moment, "if he behaves honorably, I wouldn't harm a hair of his head. If he proves malicious, he dies like any other traitor." Solomon had Adonijah brought down from the altar, and Adonijah, who had begun the day as king (in his own mind at least), did homage to the younger brother who had ascended the throne. Solomon received him quietly, and bade him return to his house. So the reign of Solomon, whom Nathan had named "beloved of God," began in peace and mercy.

# Old Scores Settled—David's Death

SOLOMON'S REIGN BEGAN in peace and mercy, but some of the warrior David's bloodshed marred its first years after all. David lay dying, and as Solomon bent over him, he gave his last instructions. "Serve Jahweh faithfully and according to the laws he gave Moses, and he will secure your throne. There are a few little things—sort of unfinished business."

"Yes, Father, what is it?"

"*Get* Joab! You know how he killed two men in peacetime to avenge a soldier's death in war. He dishonored me, and shouldn't die in peace. Let Barzillai of Gilead's sons eat at your table. They gave me aid and comfort when I fled before Absalom. Shimei is still with you too. He cursed me as I fled. *I* promised not to hurt him, but *you're* a different man. Find a way to bring his gray head down to Sheol in blood!" And Solomon promised.

David died and was buried with great love and honor in his own citadel. Forty years he had ruled over Israel—seven at Hebron, and thirty-three in Jerusalem—and his name stands as a name of blessing in Israel to this day.

After the time of mourning was over, the kingdom began to test what sort of king this Solomon really was, and first among them was the ambitious Adonijah. He still hankered after the throne, and he thought of a really sneaky way to reach for it. He went to Bathsheeba and said, "He's got it all, your Solomon, even though I should by rights have had the throne, since I'm oldest. Still, that's how it is. Jahweh's will can't be changed. But there is one small thing, if you'd ask it for me."

Bathsheeba could afford to be generous. She'd gotten her way, and was the "queen mother." Besides, it must have been sort of fun to have people flatter and fawn for favors, so she said, "What is it, Adonijah? I'll see what I can do."

"It's Abishag, the Shunemite," said Adonijah. "I'm crazy about the girl! She's a lovely thing, and besides, it's not as if the king, my father, had actually had intercourse with her. She was really only a caretaker for him. Bathsheeba, get her for me! Solomon will surely not refuse *you* if you ask."

Bathsheeba went to Solomon. King or not, he was a proper son, and he got off his throne and bowed to his mother and had a chair brought and set at his right hand for her.

"Now, Mother, what is it you want? I'll surely do what you ask, because I honor you. Not only are you my mother, but I know you secured the throne for me—you and Nathan—so ask what you will."

"It's a small thing, son," said Bathsheeba, "really a minor matter, but I promised Adonijah I'd ask. You know that pretty child Abishag from Shunem they brought to tend to your father at the last? Adonijah wants to marry her. Just let him have her for his wife, now that your father is gone."

Now, Bathsheeba was up on some of the court intrigues, but there were some finer points of political protocol that were beyond her. She really thought the request was innocent until Solomon burst out, "Mother! Why don't you just ask me to gift wrap the crown and throne for him?"

"What?" said Bathsheeba. "What's that got to do with his wanting Abishag for a wife?"

"Just this," replied her son. "If he takes the king's wife, the succession goes with her, and he knows it! He's signed his death warrant with that request!"

A shaken Bathsheeba bowed her way out of Solomon's presence, and Benaiah was dispatched to kill Prince Adonijah.

When Joab heard what had happened to Adonijah he read the signs bright and clear. Solomon might be a peaceable man, and slow to anger, but when he saw a reason, he would be as ruthless as David had ever been. Joab reasoned he had two things to fear. It's not likely David's last words hadn't reached his ears. Besides that, he was known to have been with the dead and dishonored Adonijah during his abortive attempt to snatch the throne the first time. Joab ran for the Tent of the Presence and knelt clutching the horns of the altar.

Solomon, when he heard of Joab's flight to the altar, sent word to him. "What on earth do you have a guilty conscience about that you should run for refuge before you are even accused?" Joab replied, "I was afraid of you, and I fled to God for protection."

"Go back," Solomon told Benaiah, "and strike down Joab." But Benaiah returned to Solomon to report, "I told him to come out, in the king's name, and he won't. He just clings there and says he won't do it and if he's going to die it will have to be there."

"Do as he says, and strike him down there," replied Solomon. "He unfairly tricked and murdered Abner and Amasa. He is blood guilty, and deserves no mercy. Let their blood be on his head, and let the household of David be blessed in its innocence from that crime."

Joab was killed, as Solomon had ordered, and buried on his estates. The command of Israel's forces went, not surprisingly, to Benaiah.

Now Solomon turned to Abiathar, the priest who had presided at Adonijah's crowning. "I can't see taking your life," he said. "You served my father David in all his hardships, and bore the ark before him. I can't kill you, but neither can I see keeping a traitor at court. Go home to your estates and stay out of my sight. Zadok shall be priest in your stead." With Abiathar's removal, the prophecy God gave Samuel so long ago was fulfilled. The last of the house of Eli lost the priesthood.

One final enemy remained, and Solomon called in Shimei, who had cursed David when he fled before Absalom. Shimei was virtually put under city arrest. "As long as you stay in Jerusalem, I won't touch you," Solomon said. "But if you set foot across the Kidron Brook, you're a dead man!"

For two years Shimei stayed put, and Solomon waited, then two of Shimei's slaves ran off to Gath.

"I'll just run over and get these two home," said Shimei. "Solomon won't notice, and a little country air will do me good. I'll be back before he knows it." This was exactly what the wily Solomon had counted on. Shimei could have sat in Jerusalem for twenty years if he hadn't been constrained, but draw a man a line, and there's something that goads him until he crosses it.

Shimei hadn't been home an hour before Solomon's guards were at his door. "Did I or did I not bind you by a solemn vow before Jahweh to stay in the city?" asked Solomon.

"You did," muttered the miserable Shimei, "but—"

"Your blood is on your own head," said Solomon. "You remember the evil you invoked on my father, David, when he was in distress. Now it has returned to curse you, but let David's house be blessed forever." Benaiah was given his orders, and Shimei was struck down. The last of David's dying orders was fulfilled, and Solomon settled securely to rule the kingdom.

# Solomon's Glory

WHEN THE THRONE WAS SECURELY ESTABLISHED under him, Solomon went up to Gibeon. It was the oldest and most sacred of the "high places" where the Israelites offered sacrifices before the temple was built. Solomon offered a great sacrifice to Jahweh and then he went to his rest.

God was pleased with Solomon's piety, and came to visit him in a dream. "Solomon," he said, "you have followed in your father's righteous footsteps. Ask for anything you want of me. What gift would you like?"

Solomon said, "Lord Jahweh, you have kept our family in great power and set me on my father's throne securely, but grateful as I am, one thing does worry me. Your people Israel are a huge nation, and diverse. I'm little more than a boy, and I feel so inadequate. Lord, give me a wise, discerning heart to judge your people fairly."

"That is a good request," said Jahweh. "Already you have wisdom beyond your years, and you shall have all you ask—more than any man before you, and no man shall ever be so wise again. You didn't ask for wealth or long life, but that you shall have as well. If you honor me as your father, David, did, not only will you reign for many years, but your sons and theirs shall hold the throne in my name." Solomon woke from his dream and, returning to Jerusalem, he offered sacrifices of thanksgiving to Jahweh.

It was soon evident to the people that the king had a maturity and wisdom unusual in one so young. One case in point was the baby case.

Two prostitutes who lived in the same house came in one morning wrangling bitterly. Each had borne a son, and one of the newborn infants had died in the night. "She rolled over on him is what it was!" scolded the first, "and then she had the nerve to sneak *my* son away while I slept and put her dead brat at my breast. When I woke at first daylight to suckle him I *knew* it wasn't mine. *Mine* had more hair, and a dimple just here, and—"

"You lie!" shrieked the other. "Yours was puny from the start! I *told* you he'd never make it, and now you want to snatch my fine son to replace yours that's dead!"

Solomon listened quietly and then he signed for silence. "Was there no witness? No midwife or friend?" he asked. There hadn't been. Solomon turned away a moment in thought. The living baby stirred and whimpered in the arms of the attendant who held him. The women glared at each other.

Suddenly the king said, "Bring a sword!" A sword? The court exchanged surprised looks. "Cut the child in half," ordered the king, "*precisely* in half, so that each gets her fair share."

"Good!" said one of the women. "If I can't have him, neither can she!" But as she said it, the other dropped to her knees at Solomon's feet and said, "Oh, no! Don't kill the baby! I'd rather he live as her son than to see him hurt! Please, lord king, let her have him!"

The soldier who held the sword stood hesitating, and Solomon smiled. "Put the sword away," he said. "We won't need it now. And you, my dear," he said to the woman at his feet, "take your living child and go home in peace. No true mother would see her child killed for spite."

The tale about the baby spread far and wide, and people marveled. That was one of the more spectacular, but every day of judgment brought more such decisions, and there seemed no end to his knowledge. It's said that he was so wise that the rulers of all the lands around used to come to visit just to hear him talk. Not only was Solomon wise, but there was peace on all his borders.

King Hiram of Tyre sent an embassy to Solomon when he heard of his enthronement. Hiram had been David's friend, and besides, from the rumors he heard, this youngster was someone you wanted to get on the right side of. Solomon was very pleased. Hiram's land had cedar and juniper and the means of transporting it to Jerusalem. Solomon was ready, now, to start what was to be his most enduring work. The temple David had dreamed of began to rise under Solomon's hand.

For seven years they worked on that temple and its furnishings—thousands of slaves quarried stone and hauled materials. Hundreds of artisans worked on the vessels of gold and silver and bronze, and on the weavings and vestments. So well was the whole thing planned that the stone was dressed in the quarries so no sound of metal tool should profane its rooms at building.

When the last work was finished, Solomon gathered all the elders of Israel, and with solemn joy they moved the ark of the covenant and all its furnishings up from the citadel of David to rest under the outspread wings of the cherubs in the Holy of Holies in the new temple.

When the ark had been set in place, Jahweh himself took possession of his temple and filled it with his glory in the form of a thick cloud. Solomon knelt down in the sight of all the people, and asked God's blessing on his reign and his people. For seven days the people held festival, and on the eighth Solomon dismissed them to their homes, rejoicing.

When the people had left, Jahweh came once more to Solomon as he had at Gibeon. "I'm pleased," said God. "You shall have everything you've asked for, you and your people, but Solomon, one thing—"

"Yes, Lord?"

"There's been an awful lot of trade and interchange with the heathen over this. Be careful that's all it is. My promise lasts as long as your faithfulness does. But Solomon, if you and your people run after foreign gods, I'll *blast* you. You'll be scattered and dishonored and your throne left empty. As for this temple, I'll leave it in such ruins people will make a curse of it if you desert me!"

"Lord, Jahweh," said Solomon, "I wouldn't think of it!"

Solomon turned from the temple building to raising a splendid palace for himself and quarters for his wives (for by now he had made quite a few of those convenient political liaisons). He sent trading ships far and wide and raised a force of chariots and horses to stay in outlying cities and guard the realm.

At the high point of Solomon's reign, they *do* say that the Queen of Sheba made a special trip over to hear his wisdom and marvel at his wealth. The height of the civilization Israel had attained was truly impressive. The queen looked and listened, and every question she asked, Solomon replied to with wisdom. "Jahweh your god is truly great to bless you with such wisdom and power and to make your nation so great," she said. They gave each other fabulously rich gifts and parted with great respect and admiration, and all Israel basked in Solomon's glory.

# Decline of the House of David

THE WISDOM AND WEALTH OF SOLOMON have remained the stuff of legend, even to the present time. This was the man who had *everything*—almost. As his reign lengthened to twenty and thirty years, the wisdom in judgment remained. So did the peace on the borders, and so did the wealth, but the last two cost him perhaps more than they were worth.

Remember when Israel asked Samuel for "a real king." They wanted to be like other nations, and not a theocracy. Jahweh told Samuel to anoint Saul for them, but he told him also to be sure they understood what they were getting into. A king costs money! He needs servants and soldiers and palaces and pleasure gardens. Kings don't sow and reap; they rule and tax.

The needs of Saul and David seem to have remained relatively modest. They were warrior kings for the most part, and their courts were not so different from any rich man's house of the day, with its hired servants and foreign slaves. But Solomon was different. Solomon had an "edifice complex." When the temple was built, there had to be a palace. When the palace was built, there had to be houses for his wives and concubines. (There were a thousand of them, by the way.) If there was to be foreign trade, there must be ships, and ships cost money.

We worry about the cost of our defense budget as set against the available national wealth. Would you care to imagine what the cost of one of those war chariots—with an armed charioteer and with swift, blooded horses—looked like to a small freeholder? Not only did the horses and chariot and armor have to be paid for, but the cost of maintaining these standing troops of professional soldiers wasn't chicken feed.

Men had always rallied and fought when necessary to hold the territory, but now there was forced labor. The king was actually conscripting men of Israel to work on his building projects. The mutter went around that this was too much like Egypt for comfort. Still, the temple was glorious, and Jahweh was said to be very pleased. Then, too, Solomon was *impressive* and obviously the peoples around respected Israel. That's heady stuff! So they bent their backs to the load and paid the heavier taxes and got along (as men are likely to), rather than make a fuss.

What God thought of the state of affairs isn't recorded. He seems not to have spoken directly to Solomon again, and such prophets as there were had little to say, openly at least, about the state of affairs. Besides, it's said that silver was common as pebbles in the streets of Jerusalem. Parts of the economy, at least, were really booming.

There was one thing Jahweh *did* care about, though. Remember his final warning to Solomon about not following other gods? I'm sure Solomon meant to be faithful, but you see, there were all these women. ...He wasn't any more oversexed than any man of his time. It wasn't that. The whole point of all these girls was that their fathers were kings and princes. Solomon needed their friendship and influence. He needed their goods and services. No man, he reasoned, is likely to make war on his son-in-law, the father of his grandchildren.

One after another, Solomon took wives to establish alliances. It started with Pharaoh's daughter; after that it was a Moabite, or an Edomite, or a Sidonian. Was there a diplomatic problem? No matter, just send a few emissaries to say, "I'm really mad about your lovely daughter! Why don't we see if we can do business!" It worked, and each of the girls had to have a house for her retinue and a place of worship for her gods. It wouldn't do, after all, for them to be unhappy and ruin the whole alliance.

Back at the time when God's people first moved into the Promised Land, he had warned them about this. "A wife has a powerful influence on a man," God had warned. "Not only that, but she raises the children. *Don't* marry those idol worshippers. They will lead you away from me!"

If Solomon thought of that at all, he thought simply, "Not me. Surely with Jahweh's gift of wisdom I will be immune." Besides, it was expedient.

Did you ever notice that when you plead with either "I'm special" or expediency, the ice gets thin? It did for Solomon too. First he built the temples, then he began occasionally to frequent them. Finally, Solomon turned less and less often to Jahweh, the God of his youth. It was *his* greatness he saw now, not Jahweh's. It was *his* success. Presently he became fascinated with the worship of Astarte.

"That's it!" said Jahweh. "I'll tear the kingdom from the house of David! I won't take it out of Solomon's own hand. I promised that I wouldn't. But his sons shall never hold it in its completeness, because of his evil."

As David was chosen, well before his time, to replace Saul, so God chose another man to replace Solomon. He sent the prophet Ahijah of Shiloh to Jeroboam, a young Ephriamite noble who was in charge of the forced labor on the palace millo. Ahijah met Jeroboam on the road where they were alone. Taking the cloak from his own back, Ahijah tore it into twelve strips. Ten he put in Jeroboam's hand, saying, "God says that so he will divide this kingdom. Ten tribes will be yours. Remembering his promise to David, he leaves two to Solomon's son."

Somehow Solomon got wind of the prophecy, and he set out to destroy Jeroboam. The young man fled to Egypt to remain until Solomon's death. When Solomon had reigned for forty years, God let him die in peace because of his promise to David.

When Rehoboam came to the throne in Solomon's succession, the people begged, "Lift the load of your father. The weight is more than we can bear!" There's no point in playing "iffys." To the devout Jew writing the story down with twenty-twenty hindsight, Jahweh had it all planned anyway. One might even ponder the little matter of a warped sense of values being passed from father to son. The elders tried to counsel wisdom, but Rehoboam's younger friends said, "Man, you've got it all your way! Tell them to bug off!" So he did! He told them, in fact, it was going to get twice as heavy.

The people bugged off, all right. They renounced their loyalty to the line of David, and ultimately, ten tribes crowned Jeroboam king over them. Rehoboam kept only Judah, which included the remnant of Simeon. When he tried to start up the forced labor, even with them, they stoned his overseer to death, and Rehoboam himself had to make a run for it to the safety of his palace in Jerusalem.

So the kingdom of David became history, and the history legend. To this day its earthly glory has never returned. But Jahweh continued to prepare his chosen people for their vocation, and the later prophets came to speak of a messiah who would be a "son of David." And hearts of every age long toward Isaiah's description of a peaceable kingdom, ruled over by

*A shoot springing from the stock of Jesse;*
*A scion thrusting from his roots,*
*On whom the spirit of Jahweh rests.*

# Bible Stories
# From The Old Testament

Katherine Whaley
Interviewed by her editor, Patty Sleem

# Talking Things Over with Katherine Whaley

**Q:**     **In light of all that has been written in this field, why the Old Testament?**

**KW:**     Quite simply because, like every other writer who has done it, I am fascinated with the relationships it contains. Then, too, I am a professional storyteller, and there are no stories more intriguing to tell than those of the Old Testament— perhaps because they were oral literature for centuries before anyone wrote them down.

**Q:**     **When did you get your start as an author?**

**KW:**     Do you mean when did I start writing, or when did I come to consider myself an author? I have had a love affair with spilling words on paper ever since I learned to spell C-A-T! I suppose you could say I prepared for authorship by writing voluminous letters to family, friends, and Godchildren, not to say editors, and anyone else who gave me the remotest excuse for communication. There's something positively mesmerizing to me about a piece of clean paper and a pen in my hand. The paper actually aches for words. I didn't even think of myself as being an author until I entered a poetry contest about eighteen years ago and had a modest degree of success. Like most writers, I'm a closet poet!

**Q:**     **We hear a lot about "Inspiration." Is that a factor in your work, and does it require anything special in the line of workspace or tools?**

**KW:**     I think that nothing worthwhile comes into being without inspiration—that is to say literally the breathing into it of spirit somewhere in its creation. That's as true for a book as for a painting, a pageant, or a piecrust. It must have a spark of life. I do not, however, sit about and wait for it. Once in a while, ideas hit me when I'm not sitting with pencil poised, but most of the time, I simply sit down to write, and after I begin, it comes. Sometimes I slog along for a while, and throw out what doesn't fly or sing for me, but that's part of the price. As to places and situations, I have a rocker in the sunporch, and a lapboard. This keeps me in touch with the rising bread, the grandchild running in the back door, and whatever else is happening. I need a degree of quiet for concentration, but I also need to be in the middle of who I am.

Q: **You speak fondly of pen and paper. Is that how you do all your writing?**

KW: It is still my preferred way of doing it. It's how I first became intimate with WORD, however, I am struggling to learn to communicate by computer, since it is the only way the work can be transmitted to publisher and reader. Sometimes, though, I still return to my corner, and mull over a difficult or tender passage with my pen. All my poetry is done that way. It's one of my little luxuries! Much of the other work is now done in the computer room, which, being the upstairs sunporch, is a bright nest among the dogwood and pecan trees. There's just something about sunporches—. The grandkids know where to look for me, and I get my exercise running downstairs to check on the rising bread.

Q: **Why did the book stop where it did with Solomon's death and his son's misjudgments?**

KW: Because it had to stop somewhere, and most of the kings after that seemed petty and uninteresting against the patriarchs, judges, and monarchs before them. There are some great tales left to be told, though, and believe me, my writing hand itches when I think of it.

**Q:** **Is all of your writing pretty much Bible oriented?**

**KW:** Far from it. I really enjoy writing nostalgic stuff, and I have more of that published (one tale at a time) than anything else. I also write fairy tales—some for children and some for adults, Christmas "legends," and small children's stories for grandchildren and smallfry I tell stories to at schools and parties. And I write some stories for myself. They help to explain to me who I am and why. And I've come to find out that stories make delightful presents. They are a uniquely personal gift.

**Q:** **What do you do when you're not writing?**

**KW:** I'm a Matriarch and Homemaker. That's my chief calling. We have four grown children, four grandchildren, and a number of "godfamily" members who belong to the household in varying ways. All are very important to my life. And, yes, of course, there is a Patriarch to whom I've been married for over forty years. In addition, I'm a church mouse. I enjoy singing in choir, being an acolyte director, lending other skills as needed. Anything to do with kids hooks me— hence the acolytes—and weekly tutoring in a latchkey program. And I'm a church vestment maker. I enjoy designing banners and priest's vestments.

**Q:** **Who is your all-time favorite Old Testament character?**

**KW:** The one I'm writing or telling about at any given time. They are all fascinating to me—even those who are somewhat villainous. They are so terribly human. I feel as if I knew them personally. I guess that's why I keep figuring what people think or why they do what they do in the stories. I live with the people while I'm writing. They feel as real to me as, say, you do.

Q:     **Do you believe in this Jahweh you speak about so intimately?**

KW:    I've bet my life on that belief! I don't always live as if that were the case, but when I don't that's my mistake. None of the people in the book did it perfectly either, yet they believed and trusted him. Perhaps that is one of the reasons I find their company so congenial.

# Reading Group Questions and Discussion Topics

1. What is different about the creation of humankind from the other creatures?

2. Why do you think God knowingly created a no-no in the trees of life and knowledge?

3. In what ways are you and I like Cain?

4. Pretend you are Noah, and God gave you those instructions—here—now.

5. What was God's first promise to Abraham that made him leave Haran after Terah's death? Would that have been enough to make you pull up stakes and go?

6. The sacred law of hospitality to strangers enters these accounts heavily. Do you think it is still in effect? If so, in what ways is it the same, and in what ways changed?

7. Lot seems to have chosen a pretty rough neighborhood to live in! How has he managed to get along there until now? How do we get along with "the world?" Is this accommodation bad, good, or both? Why?

8. Does it surprise you that Abraham, who haggled with God at length over Sodom's destruction, doesn't protest at all over the demand for Isaac's life? Why do you think he reacts in this way?

9.      Some theologians picture Isaac as knowledgeable and willing to be sacrificed, comparing this to Jesus' crucifixion. The author does not tell it that way. How much difference does this make to the significance of the story?

10.     When Rebekah offered to water the camels for Abraham's servant, do you think God simply nudged her into the "right" response, or was she truly the kind of girl who would respond that generously? Is this important to God's plan?

11.     Why is Rebekah uneasy with the prophecy that "the younger shall rule the elder?" Do you think that she has come to agree with it by the time she helps Jacob steal the birthright blessing? Why was Jacob a better bet for a patriarch to found God's people than Esau?

12.     Discuss the irony of Jacob's being "taken" by Laban in his very first deal on his own. If you are Leah, how do you feel about being put in this position? Advantages? Disadvantages? How do you feel after several children are born? If you are Rachel, how do you feel?

13.     What does Laban's not harming Jacob say about a man we haven't seen much good in before?

14.     How much does the fact that there must have been animosity among their four mothers affect the situation among the brothers?

15.     Why do you suppose God let Joseph stay in prison for so long a time? What does Joseph's relationship to God seem to be at this time in his life?

16.     Imagine you are Joseph going to bed the night after you have interpreted Pharaoh's dream. What are your thoughts?

17. Why do you think that Joseph arranges the much more intimate situation of dining with his brothers before he reveals himself?

18. Why does Joseph try to trap his brothers? Would Joseph have kept Benjamin for theft of the cup had the others let him? Why do the brothers feel Joseph will be vindictive, and why isn't he?

19. How does Moses' life before he leaves Egypt prepare him for what God means him to do? Do you think Moses is really worried about his speech, or is he looking for an excuse?

20. What purposes do you suppose God means the "Passover" meal to serve for his people? Why do you suppose God uses very visible and spectacular means to rescue this enslaved people?

21. Why do you think that Jahweh didn't let this attack on the Promised Land succeed but instead turned the tribes back to wandering?

22. Why do you think God makes a big point of arranging both Moses' and Aaron's deaths ceremonially? If you are Moses, how do you feel when you see Aaron lie down to die? What are your thoughts and emotions when God shows you the Promised Land, and you know that you, too, are dying?

23. The words "hallel lu Jah" which the author has put as a battle cry in the mouths of the men of Israel mean praise to God. If you are in Israel's troops at that instant, do you think this might seem appropriate? Is it a good battle cry for Israel, knowing their history as we do? Have you ever been in a position where you think this "battle cry" (either spoken, or unspoken) might have been appropriate?

24. If you are Jael, why might you break the general law of hospitality to kill Sisera even though this isn't your battle?

25. When a people's situation changes from insecure to secure, or from nomadic to settled, or from isolated to mingling with other people of different mores, changes occur. Point out some in these stories. Can you name any modern parallels? Are all the changes bad, or can you name some good ones as well?

26. Who would you rather have for a neighbor, Manoah or Samson? Why? Do you think God approved of the way Samson's parents raised him? If Samson was, as the author suggests, spoiled badly, was that God's intention, or did he just use it to further his plans?

27. If Samson had been a modest, quiet man, how might this story have read? Would he still have been a judge? Did God actually approve of what Samson was and did? What things in Samson's life would you consider chief vices that led to his downfall?

28. There was no doubt in these times that the request for a child had more potency in a "holy place." Is that belief still in existence? Do we believe it in any sense?

29. Discuss the importance of the Ark of the Covenant as a national symbol. The Ark was considered holy. What does that word mean to you?

30. Elimelech and Naomi moved for very practical reasons, but this took them away from family support. In what ways is that much like today's family situations? What does the fact that Ruth had converted to belief in Jahweh say about Naomi and her sons?

31. Besides her first marriage to Mahlon, Ruth is involved in three "love stories." What are they, and discuss how they affected each other.

32. The book of Esther takes place in a Jewish community that is away from the homeland of the Jews. In what ways does this make her position in a gentile household different? Has government intrigue changed much over the centuries? In what ways is it different? The same?

33. It's a question as old as the ages. Why do you think God lets Job, or any good person, suffer disaster? Do you accept the Biblical writer's interpretation that Satan talked God into it?

34. What sort of prophet would you be if you heard God's call? Are people ever called to be prophets in this day and time and place? What is a prophet, anyway?

35. God seems to have an odd habit of passing over older sons in favor of younger sons in these stories. Can you see any reason why that might be? As compared to Jacob's sons, how did Jesse's do in response to the younger being promoted over the elder?

36. Do you think that the behavior of Jonathan and Michal is wrong in getting David away from Saul? If you were either, how might you justify your behavior? Are there still times when God calls people to put another person's welfare before family loyalty? If so, what are the marks that distinguish them?

37. Is Saul really repentant when he speaks to David? If so, why does he return to the hunt later? Can you think of a time and place where someone clearly went back on their repentance? Is this ever justified? Was it in Saul's case?

38. Have you ever felt, like Nabal, that you were being asked to give more than was fair, or for a questionable cause? Does God mean us to be discriminating about our gifts? If so, how do we know how to draw the line?

39. Why do you suppose Abigail chose to live in David's wilderness camp over whatever her widowhood might bring in more civilized surroundings?

40. David was a vicious raider, yet he was lavishly generous to the young Egyptian slave who led them to the raiders of Ziklag. What does that tell us about David's personality? Was David a fair man? On what do you base your conclusions?

41. Christians profess to believe, as did Saul, that seeking signs anywhere other than from God about what is to happen in the future is wrong. What ways of manipulating the future are still practiced and easily available to us? Are they wrong? If so, why do you think so?

42. In returning to Hebron, David is ensuring rule over the part of the kingdom he knows he can get. What do you suppose his thoughts are about splitting the kingdom? Does Abner's question *Shall the sword eat its fill forever?* still apply to today's world?

43. Was it right for Joab to avenge Asahel? Can you understand why he did it? The killers of Ishbaal were summarily executed, but Joab got off with what amounted to a reprimand. Why do you suppose this was?

44. When David dances before the Ark, and Michal objects so angrily, what do you think her thoughts are? What are David's thoughts? Do you agree with the writer that he put her away?

45. In an era of arranged marriages, what do you think Bathsheeba's thoughts were when David summoned her to the palace as his wife? In light of these two tales about David and Bathsheeba, what sort of man is David, anyway? Are we very different? Are our leaders?

46. Had David disciplined Amnon, how might the monarchy have been changed? Asking that Absalom be spared is not good statesmanship, but is it understandable? Why does Joab disregard the order, and why is his punishment literally a slap on the wrist?

47. The crowning of Solomon is the end of David's reign—not his physical death. Why does Israel celebrate David as its greatest king? Do you think that this is justified?

48. Solomon was permitted by God to build the temple David had been forbidden to because David was a man of war. Was Solomon a better man than David in the long run? Which would you prefer as king?

49. Discuss the irony of the fact that as David was anointed to replace Saul in Saul's lifetime, Jeroboam was anointed to replace Solomon in Solomon's lifetime. How was Rehoboam like his father? In what ways was he different?

50. What thoughts occur to you when Jesus is referred to as "Son of David?"

# About The Author

Katherine Whaley is a former high school teacher with four grown children and four grandchildren. She has been a professional story-teller in all age groups, from pre-schoolers to the elderly, for seventeen years. The first edition of this book, *Bible Stories Of Long Ago*, was published by Prentice Hall in 1984 and was Whaley's first book. She has written for various publications, such as *Cross Currents* (Diocese of Eastern North Carolina) and the *American Poetry Anthology*. She enjoys ballroom dancing, baking yeast breads and (at the drop of a hint) millions of cupcakes, making her own rather singular clothes, and reading anything she can get her hands on (including the phone book and old bills if nothing else presents itself).

# ALSO BY PREP PUBLISHING

BACK IN TIME
*Patty Sleem*

SECOND TIME AROUND
*Patty Sleem*

WHAT THE BIBLE SAYS ABOUT ...
Words That Can Lead To Success And Happiness
*Patty Sleem*

A GENTLE BREEZE FROM GOSSAMER WINGS
*Gordon Beld*

COVER LETTERS THAT BLOW DOORS OPEN
*Anne McKinney*

RESUMES AND COVER LETTERS THAT HAVE WORKED
*Anne McKinney*

RESUMES AND COVER LETTERS THAT HAVE WORKED
FOR MILITARY PROFESSIONALS
*Anne McKinney*

LETTERS FOR SPECIAL SITUATIONS
*Anne McKinney*

GOVERNMENT JOB APPLICATIONS AND FEDERAL RESUMES
*Anne McKinney*

RESUMES AND COVER LETTERS FOR MANAGERS
*Anne McKinney*

# PREP Publishing Order Form

You can order any of our titles from your favorite bookseller! Or just send a check or money order or your credit card number for the total amount*, plus $3.20 postage and handling, to PREP, Box 66, Fayetteville, NC 28302. If you have a question about any of our titles, feel free to e-mail us at preppub@aol.com and visit our website at http://www.prep-pub.com

Name: _____

Phone #: _____

Address: _____

E-mail address: _____

Payment Type: ☐ Check/Money Order  ☐ Visa  ☐ MasterCard

Credit Card Number: _____ Expiration Date: _____

Check items you are ordering:

☐ $25.00—RESUMES AND COVER LETTERS THAT HAVE WORKED. Anne McKinney

☐ $25.00—RESUMES AND COVER LETTERS THAT HAVE WORKED FOR MILITARY PROFESSIONALS. Anne McKinney

☐ $25.00—RESUMES AND COVER LETTERS FOR MANAGERS. Anne McKinney

☐ $25.00—GOVERNMENT JOB APPLICATIONS AND FEDERAL RESUMES: Federal Resumes, KSAs, Forms 171 and 612, and Postal Applications. Anne McKinney

☐ $25.00—COVER LETTERS THAT BLOW DOORS OPEN. Anne McKinney

☐ $25.00—LETTERS FOR SPECIAL SITUATIONS. Anne McKinney

☐ $16.00—BACK IN TIME. Patty Sleem

☐ $17.00—(trade paperback) SECOND TIME AROUND. Patty Sleem

☐ $25.00—(hardcover) SECOND TIME AROUND. Patty Sleem

☐ $18.00—A GENTLE BREEZE FROM GOSSAMER WINGS. Gordon Beld

☐ $18.00—BIBLE STORIES FROM THE OLD TESTAMENT. Katherine Whaley

☐ $20.00—(hardcover) WHAT THE BIBLE SAYS ABOUT... *Words that can lead to success and happiness.* Patty Sleem

_____ **TOTAL ORDERED (add $3.20 for postage and handling)**

*Volume discounts on large orders. Call (910) 483-6611 for more information.